THE MEN WERE FROM THE SLAMMERS, AND THEY WERE MAGNIFICENT

My Lady Miriam and her entourage rushed back from the barred windows of the women's apartments on the second floor, squealing for effect. The tanks were so huge that the mirror-helmeted men watching from the turret hatches were nearly on a level with the upper story of the palace.

The Baron's soldiers had boasted that they were better men than the mercenaries if it ever came down to cases. The fear that the women had mined from behind stone walls seemed real enough now to the soldiers whose bluster and assault rifles were insiginificant against the iridium titans which entered the courtyard.

Even at idle speed, the tanks roared as their fans maintained the cushions of air that slid them over the ground. Three of the Baron's men dodged back through the palace doorway, their curses inaudible over the intake whine of the approaching vehicles.

They did not need to respect us. They were

DAVID DRAKE
HAMMER'S
Slammers

BAEN
BOOKS

HAMMER'S SLAMMERS

Copyright © 1987 by David Drake.

Introduction copyright © 1979 by Jerry Pournelle.

A shorter version of this book was published by Ace Books, copyright © 1979.

A Baen Books Original

Baen Publishing Enterprises
260 Fifth Avenue
New York, N.Y. 10001

First printing, April 1987

ISBN: 0-671-65632-5

Cover art by Paul Alexander

Printed in the United States of America

Distributed by
SIMON & SCHUSTER
1230 Avenue of the Americas
New York, N.Y. 10020

CONTENTS

Introduction

Mercenaries and Military Virtue

by

Jerry Pournelle

IN EUROPE and especially in England, military history is a respected intellectual discipline. Not so here. I doubt there are a dozen academic posts devoted to the study of the military arts.

The public esteem of the profession of arms is at a rather low ebb just now—at least in the United States. The Soviet Union retains the pomp and ceremony of military glory, and the officer class is highly regarded, if not by the public (who can know the true feelings of Soviet citizens?) then at least by the rulers of the Kremlin. Nor did the intellectuals always despise soldiers in the United States. Many of the very universities which delight in making mock of uniforms were endowed by land grants and were founded in the expectation that they would train officers for the state militia. It has not been all that many years since U.S. combat troops were routinely expected to take part in parades; when soldiers were proud to wear uniform off post, and when my uniform was sufficient for free entry into movie houses, the New York Museum of Modern Art, the New York Ballet, and as I recall the Met (as well as to other establishments catering to less cultural needs of the soldier).

But now both the military and anyone who studies war are held in a good deal of contempt.

I do not expect this state of affairs to last—in fact, I am certain that it cannot. A nation which despises its soldiers will all too soon have a despicable army.

The depressing fact is that history is remarkably clear on one point: wealthy republics do not last long. Time after time they have risen to wealth and freedom; the citizens become wealthy and sophisticated; unwilling to volunteer to protect themselves, they go to conscription; this too becomes intolerable; and soon enough they turn to mercenaries.

Machiavelli understood that, and things have not changed much since his time—except that Americans know far less history than did the rulers of Florence and Milan and Venice.

For mercenaries are a dangerous necessity. If they are incompetent, they will ruin you. If they are competent there is always the temptation to rob the paymaster.

Why should they not? They know their employers will not fight. They may, if called a national army, retain loyalty to the country—but if the nation despises them, and takes every possible opportunity to let them know it, then that incentive falls as well—and they have a monopoly on the means of violence.

After all, it should be fairly clear that no one fights purely for money; that anyone who does is probably not worth hiring. As Montesquieu put it, "a rational army *would* run away." To stand on the firing parapet and expose yourself to danger; to stand and fight a thousand miles from home when you're all alone and outnumbered and probably beaten; to spit on your hands and lower the pike; to stand fast over the body of Leonidas the King; to be rear guard at Kunu-ri; to stand and be still to the Birkenhead drill; these are not rational acts.

They are often merely necessary.

Through history, through painful experience, military professionals have built up a specialized knowledge: how to induce men (including most especially themselves) to fight, aye, and to die. To charge the guns at Breed's Hill and New Orleans, at Chippewa and at Cold Harbor; to climb the wall of the Embassy Compound at Peking; to go ashore at Betio and Saipan; to load and fire with precision and accuracy while the *Bon Homme Richard* is sinking; to fly in that thin air five miles above a hostile land and bring the ship straight and level for thirty seconds over Regensberg and Ploesti; to endure at Heartbreak Ridge and Porkchop Hill and the Iron Triangle and Dien Bien Phu and Hue and Firebase 34 and a thousand nameless hills and villages.

It's a rather remarkable achievement, when you think about it. It's even more remarkable when you look closer and see just how many mercenary units have performed creditably, honorably, even gallantly; how many of those who have changed history on the battlefield have been professional soldiers. For despite the silly sayings about violence never settling anything, history IS changed on the battlefield: ask the National Socialist German Workers' Party, or the Carthaginians, or the Confederate States of America, Pompey and Richard III and Harold of Wessex, Don Juan of Austria and Aetius the last Roman. Yet you could search through the armies of history and you would find few competent troopers who fought for money and money alone.

This is the mistake so often made by those who despise the military, and because they despise it refuse to understand it: they fail to see that few are so foolish as to give their lives for money; yet an army whose soldiers are not willing to die is an army that wins few victories.

Yet certainly there have always existed mercenary soldiers.

We can piously hope that there will be no armies in the future. It is an unlikely hope; at least history is against it. On the evidence, peace is a purely theoretical state of affairs whose existence we deduce because there have been intervals between wars. But I did not speak contemptuously when I spoke of pious hopes; nor do I find it an irony that the Strategic Air Command, whose commanders hold leashed more firepower than has been expended by all the armies of all time, has as its motto "Peace is our profession." Most of those young men who guard us as we sleep believe in that, believe it wholeheartedly and give up a very great deal for it. I too can piously hope for peace; that we shall heed the advice of the carol we sing annually and "hush the noise, ye men of strife, and hear the angels sing."

But to hope is nothing. When Appius Claudius told the Senate of Rome that "If you would have peace, be thou then prepared for war" he said nothing that history has not repeatedly affirmed. It may be wrong advice. Certainly there is an argument against it. But I think there is no argument at all against a similar aphorism: "If you would have peace, then understand war."

Which is to say, understand armies; understand

why men fight; understand the organization of violence.

And that, at last, brings us to this book.

Military science fiction is a highly specialized art form. It is attempted often, but there are few writers who know science, society, and the military well enough to write a good story of war in the future.

This is unfortunate: although science fiction, like all literature, must entertain and divert if it is to have readers, it often has a serious purpose as well: to look at future societies, and the impact of technology on history. Any attempt to look into the future while ignoring war and the military is probably doomed to failure: if five thousand years of recorded history have given us no formula for controlling violence and greed, we would be fortunate indeed if this generation has indeed fought the war to end all wars; if the armies that exist today were the last this planet will ever see.

Hammer's Slammers is a serious book. This is not to say it is not a whacking good story, with real people fighting real conflicts, for it is all of that; nor is it a tract, preachifying for or against war. It is a serious book because while it tells a good story it depicts much of the reality of conflict. It is a book by a man who has been there, and who has studied enough military history to understand, incompletely, as all of us understand only incompletely, why men fight; a book about a man who has that intangible but very real quality, the ability to lead men into Hell.

But like many of the great conquerors, Hammer is despised by those who employ him; his country has no use for his talents. He is not often admirable, except to his own men, and not always to them. Like all the great warriors, real and imaginary, he may be seen, as you wish, as a saint or a fiend. That is true of my own John Christian Falkenberg, of Dickson's Donal Graeme and Drake's Alois Hammer, of Patton and MacArthur and Guderian and Robert E. Lee and Ulysses Simpson Grant, Caesar and Alexander of Macedon and all the others: for the essence of war is violence, and those who make it their profession must be stained by it; yet for all that they have, they *must* have, that peculiar and elusive quality known as military virtue. And make no mistake, the military virtues are real, and they are indeed virtues—although one might make the case that they are perversions of the truly human virtues, and thus worse than vices. But perversions or no, the great commanders whose company Alois Hammer now joins truly hold and revere the military virtues. They must have them, for without them they would not be great captains; without them their men would not follow them to Hell.

For all great captains there is the great temptation; for those who can lead men to Hell, there is the vision that they might lead them to Paradise. Hammer is no exception: but history records few instances of success.

Of course Hammer knows that. All the great warrior captains have. But humility has never been a military virtue. . . .

But Loyal to His Own

"IT JUST BLEW UP. Hammer and his men knew but they didn't say a thing," blurted the young captain as he looked past Secretary Tromp, his gaze compelled toward the milky noonday sky. It was not the sky of Friesland and that bothered Captain Stilchey almost as much as his near-death in the ambush an hour before. "He's insane! They all are."

"Others have said so," the councillor stated with the heavy ambiguity of an oracle replying to an ill-phraséd question. Tromp's height was short of two meters by less than a hand's breadth, and he was broad in proportion. That size and the generally dull look on his face caused some visitors looking for Friesland's highest civil servant to believe they had surprised a retired policeman of some sort sitting at the desk of the Secretary to the Council of State.

Tromp did not always disabuse them.

Now his great left hand expanded over the grizzled fringe of hair remaining at the base of his skull. "Tell me about the ambush," he directed.

"He didn't make any trouble about coming to you here at the port," Stilchey said, for a moment watching his fingers writhe together rather than look at his superior. He glanced up. "Have you met Hammer?"

"No, I kept in the background when plans for the Auxiliary Regiment were drafted. I've seen his picture, of course."

"Not the same," the captain replied, beginning to talk very quickly. "He's not big but he, he moves, he's alive and it's like every time he speaks he's training a gun on you, waiting for you to slip. But he came along, no trouble—only he said we'd go with a platoon of combat cars instead of flying back, he wanted to check road security between Southport and the firebase where we were. I said sure, a couple hours wasn't crucial. . . ."

Tromp nodded. "Well done," he said. "Hammer's cooperation is very important if this . . . business is to be concluded smoothly. And"—here the councillor's face hardened without any noticeable shift of muscles—"the last thing we wanted was for the good colonel to become concerned while he was still with his troops. He is not a stupid man."

Gratification played about the edges of Stilchey's mouth, but the conversation had cycled the captain's mind back closer to the blast of cyan fire. His stomach began to spin. "There were six vehicles in the patrol, all but the second one open combat cars. That was a command car, same chassis and ground-effect curtain, but enclosed, you see? Better commo gear and an air-conditioned passenger compartment. I started toward it but Hammer said, no, I was to get in the next one with him and Joachim."

Stilchey coughed, halted. "That Joachim's here with

him now; he calls him his aide. The bastard's queer,
he tried to make me when I flew out. . . ."

Puzzlement. "Colonel Hammer is homosexual, Captain? Or his aide, or . . . ?"

"No, Via! Him, not the—I don't know. Via, maybe
him too. The bastard scares me, he really does."

To statesmen patience is a tool; it is a palpable
thing that can grind necessary information out of a
young man whose aristocratic lineage and sparkling
uniform have suddenly ceased to armor him against
the universe. "The ambush, Captain." Tromp pressed
stolidly.

With a visible effort, Stilchey regained the thread
of his narrative.

"Joachim drove. Hammer and I were in the back
along with a noncom from Curwin—Worzer, his
name was. He and Joachim threw dice for who had
to drive. The road was supposed to be clear but
Hammer made me put on body armor. I thought it
was cop, you know—make the staffer get hot and
dusty.

"Via," he swore again, but softly this time. "I was
at the leftside powergun but I wasn't paying much
attention; nothing really to pay attention to. Hammer was on the radio a lot, but my helmet only had
intercom so I didn't know what he was saying. The
road was stabilized earth, just a gray line through
hectares of those funny blue plants you see all over
here, the ones with the fat leaves."

"Bluebrights," the older man said dryly. "Melpomone's only export; as you would know from the
briefing cubes you were issued in transit, I should
think."

"Would the Lord I'd never *heard* of this damned
place!" Stilchey blazed back. His family controlled
Karob Trading; no civil servant—not even Tromp,

the Gray Eminence behind the Congress of the Republic—could cow him. But he was a soldier, too, and after a moment he continued, "Bluebrights in rows, waist high and ugly, and beyond that nothing but the soil blowing away as we passed.

"We were half an hour out from the firebase, maybe half the way to here. The ground was dimpled with frost heaves. A little copse was in sight ahead of us, trees ten, fifteen meters high. Hammer had the forward gun, and on the intercom he said, 'Want to double the bet, Blackie?' Then they armed their guns—I didn't know why—and Worzer said, 'I still think they'll be in the draw two kays south, but I won't take any more of your money.' They were laughing and I thought they were going to just . . . clear the guns, you know?"

The captain closed his eyes. He remembered how they had stared at him, two bulging circles and the hollow of his screaming mouth below them, reflected on the polished floorplate of the combat car. "The command car blew up just as we entered the trees. There was a flash like the sun and it *ate* the back half of the car, armor and all. The front flipped over and over into the trees, and the air *stank* with metal. Joachim laid us sideways to follow the part the mine had left, cutting in right behind when it hit a tree and stopped. The driver raised his head out of the hatch and maybe he could have got clear himself . . . but Hammer jumped off our deck to his and jerked him out, yanked him up in his armor as small as he is. Then they were back in our car. They were firing, everybody was firing, and we turned right, into the trees, into the guns."

"There were Mel troops in the grove, then?" Tromp asked.

"Must have been," Stilchey replied. He looked

straight at the older man and said, very simply, "I was behind the bulkhead. Maybe if I'd known what to expect. . . . The other driver was at my gun, they didn't need me." Stilchey swallowed once, continued, "Some shots hit on my side. They didn't come through, but they made the whole car ring. The empties kept spattering me and the car was bouncing, jumping downed trees. Everything seemed to be on fire. We cleared the grove into another field of bluebrights. Shells from the firebase were already landing in the trees; the place was targeted. And Worzer pulled off his helmet and he spat and said, 'Cold meat, Colonel, you couldn't a called it better.' Vial!"

"Well, it does sound like they reacted well to the ambush," Tromp admitted, puzzled because nothing Stilchey had told him explained the captain's fear and hatred of Hammer and his men.

"Nice extempore response, hey?" the aide suggested with bitter irony. "Only Hammer, seeing I didn't know what Worzer meant, turned to me, and said, 'We let the Mels get word that me and Secretary Tromp would take a convoy to Southport this morning. They still had fifty or so regulars here in Region 4 claiming to be an infantry battalion, and it looked like a good time to flush them for good and all.' "

Tromp said nothing. He spread his hands carefully on the citron-yellow of his desk top and seemed to be fixedly studying the contrast. Stilchey waited for a response. At last he said, "I don't like being used for bait, Secretary. And what if you'd decided to go out to the firebase yourself? I was all right for a stand-in, but do you think Hammer would have cared if you were there in person? He won't let anything stand in his way."

"Colonel Hammer does seem to have some unconventional attitudes," Tromp agreed. A bleak smile edged his voice as he continued, "But at that, it's rather fortunate that he brought a platoon in with him. We can begin the demobilization of his vaunted Slammers with them."

The dome of the Starport Lounge capped Southport's hundred-meter hotel tower. Its vitril panels were seamless and of the same refractive index as the atmosphere. As a tactician, Hammer was fascinated with the view: it swept beyond the equipment-thronged spaceport and over the shimmering billows of bluebright, to the mountains of the Crescent almost twenty kilometers away. But tankers' blood has in it a turtle component that is more comfortable on the ground than above it, and the little officer felt claws on his intestines as he looked out.

No similar discomfort seemed to be disturbing the other men in the room, all in the black and silver of the Guards of the Republic, though in name they were armor officers. "Had a bit of action today, Colonel?" said a cheerful, fit-looking major. Hammer did not remember him even though a year ago he had been Second in Command of the Guards.

"Umm, a skirmish," Hammer said as he turned. The Guardsman held out to him one of the two thimble-sized crystals he carried. In the heart of each flickered an azure fire. "Why, thank you—" the major's name was patterned in the silver highlights below his left lapel—"Mestern."

"No doubt you have seen much worse with your mercenaries, eh, Colonel?" a voice called mockingly from across the room.

Karl August Raeder lounged in imperial state in the midst of a dozen admiring junior officers. He had been the executive officer of the Guards for the past year—ever since Hammer took command of the foreign regiment raised to smash the scattered units of the Army of Melpomone.

"Mercenaries, Karl?" Hammer repeated. A threat rasped through the surface mildness of his tone. "Yes, they cash their paychecks. There may be a few others in this room who do, hey?"

"Oh . . . ," someone murmured in the sudden quiet, but there was no way to tell what he meant by it. Raeder did not move. The blood had drawn back to yellow his smooth tan, and where the cushions had borne his languid hands they now were dimpled cruelly. Two men in the lounge had reached officer status in the Guards without enormous family wealth behind them. Hammer was one, Raeder was the other.

He strained at a breath. In build, he and Hammer were not dissimilar: the latter brown-haired and somewhat shorter, a trifle more of the hourglass in his shoulders and waist; Raeder blond and trim, slender in a rapier sort of way and quite as deadly. His uniform of natural silk and leather was in odd contrast to Hammer's khaki battledress, but there was nothing of fop or sloven in either man.

"Pardon," the Guardsman said, "I would not have thought this a company in which one need explain patriotism; there are men who fight for their homelands, and then there are the dregs, the guttersweepings of a galaxy, who fight for the same reason they pimped and sold themselves before our government—let me finish, please!" (though only Hammer's smile had moved) "—misguidedly, I submit, offered them more money to do what Friesland citizens could have done better!"

"My boys are better citizens than some born on Friesland who stayed there wiping their butts—"

"A soldier goes where he is ordered!" Raeder was standing.

"A *soldier*—"

Dead silence. Hammer's sentence broke like an axed cord. He looked about the lounge at the twenty-odd men, most of them his ex-comrades and all, like Raeder, men who had thought him mad to post out of the Guards for the sake of a combat command. Hammer laughed. He inverted the stim cone on the inside of his wrist and said approvingly, "Quite a view from up here. If it weren't such a good target, you could make it your operations center." As if in the midst of a normal conversation, he faced back toward the exterior and added, "By the way, what sort of operations are you expecting? I would have said the fighting here was pretty well over, and I'd be surprised at the government sending the Guards in for garrison duty."

The whispering that had begun when Hammer turned was stilled again. It was Raeder who cleared his throat and said in a tone between triumph and embarrassment, "Colonel Rijsdal may know. He . . . he has remained in his quarters since we landed." Rijsdal had not had a sober day in the past three years since he had acceded to an enormous estate on Friesland. "No doubt we are to provide proper, ah, background for such official pronouncements as the Secretary will make to the populace."

Hammer nodded absently as if he believed the black and silver of a parade regiment would over-awe the Mels more effectively than could his own scarred killers, the men who had rammed Frisian suzerainty down Mel throats after twelve regiments of regulars had tried and failed. But the Guards were impres-

sively equipped . . . and all their gear had been
landed.

Five hundred worlds had imported bluebright
leaves, with most of the tonnage moving through
Southport. The handful of Frisian vessels scattered
on the field looked lost, but traffic would pick up
now that danger was over. For the moment, hundreds of Guard vehicles gave it a specious life. In the
broad wedge of his vision Hammer could see two
rocket batteries positioned as neatly as chess pieces
on the huge playing surface. The center of each
cluster was an ammunition hauler, low and broad-
chassied. Within their thin armor sheetings were the
racks of 150 mm shells; everything from armor-pierc-
ing rounds with a second stage to accelerate them
before impact, to antipersonnel cases loaded with
hundreds of separate bomblets. The haulers rested
on the field; no attempt had been made to dig them
in.

The six howitzers of each battery were sited about
their munitions in a regular hexagon, each joined to
its hauler by the narrow strip of a conveyor. In action
the hogs could kick out shells at five-second intervals, so the basic load of twenty rounds carried by
the howitzer itself needed instant replenishment from
the hauler's store. Their stubby gun-tubes gave them
guidance and an initial boost, but most of the accel-
eration came beyond the muzzle. They looked grim
and effective; still, it nagged Hammer to see that
nobody had bothered to defilade them.

"A pretty sight," said Mestern. Conversation in
the lounge was back to a normal level.

Hammer squeezed the last of his stim cone into
the veins of his wrist and let the cool shudder pass
through him before saying, "The Republic buys the
best, and that's the only way to go when a battle's

hanging on it. Not that you don't need good crews to man the gear."

Mestern pointed beyond the howitzers, toward a wide-spaced ring of gun trucks. "Latest thing in arty defense," he said. "Each of those cars mounts an eight-barrel powergun, only 30 mm but they're high-intensity. They've got curst near the range of a tank's 200—thirty, forty kilometers if you've that long a sight line. With our radar hook-up and the satellite, we can just about detonate a shell as soon as it comes over the horizon."

"Nice theory," Hammer agreed. "I doubt you can swing the rig fast enough to catch the first salvo, but maybe placing them every ten degrees like that . . . where you've got the terrain to allow it. The Mels never had arty worth cop anyway, of course."

He paused, not sure he wanted to comment further. The grounded tanks and combat cars of the regiment were in an even perimeter at the edge of the circular field. Their dull iridium armor was in evident contrast to the ocher soil on which they rested. "You really ought to have dug in," Hammer said at last.

"Oh, the field's been stabilized to two meters down," the major protested innocently, "and I don't think the Mels are much of a threat now."

Hammer shook his head in irritation. "Lord!" he snorted, "the Mels aren't any threat at all after this morning. But just on general principles, when you set up in a war zone—*any* war zone—you set up as if you were going to be hit. Via, you may as well park your cars on Friesland for all the good they'd do if it dropped in the pot."

"The good colonel has been away from soldiers too long," whipped Raeder savagely. "Major Mestern, would you care to enlighten him as to how operations can be conducted by a real regiment—even though a gutter militia would be incapable of doing so?"

"I don't . . . think . . . ," Mestern stuttered in embarrassment. His fingers twiddled an empty stim cone.

"Very well, then I will," the blond XO snapped. Hammer was facing him again. This time the two men were within arm's length. "The Regiment of Guards is using satellite reconnaissance, Colonel," Raeder announced sneeringly. "The same system in operation when you were in charge here, but we are *using* it, you see."

"We used it. We—"

"Pardon, Colonel, permit me to explain and there will be fewer needless questions."

Hammer relaxed with a smile. There was a tiger's certainty behind its humor. "No, your pardon. Continue."

Hammer had killed two men in semi-legal duels fought on Friesland's moon. Raeder chuckled, unconcerned with his rival's sudden mildness. "So," he continued, "no Mel force could approach without being instantly sighted."

He stared at Hammer, who said nothing. If the Guardsman wanted to believe no produce truck could drop a Mel platoon into bunkers dug by a harvesting crew—spotting the activity was no problem, interpreting it, though—well, it didn't matter now. But it proved again what Hammer had known since before he was landed, that a lack of common sense was what had so hamstrung the regular army that his Slammers had to be formed.

Of course, "common sense" meant to Hammer doing what was necessary to complete a task. And that sometimes created problems of its own.

"Our howitzers can shatter them ninety kilometers distant," Raeder lectured on, "and our tanks can pierce all but the heaviest armor at line of sight, Colonel." He gestured arrogantly toward the skyline behind Hammer. "Anything that can be seen can be destroyed."

"Yeah, it's always a mistake to underrate technology," agreed the man in khaki.

"So," Raeder said with a crisp nod. "It is possible to be quite efficient without being—" his eyes raked Hammer's stained, worn coveralls—"shoddy. When we hold the review tomorrow, it will be interesting to consider your . . . force . . . beside the Guard."

"Via, only two of my boys are in," Hammer said, "though for slickness I'd bet Joachim against anybody you've got." He looked disinterestedly at the drink dispenser. "We'll all be back in the field, as soon as I see what Tromp wants. We've got a clean-up operation mounted in the Crescent."

"There is a platoon present now," the Guardsman snapped. "It will remain, as you will remain, until you receive other orders."

Hammer walked away without answering. Bigger men silently moved aside, clearing a path to the dispenser. Raeder locked his lips, murder-tense; but a bustle at the central dropshaft caused him to spin around. His own aide, a fifteen-year-old scion of his wife's house, had emerged when the column dilated. Rather than use the PA system built into the lounge before it was commandeered as an officer's club, messages were relayed through aides waiting on the floor below. Raeder's boy carried a small flag bearing the hollow rectangle of Raeder's rank, his ticket to enter the lounge and to set him apart from the officers. The boy might well be noble, but as yet he did not have a commission. He was to be made to remember it.

He whispered with animation into Raeder's ear, his own eyes open and fixed on the mercenary officer. Hammer ignored them both, talking idly as he blended another stim cone into his blood. The blond man's face slowly took on an expression of ruddy, mottled fury.

"Hammer!"

"The next time you determine where my boys will be, Colonel Raeder, I recommend that you ask me about it."

"You traitorous scum!" Raeder blazed, utterly beyond curbing his anger. "I closed the perimeter to everyone, *everyone!* And you bull your way through my guards, get them to pass—"

"Pass *my* men, Lieutenant-Colonel!" Hammer blasted as if he were shouting orders through the howling fans of a tank. All the tension of the former confrontation shuddered in the air again. Hammer was as set and grim as one of his war cars.

Raeder raised a clenched fist.

"Touch me and I'll shoot you where you stand," the mercenary said, and he had no need to raise his voice for emphasis. As if only Raeder and not the roomful of officers as well was listening, he said, "You give what orders you please, but I've still got an independent command. As of this moment. That platoon is blocking a pass in the Crescent, because that's what I want it to do, not sit around trying to polish away bullet scars because some cop-head thinks that's a better idea than fighting."

His body still as a gravestone, Raeder spoke; "*Now* you've got a command," he said thickly.

The wing of violence lifted from the lounge. Given time to consider, every man there knew that the battle was in other hands than Raeder's now—and that it would be fought very soon.

The dropshaft hissed again.

Joachim Steuben's dress was identical in design to his colonel's, but was in every other particular far superior. The khaki was unstained, the waist-belt genuine leather, polished to a rich chestnut sheen, and the coveralls themselves tapered to follow the lines of his boyish-slim figure. Perhaps it was the very beauty of the face smoothly framing Joachim's liquid eyes that made the aide look not foppish, but softly feminine.

There was a rich urbanity as well in his careful elegance. Newland, his homeworld, was an old colony with an emphasis on civilized trappings worthy of Earth herself. Just as Joachim's uniform was of a synthetic sleeker and less rugged than Hammer's, his sidearm was hunched high on his right hip in a holster cut away to display the artistry of what it gripped. No weapon in the lounge, even that of Captain Ryssler—the Rysslers on whose land Friesland's second starport had been built—matched that of the Newlander for gorgeous detail. The receiver of the standard service pistol, a 1 cm powergun whose magazine held ten charged-plastic disks, had been gilded and carven by someone with a penchant for fleshy orchids. The stems and leaves had been filled with niello while the veins remained in a golden tracery. The petals themselves were formed from a breathtakingly purple alloy of copper and gold. It was hard for anyone who glanced at it to realize that such a work of art was still, beneath its chasing, a lethal weapon.

"Colonel," he reported, his clear tenor a jewel in the velvet silence, "Secretary Tromp will see you now." Neither he nor Hammer showed the slightest concern as to whether the others in the lounge were listening. Hammer nodded, wiping his palms on his thighs.

Behind his back, Joachim winked at Colonel Raeder before turning. The Guardsman's jaw dropped and something mewled from deep in his chest.

It may have been imagination that made Joachim's hips seem to rotate a final purple highlight from his pistol as the dropshaft sphinctered shut.

When the Guards landed, all but the fifteenth story of the Southport Tower was taken over for officers' billets. That central floor was empty save for Tromp, his staff, and the pair of scowling Guardsmen confronting the dropshaft as it opened.

"I'll stay with you, sir," Joachim said. The guards were in dress blacks but they carried full-sized shoulder weapons, 2 cm powerguns inferior only in rate of fire to the tribarrels mounted on armored vehicles.

"Go on back to our quarters," Hammer replied. He stepped off the platform. His aide showed no signs of closing the shaft in obedience. "Martyrs' *blood*!" Hammer cursed. "Do as I say!" He wiped his palms again and added, more mildly, "That's where I'll need you, I think."

"If you say so, sir." The door sighed closed behind Hammer, leaving him with the guards.

"Follow the left corridor to the end—sir," one of the big men directed grudgingly. The colonel nodded and walked off without comment. The two men were convinced their greatest worth lay in the fact that they were Guardsmen. To them it was an insult that another man would deliberately leave the Regiment, especially to take service with a band of foreign scum. Hammer could have used his glass-edged tongue on the pair as he had at the perimeter when he sent his platoon through, but there was no need. He was not the man to use any weapon for entertainment's sake.

The unmarked wood-veneer door opened before he could knock. "Why, good afternoon, Captain," the mercenary said, smiling into Stilchey's haggardness. "Recovering all right from this morning?"

"Go on through," the captain said. "He's expecting you."

Hammer closed the inner door behind him, making a soft echo to the thump of the hall panel. Tromp rose from behind his desk, a great gray bear confronting a panther.

"Colonel, be seated," he rumbled. Hammer nodded cautiously and obeyed.

"We have a few problems which must be cleared up soon," the big man said. He looked the soldier full in the face. "I'll be frank. You already know why I'm here."

"Our job's done," Hammer said without inflection. "It costs money to keep the Sl—the auxiliary regiment mobilized when it isn't needed, so it's time to bring my boys home according to contract, hey?"

The sky behind Tromp was a turgid mass, gray with harbingers of the first storm of autumn. It provided the only light in the room, but neither man moved to turn on the wall illuminators. "You were going to say 'Slammers,' weren't you?" Tromp mused. "Interesting. I had wondered if the newscasters coined the nickname themselves or if they really picked up a usage here. . . ."

"The boys started it. . . . It seemed to catch on."

"But I'm less interested in that than another word," Tromp continued with the sudden weight of an anvil falling. " 'Home.' And that's the problem, Colonel. As you know."

"The only thing I could tell you is what I tell recruits when they sign on," Hammer said, his voice quiet but his forehead sweat-gemmed in the cool air. "By their contract, they became citizens of Friesland with all rights and privileges thereof. . . . Great Dying *Lord*, sir, that's what brought most of my boys here! Look, I don't have to tell you what's been happening everywhere the past ten years, twenty— there are thousands and thousands of soldiers, good soldiers, who wound up on one losing side or another. If everybody that fought alongside them had been as good, and maybe if they'd had the equipment Friesland could buy for them . . . I tell you, sir, there's no one in the galaxy to match them. And what they fight for isn't me, I don't care what cop you've heard, it's that chance at peace, at stability that their fathers had and their father's fathers, but they lost somewhere when everything started to go wrong. They'd *die* for that chance!"

"But instead," Tromp stated, "they killed for it."

"Don't give *me* any cop about morals!" the soldier snarled. "Whose idea was it that we needed control of bluebright shipments to be sure of getting metals from Taunus?"

"Morals?" replied Tromp with a snort. "Morals be hanged, Colonel. This isn't a galaxy for men with morals, you don't have to tell me that. Oh, they can moan about what went on here and they have—but nobody, not even the reporters, has been looking very hard. And they wouldn't find many to listen if they had been. You and I are paid to get things done, Hammer, and there won't be any blame except for failure."

The soldier hunched his shoulders back against the chair. "Then it's all right?" he asked in wonder.

"After all I worried, all I planned, my boys can go back to Friesland with me?"

Tromp smiled. "Over my dead body," he said pleasantly. The two men stared at each other without expression on either side.

"I'm missing something," said Hammer flatly. "Fill me in."

The civilian rotated a flat datavisor toward Hammer and touched the indexing tab with his thumb. A montage of horror flickered across the screen—smoke drifting sullenly from a dozen low-lying buildings; a mass grave, reopened and being inspected by a trio of Frisian generals; another village without evident damage but utterly empty of human life—

"Chakma," Hammer said in sudden recognition. "Via, you ought to thank me for the way we handled that one. I'd half thought of using a nuke."

"Gassing the village was better?" the councillor asked with mild amusement.

"It was quiet. No way you could have kept reporters from learning about a nuke," Hammer explained.

"And the convoy runs you made with hostages on each car?" Tromp asked smilingly.

"The only hostages we used were people we knew—and they knew we knew—" Hammer's finger slashed emphasis—"were related to Mel soldiers who hadn't turned themselves in. We cut ambushes by a factor of ten, and we even had some busted when a Mel saw his wife or a kid riding the lead car. Look, I won't pretend it didn't happen, but I didn't make any bones about what I planned when I put in for transfer. This is bloody late in the day to bring it up."

"Right, you did your duty," the big civilian agreed. "And I'm going to do mine by refusing to open Friesland to five thousand men with the training you gave them. Lord and Martyrs, Colonel, you tell me we're going through a period when more governments are breaking up than aren't—what would happen to *our* planet if we set your animals loose in the middle of it?"

"There's twelve regiments of regulars here," Hammer argued.

"And if they were worth the cop in their trousers, we wouldn't have needed your auxiliaries," retorted Tromp inflexibly. "Face facts."

The colonel sagged. 'OK," he muttered, turning his face toward the sidewall, "I won't pretend I didn't expect it, what you just said. I owed it to the boys, they . . . they believe when they ought to have better sense, and I owed them to try. . . ." The soldier's fingers beat a silent tattoo on the yielding material of his chair. He stood before speaking further. "There's a way out of it, Secretary," he said.

"I know there is."

"No!" Hammer shouted, his voice denying the flat finality of Tromp's as he spun to face the bigger man again. "No, there's a better way, a way that'll work. You didn't want to hire one of the freelance regiments you could have had because they didn't have the equipment to do the job fast. But it takes a government and a curst solvent one to equip an armored regiment—none of the privateers had that sort of capital."

He paused for breath. "Partly true," Tromp agreed. "Of course, we preferred to have a commander—" he smiled—"whose first loyalty was to Friesland."

Hammer spoke on, choking with his effort to convince the patient, gray iceberg of a man across from him. "Friesland's always made her money by trade. Let's go into another business—let's hire out the best equipped, best trained—by the Lord, *best*—regiment in the galaxy!"

"And the reason that won't work, Colonel," Tromp rumbled coolly, "is not that it would fail, but that it would succeed. It takes a very solvent government, as you noted, to afford the capital expense of maintaining a first-rate armored regiment. The Melpomonese, for instance, could never have fielded a regiment of their own. But if . . . the sort of unit you suggest was available, they could have hired it for a time, could they not?"

"A few months, sure," Hammer admitted with an angry flick of his hands, "But—"

"Nine months, perhaps a year, Colonel," the civilian went on inexorably. "It would have bankrupted them, but I think they would have paid for the same reason they resisted what was clearly overwhelming force. And not even Friesland could have economically taken Melpomone if the locals were stiffened by—by your Slammers, let us say."

"Lord!" Hammer shouted snapping erect, "Of course we wouldn't take contracts against Friesland."

"Men change, Colonel," Tromp replied, rising to his own feet. "Men die. And even if they don't, the very existence of a successful enterprise will free the capital for others to duplicate it. It won't be a wild gamble any more. And Friesland will *not* be the cause of that state of affairs while I am at her helm. If you're the patriot we assumed you were when we gave you this command, you will order your men to come in by platoons and be disarmed."

The smaller man's face was sallow and his hands shook until he hooked them in his pistol belt. "But you can't even let them go then, can you?" he whispered. "It might be all right on Friesland where there wouldn't be any recruiting by outsiders. But if you just turn my boys loose, somebody else will snap them up, somebody else who reads balance sheets. Maybe trained personnel would be enough of an edge to pry loose equipment on the cuff. Life's rough, sure, and there are plenty of people willing to gamble a lot to make a lot more. Then we're where you didn't want us, aren't we? Except that the boys are going to have some notions of their own about Friesland. . . . What do you plan, Secretary? Blowing up the freighter with everybody aboard? Or will you just have the Guards shoot them down when they've been disarmed?"

Tromp turned away for the first time. Lightning was flashing from cloud peak to cloud peak, and the mass that lowered over the Crescent was already linked to the ground by a haze of rain. "They put us in charge of things because we see them as they are, Colonel," Tromp said. The vitril sheet in front of him trembled to the distant thunder. "Friesland got very good value from you, because you didn't avoid unpleasant decisions; you saw the best way and took it—be damned to appearances.

"I would not be where I am today if I were not the same sort of man. I don't ask you to like this course of action—I don't like it myself—but you're a pragmatist too, Hammer, you see that it's the only way clear for our own people."

"Secretary, anything short of having my boys killed, but—"

"Curse it, man!" Tromp shouted. "Haven't you taken a look around you recently? Lives are cheap, Colonel, lives are very cheap! You've got to have loyalty to something more than just men."

"No," said the man in khaki with quiet certainty. Then, "May I be excused sir?"

"Get out of here."

Tromp was seated again, his own face a mirror of the storm, when Captain Stilchey slipped in the door through which Hammer had just exited. "Your lapel mike picked it all up," the young officer said. He gloated conspiratorially. "The traitor."

Tromp's face forced itself into normal lines. "You did as I explained might be necessary?"

"Right. As soon as I heard the word 'disarmed' I ordered men to wait for Hammer in his quarters." Stilchey's gleeful expression expanded to a smile of real delight. "I added a . . . refinement, sir. There was the possibility that Hammer would—you know how he is, hard not to obey—tell the guards be cursed and leave them standing. So I took the liberty of suggesting to Colonel Raeder that he lead four men himself for the duty. I used your name, sir, but I rather think the colonel would have gone along with the idea anyway."

The captain's laughter hacked loudly through the suite before he realized that Tromp still sat in iron gloom, cradling his chin in his hands.

The room was a shifting bowl of reds and hot orange in which the khaki uniforms of Worzer and Steuben seemed misplaced. The only sound was a faint buzzing, the leakage of the bone-conduction speakers implanted in either man's right mastoid. Hammer, like Tromp, had left his lapel mike keyed to his aides.

"Get us a drink, Joe," Worzer asked. With the Slammers, you either did your job or you left, and nobody could fault Joachim's effectiveness. Still, there was a good deal of ambivalence about the Newlander in a unit made up in large measure of ex-farmers whose religious training had been fundamental if not scholarly. Tense, black-bearded Worzer got along with him better than most, perhaps because it had been a Newland ship which many years before had lifted him from Curwin and the Security Police with their questions about a bombed tax office.

Joachim stood and stretched, his eyes vacant. The walls and floor gave him a satanic cruelty that would have struck as incongruous those who knew him slightly. Yawning, he touched the lighting control, a slight concavity in the wall. The flames dulled, faded to a muted pattern of grays. The room was appreciably darker.

"Wanted you to do that all the time," Worzer grumbled. He seated himself on a bulging chair that faced the doorway.

"I liked it," Joachim said neutrally. He started for the kitchen alcove, then paused. "You'd best take your pistol off, you know. They'll be jumpy."

"You're the boss," Worzer grunts. Alone now in the room, he unlatches his holstered weapon and tosses the rig to the floor in front of him. It is a fixed blackness against the grays that shift beneath it. Glass tinkles in the kitchen. Men on every world have set up stills, generally as their first constructions. Even in a luxury hotel, Worzer's habits are those of a lifetime. Hammer's microphone no longer broadcasts voices.

The door valves open.

"Freeze!" orders the first man through. He is small and blond, his eyes as cold as the silver frosting his uniform. The glowing tab of a master door key is in his left hand, a pistol in his right. The Guardsmen fanning to each side of him swing heavy powerguns at waist level, the muzzles black screams in a glitter of iridium. Two more men stand beyond the door, facing either end of the hallway with their weapons ready.

"Move and you're dead," the officer hisses to Worzer. Then, to his tight-lipped subordinates, "Watch for the other one—the deviate."

The kitchen door rotates to pass Joachim. His left hand holds a silver tray with a fruit-garnished drink on it. Reflections shimmer from the metal and the condensate on the glass. He smiles.

"You foul *beast!*" says the officer and his pistol turns toward the aide of its own seeming will. The enlisted men wait, uncertain.

"Me, Colonel Raeder?" Joachim's voice lilts. He is raising the tray and it arcs away from his body in a gentle movement that catches Raeder's eyes for the instant that the Newlander's right hand dips and—a cyan flash from Joachim's pistol links the two men. Raeder's mouth is open but silent. His eyeballs are bulging outward against the pressure of exploding nerve tissue. There is a hole between them and it winks twice more in the flash of Joachim's shots. Two spent cases hang in the air to the Newlander's right; a third is jammed, smeared across his pistol's ejection port. None of the Guardsmen have begun to fall, though a gout of blood pours from the neck of the right-hand man.

It is two-fifths of a second from the moment Joachim reached for his pistol.

Worzer had been ready. He leaped as Steuben's shots flickered across the room, twisting the shoulder weapon from a Guardsman who did not realize he was already dead. The stocky Curwinite hit the floor on his right side, searching the doorway with the powergun. In the hall, a guard shouted as he spun himself to face the shooting. Joachim's jammed pistol had thudded on the floor but Worzer wasted no interest on what the aide might do—you didn't worry about Joachim in a firefight, he took care of himself. The noncom had been squeezing even as he fell, and only a feather of trigger pressure was left to take up when the Guardsman's glittering uniform sprouted above the sights.

Heated air thumped the walls of the room. The body ballooned under the cyan impact. The big-bore packed enough joules to vaporize much of a man's abdomen at that range, and the Frisian hurtled back against the far wall. His tunic was afire and spilling coils of intestine.

The boots of the remaining Guardsman clattered on the tile as he bolted for the dropshaft. Joachim snaked his head and the pistol he had snatched from Raeder through the doorway. Worzer and the big gun plunged into the corridor low to cover the other end. The shaft entrance opened even before the Frisian's outflung arm touched the summoning plate. Hammer, standing on the platform, shot him twice in the chest. The Guardsman pitched into the wall. As he did so, Joachim shot him again at the base of the skull. Joachim generally doubted other men's kills, a practice that had saved his life in the past.

Hammer glanced down at the jellied skull of the last Guardsman and grimaced. "Didn't anybody tell you about aiming at the body instead of getting fancy?" he asked Joachim. Neither man commented that the final shot had been aimed within a meter of Hammer.

The Newlander shrugged. "They should've been wearing body armor," he said offhandedly. "Coppy fools."

The colonel scooped up both the powerguns from the corridor and gestured his men back into the room. The air within stank of blood and hot plastic. Death had been too sudden to be prefaced with pain, but the faces of the Guardsmen all held slack amazement. Hammer shook his head. "With five thousand of you to choose from," he said to Joachim, "didn't they think I could find a decent bodyguard?"

The Newlander smiled. After his third quick shot, the expended disk had been too hot to spin out whole and had instead flowed across the mechanism when struck by the jet of ejection gas. Joachim was carefully chipping away at the cooled plastic with a stylus while the pistol he had taken from his first victim lay on the table beside him. Its muzzle had charred the veneer surface. "There isn't enough gas in a handgun ejector to cool the chamber properly," he said, pretending to ignore his colonel's indirect praise.

"Via, you hurried 'cause you wanted all of them," Worzer laughed. He thumbed a loaded round into the magazine of the shoulder gun he had appropriated. "What's the matter—don't you want the colonel to bother bringing me along the next time 'cause I scare away all your pretty friends?"

Hammer forced a smile at the interchange, but it was only a shimmer across lines of fear and anger. On one wall was a communicator, a flat, meter-broad screen whose surface was an optical pickup as well as a display. Hammer stepped in front of it and drew the curtain to blank the remainder of the room. His fingers flicked the controls, bringing Captain Stilchey into startled focus. Tromp's aide blinked, but before he could speak the colonel said, "We've got three minutes, Stilchey, and there's no time to cop around. Put me through."

Stilchey's mouth closed. Without comment he reached out and pressed his own control panel. With liquid abruptness his figure was replaced by the hulking power of Secretary Tromp, seated against the closing sky.

"Tell the Guard to ground arms, Secretary," Hammer ordered in a voice trembling with adrenalin. "Tell them now and I'll get on the horn to my boys—it'll be close."

"I'm sorry for the necessity of your arrest, Colonel," the big man began, "but—"

"Idiot!" Hammer shouted at the pickup, and his arm slashed aside the drapes to bare the room. "I heard your terms—now listen to mine. I've arranged for a freighter to land tomorrow at 0700 and the whole regiment's leaving on it. I'll leave you an indenture for the fair value of the gear, and it'll be paid off as soon as contracts start coming in. But the Lord help you, Tromp, if anybody tries to stop my boys."

"Captain Stilchey," Tromp ordered coolly, "sound general quarters. As for you, Colonel," he continued without taking verbal notice of the carnage behind the small officer, "I assure you that the possibility you planned something like this was in my mind when I ordered the Guards landed with me."

"Secretary, we planned what we'd do if we had to a month and a half ago. Don't be so curst a fool to doubt my boys can execute orders without me to hold their hands. If I don't radio in the next few seconds, you won't have the Guards to send back. Lord and *Martyrs*, man, don't you understand what you see back of me? This isn't some coppy parade!"

"Sir," came Stilchey's thin voice from offscreen, "Fire Central reports all satellite signals are being jammed. The armored units in the Crescent began assembling thirty—Lord! Lord! *Sir!*"

A huge scarlet dome swelled upward across the vitril behind Tromp. The window powdered harmlessly an instant later as the shock wave threw man and desk toward Hammer's image. The entire hotel shuddered to the blast.

"They're blowing up the artillery," the captain bleated. "The ammunition—" His words were drowned in the twin detonations of the remaining batteries.

Hammer switched the communicator off. "Early," he muttered. "Not that it mattered!" His face was set like that of a man who had told his disbelieving mechanic that something was wrong with the brakes, and who now feels the pedal sink to the firewall to prove him fatally correct. "Don't go to sleep," he grunted to his companions. "Tromp knows he's lost, and I'm not sure how he'll react."

But only Worzer was in the room with him.

Though Tromp was uninjured, he rose only to his knees. He had seen Captain Stilchey when the jagged sheet of iridium buzz-sawed into the suite and through him. Scuttling like a stiff-legged bear, the civilian made his way to the private dropshaft built into the room. He pretended to ignore the warm greasiness of the floor, but by the time the platform began to sink his whole body was trembling.

Ground floor was a chaos of half-dressed officers who had been on the way to their units when fire raked the encampment. Tromp pushed through a trio of chattering captains in the branch corridor; the main lobby of bronze and off-planet stonework was packed and static, filled with men afraid to go out and uncertain where to hide. The councillor cursed. The door nearest him was ajar and he kicked it fully open. The furniture within was in sleep-mode, the self-cleaning sheets rumpled on the bed, but there was no one present. The vitril outer wall had pulverized; gouges in the interior suggested more than a shock wave had been responsible for the damage.

Seen through it, the starport had become a raving hell.

Four hundred meters from the hotel, one of the anti-artillery weapons was rippling sequential flame skyward from its eight barrels. High in a boiling thunderhead at its radar-chosen point of aim, man-made lightning flared magenta: high explosive caught in flight. Almost simultaneously a dart of cyan more intense than the sun lanced into the Guard vehicle. Metal heated too swiftly to melt and sublimed in a glowing ball that silhouetted the gun crew as it devoured them. Hammer's tanks, bunkered in the Crescent, were using satellite-computed deflections to rake the open Guard positions. Twenty kilometers and the thin armor of the lighter vehicles were no defense against the 200 mm powerguns.

Tromp stepped over the low sill and began to run. The field was wet and a new slash of rain pocked its gleam. Three shells popped high in the air. He ignored them, pounding across the field in a half-crouch. For a moment the whistling beginning to fill the sky as if from a thousand tiny mouths meant nothing to him either—then realization rammed a scream from his throat and he threw himself prone. The bomblets showering down from the shells went off on impact all across the field, orange flashes that each clipped the air with scores of fragments. Panic and Hammer's tanks had silenced the Guard's defensive weaponry. Now the rocket howitzers were free to rain in wilful death.

But the tanks, Tromp thought as he stumbled to his feet, they can't knock out the tanks from twenty kilometers and they can't capture the port while the Guard still has that punch. The surprise was over now. Lift fans keened from the perimeter as the great silvery forms of armored vehicles shifted from their targeted positions. The combatants were equal, and a stand-off meant disaster for the mercenaries.

Much of the blood staining Tromp's clothing was his own, licked from his veins by shrapnel. Incoming shells were bursting at ten-second intervals. Munitions shortages would force a slowdown soon, but for the moment anyone who stood to run would be scythed down before his third step. Even flat on his belly Tromp was being stung by hot metal. His goal, the ten-place courier vessel that had brought him to Melpomone, was still hopelessly far off. The remains, however, of one of the Guard's self-propelled howitzers lay like a cleat-kicked drink-can thirty meters distant. Painfully the councillor crawled into its shelter. Hammer's punishing fire had not been directed at the guns themselves but at the haulers in the midst of each battery. After three shots, the secondary explosions had stripped the Guard of all its ill-sited artillery.

A line of rain rippled across the field, streaking dried blood from Tromp's face and whipping the pooled water. He was not running away. There was one service yet that he could perform for Friesland, and he had to be home to accomplish it. After that—and he thought of it not as revenge but as a final duty—he would not care that reaction would assuredly make him the scapegoat for the catastrophe now exploding all around him. It was obvious that Hammer had ordered his men to disturb the spaceport as little as possible so that the mercenaries would not hinder their own embarkation. The lightly rattling shrapnel crumpled gun crews and the bewildered Guard infantry, but it would not harm the port facilities themselves or the ships docked there.

For the past several minutes no powerguns had lighted the field. The bunkered mercenaries had either completed their programs or ceased fire when a lack of secondary explosions informed them that the remaining Guard vehicles had left their targeted positions. The defenders had at first fired wild volleys at no better target than the mountain range itself, but a few minutes' experience had taught them that the return blasts aimed at their muzzles were far more effective than their own could possibly be. Now there was a lull in the shelling as well.

Tromp eased a careful glance beyond the rim of his shelter, the buckled plenum chamber of the gun carriage. His ship was a horizontal needle three hundred meters distant. The vessel was unlighted, limned as a gray shadow by cloud-hopping lightning. The same flashes gleamed momentarily on the wet turtle-backs of a dozen tanks and combat cars in a nearby cluster, their fans idling. All the surviving Guard units must be clumped in similar hedgehogs across the port.

The big man tensed himself to run; then the night popped and crackled as a Guard tank began firing out into the storm. Tromp counted three shots before a cyan dazzle struck the engaged vehicle amidships and its own ammunition went off with an electric crash. The clustered vehicles were lit by a blue-green fire that expanded for three seconds, dissolving everything within twenty meters of its center. One of the remaining combat cars spun on howling fans, but it collapsed around another bolt before it could pull clear. There were Guardsmen on the ground now, running from their vehicles. Tromp's eyes danced with afterimages of the exploding tank, and for the first time he understood why Stilchey had been so terrified by the destruction of the car he might have ridden in.

Half a dozen shots ripped from beyond the perimeter and several struck home together. All the Guard blowers were burning now, throwing capering shadows beyond the councillor's shelter. Then, thread-

ing their way around the pools of slag, the steam and
the dying fires, came a trio of tanks. Even without
the scarlet wand wavering from each turret for iden-
tification, Tromp would have realized these were not
the polished beauties of the Guard. The steel skirts
of their plenum chambers were rusty and brushworn.
One's gouged turret still glowed where a heavy
powergun had hit it glancingly; the muzzle of its own
weapon glowed too, and the bubbling remains of the
perimeter defense left no doubt whose bolts had
been more accurately directed. The fighting had been
brief, Hammer's platoons meeting the disorganized
Guardsmen with pointblank volleys. The victors'
hatches were open and as they swept in toward the
central tower, Tromp could hear their radios crackling triumphant instructions. Other wands floated
across the immense field, red foxfire in the rain.

The shooting had stopped. Now, before the combat cars and infantry followed up the penetrations
their tanks had made, Tromp stood and ran to his
ship. His career was ruined, of that he had no doubt.
No amount of deceit would cover his role in the
creation of the Slammers or his leadership in the
attempted suppression. All that was left to Nicholas
Tromp was the sapphire determination that the national power which he had worked four decades to
build should not fall with him. They could still smash
Hammer before he got started, using Friesland's own
fleet and the fleets of a dozen other worlds. The cost
would leave even Friesland groaning, but they could
blast the Slammers inexorably from space wherever
they were landed. For the sake of his planet's future,
the excision had to be made, damn the cost.

And after Tromp fell in disgrace in the next week
or two weeks at most, there would be no man left
with the power to force the action or the foresight to

see its necessity. Panting, he staggered through his vessel's open lock. The interior, too, was unlighted. That was not surprising in view of the combat outside, but one of the three crewmen should have been waiting at the lock. "Where are you?" Tromp called angrily.

The lights went on. There was a body at the big Frisian's feet. From the cockpit forward stretched another hairline of blood still fresh enough to ooze. "I'm here," said a cultured voice from behind.

Tromp froze. Very slowly, he began to turn his head.

"People like you," the voice continued, "with dreams too big for men to fit into, don't see the same sort of world that the rest of us do. And sometimes a fellow who does one job well can see where his job has to be done, even though a better man has overlooked it. Anyhow, Secretary, there always was one thing you and I could agree on—lives *are* cheap."

Surely Joachim's wrists were too slim, Tromp thought, to raise his heavy pistol so swiftly.

Interlude:
Supertanks

TANKS WERE BORN in the muck and wire of World War One. Less than sixty years later, there were many who believed that technology had made the behemoths as obsolete as horse cavalry. Individual infantrymen of 1970 carried missiles whose warheads burned through the armor of any tank. Slightly larger missiles ranged kilometers to blast with pinpoint accuracy vehicles costing a thousand times as much. Similar weaponry was mounted on helicopters which skimmed battlefields in the nape of the earth, protected by terrain irregularities. At the last instant the birds could pop up to rip tanks with their missiles. The future of armored vehicles looked bleak and brief.

Technology had dragged the tank to the brink of abandonment. Not surprisingly, it was technology again which brought the panzers back. The primary breakthrough was the development of portable fusion power plants. Just as the gasoline engine with its high horsepower-to-weight ratio had been necessary before the first tanks could take the field, so the fusion unit's almost limitless output was required to move the mass which made the new supertanks viable. Fusion units were bulky and moderately heavy themselves, but loads could be increased on a fusion-powered chassis with almost no degradation of performance. Armor became thick—and thicker. With the whole galaxy available as a source of ores, iridium replaced the less effective steels and ceramics without regard for weight.

Armor alone is not adequate protection. Stationary fortresses can always be battered down—as the French learned in 1940, having forgotten the lesson Caesar taught their ancestors at Alesia two millennia before. Caterpillar treads had given the first tanks cross-country ability; but at the cost of slow speed, frequent breakage, and great vulnerability to attack. Now that power was no longer a factor, even the armored bulk of a tank could be mounted on an air cushion.

The air cushion principle is a very simple one. Fans fill the plenum chamber, a solid-skirted box under a vehicle, with air under pressure. To escape, the air must lift the edges of the skirts off the ground—and with the skirts, the whole vehicle rises. Fans tilt with the velocity and angle of attack of the blades determine the amount and direction of thrust. The vehicle skims over surfaces it does not touch.

On tanks and combat cars, the lift was provided by batteries of fans mounted on the roof of the plenum chamber. Each fan had its own armored nacelle. Mines could still do considerable damage; but while a single broken track block would deadline a tracked vehicle, a wrecked fan only made a blower a little more sluggish.

Successful protection for the supertanks went beyond armor and speed. Wire-guided missiles are still faster, and their shaped-charge warheads can burn holes in any practical thickness of any conceivable material—if they are allowed to hit. Reconnaissance satellites, computer fire control, and powerguns combined to claw missiles out of the air before they were dangerous. The satellites spotted missile launchers, usually before they fired and never later than the moment of ignition. Fire control computers, using data from the satellites, locked defensive weaponry on the missiles in microseconds. And a single light-swift tribarrel could hose any missile with enough fire in its seconds of flight to disintegrate it.

Hand-launched, unguided rockets—buzzbombs—were another problem, and in some ways a more dangerous one despite their short range and small bursting charges. Individual infantrymen fired them from such short ranges that not even a computer had time enough to lay a gun on the little rockets. But even here there was an answer—beyond the impossible one of killing every enemy before he came within two hundred meters.

Many armored vehicles were already fitted with a band of anti-personnel directional mines just above the skirts. Radar detonated the mines when an object came within a set distance. Their blast of shrapnel was designed to stop infantry at close quarters. With only slight modification, the system could be adapted against buzzbombs. It was not perfect, since the pellets were far less destructive than powergun bolts, and the mines could not be used in close terrain which would itself set them off. Still, buzzbombs were apt to be ill-aimed in the chaos of battle, and a tank's armor could shrug off all but a direct hit by the small warheads.

So tanks roamed again as lords of battle, gray-gleaming phoenixes on air cushions. Their guns could defeat the thickest armor, their armor could blunt all but the most powerful attacks. They were fast enough to range continents in days, big enough to carry a battery of sensors and weaponry which made them impossible to escape when they hunted. The only real drawback to the supertanks was their price.

A tank's fire control, its precisely metered lift fans, the huge iridium casting that formed its turret—all were constructs of the highest sophistication. In all the human galaxy there were probably no more than a dozen worlds capable of manufacturing war tools as perfect as the panzers of Hammer's tank companies.

But Hammer paid for the best, man and tank alike; and out of them he forged the cutting edge of a weapon no enemy seemed able to stop.

The Butcher's Bill

"YOU CAN go a thousand kays any direction there and there's nothing to see but the wheat," said the brown man to the other tankers and the woman. His hair was deep chestnut, his face and hands burnt umber from the sun of Emporion the month before and the suns of seven other worlds in past years. He was twenty-five but looked several years older. The sleeves of his khaki coveralls were slipped down over his wrists against the chill of the breeze that had begun at twilight to feather the hillcrest. "We fed four planets from Dunstan—Hagener, Weststar, Mirage, and Jackson's Glade. And out of it we made enough to replace the tractors when they wore out, maybe something left over for a bit of pretty. A necklace of fireballs to set off a Lord's Day dress, till the charge drained six, eight months later. A static cleaner from Hagener, it was one year, never quite

50

worked off our powerplant however much we tinkered with it. . . .

"My mother, she wore out too. Dad just kept grinding on, guess he still does."

The girl asked a question from the shelter of the tank's scarred curtain. Her voice was too mild for the wind's tumbling, her accent that of Thrush and strange to the tanker's ears. But Danny answered, "Hate them? Oh, I know about the Combine, now, that the four of them kept other merchants off Dunstan to freeze the price at what they thought to pay. But Via, wheat's a high bulk cargo, there's no way at all we'd have gotten rich on what it could bring over ninety minutes' transit. And why shouldn't I thank Weststar? If ever a world did me well, it was that one."

He spat, turning his head with the wind and lofting the gobbet invisibly into the darkness. The lamp trembled on its base, an overturned ration box. The glare skippered across the rusted steel skirts of the tank, the iridium armor of hull and turret; the faces of the men and the woman listening to the blower chief. The main gun, half shadowed by the curve of the hull, poked out into the night like a ghost of itself. Even with no human in the tank, at the whisper of a relay in Command Central the fat weapon would light the world cyan and smash to lava anything within line of sight of its muzzle.

"We sold our wheat to a Weststar agent, a Hindi named Sarim who'd lived, Via, twenty years at least on Dunstan but he still smelled funny. Sweetish, sort of; you know? But his people were all back in Ongole on Weststar. When the fighting started between the Scots and the Hindi settlers, he raised a battalion of farm boys like me and shipped us over in the hold of a freighter. Hoo Lordy, that was a transit!

"And I never looked back. Colonel Hammer docked in on the same day with the Regiment, and he took us all on spec. Six years, now, that's seven standard . . . and not all of us could stand the gaff, and not all who could wanted to. But I never looked back, and I never will."

From the mast of Command Central, a flag popped unseen in the wind. It bore a red lion rampant on a field of gold, the emblem of Hammer's Slammers, the banner of the toughest regiment that ever killed for a dollar.

"Hotel, Kitchen, Lariat, Michael, move to the front in company columns and advance."

The tiny adamantine glitter winking on the hilltop ten kays distant was the first break in the landscape since the Regiment had entered the hypothetical war zone, the Star Plain of Thrush. It warmed Pritchard in the bubble at the same time it tightened his muscles. "Goose it, Kowie," he ordered his driver in turn, "they want us panzers up front. Bet it's about to drop in the pot?"

Kowie said nothing, but the big blower responded with a howl and a billow of friable soil that seethed from under the ground effect curtain. Two Star in the lead, H Company threaded its way in line ahead through the grounded combat cars and a company from Infantry Section. The pongoes crouched on their one-man skimmers, watching the tanks. One blew an ironic kiss to Danny in Two Star's bubble. Moving parallel to Hotel, the other companies of Tank Section, K, L, and M, advanced through the center and right of the skirmish line.

The four man crew of a combat car nodded unsmilingly from their open-topped vehicle as Two Star boomed past. A trio of swivel-mounted powerguns,

2 cm hoses like the one on Danny's bubble, gave them respectable firepower; and their armor, a sandwich of ceramics and iridium, was in fact adequate against most hand weapons. Buzzbombs aside, and tankers didn't like to think about those either. But Danny would have fought reassignment to combat cars if anybody had suggested it—Lord, you may as well dance in your skin for all the good that hull does you in a firefight! And few car crewmen would be caught dead on a panzer—or rather, were sure that was how they would be caught if they crewed one of those sluggish, clumsy, blind-sided behemoths. Infantry Section scorned both, knowing how the blowers drew fire but couldn't flatten in the dirt when it dropped in on them.

One thing wouldn't get you an argument, though: when it was ready to drop in the pot, you sent in the heavies. And nothing on the Way would stop the Tank Section of Hammer's Slammers when it got cranked up to move.

Even its 170 tonnes could not fully dampen the vibration of Two Star's fans at max load. The oval hull, all silvery-smooth above but of gouged and rusty steel below where the skirts fell sheer almost to the ground, slid its way through the grass like a boat through yellow seas. They were dropping into a swale before they reached the upgrade. From the increasing rankness of the vegetation that flattened before and beside the tank, Pritchard suspected they would find a meandering stream at the bottom. The brow of the hill cut off sight of the unnatural glitter visible from a distance. In silhouette against the pale bronze sky writhed instead a grove of gnarled trees.

"Incoming, fourteen seconds to impact," Command Central blatted. A siren in the near distance underscored the words. "Three rounds only."

The watercourse was there. Two Star's fans blasted its surface into a fine mist as the tank bellowed over it. Danny cocked his powergun, throwing a cylinder of glossy black plastic into the lowest of the three rotating barrels. There was shrieking overhead.

WHAM

A poplar shape of dirt and black vapor spouted a kay to the rear, among the grounded infantry.

WHAM WHAM

They were detonating underground. Thrush didn't have much of an industrial base, the rebel portions least of all. Either they hadn't the plant to build proximity fuses at all, or they were substituting interference coils for miniature radar sets, and there was too little metal in the infantry's gear to set off the charges. With the main director out, Central wasn't even bothering to explode the shells in flight.

"Tank Section, hose down the ridge as you advance, they got an OP there somewhere."

"Incoming, three more in fourteen." The satellite net could pick up a golf ball in flight, much less a two hundred kilo shell.

Pritchard grinned like a death's head, laying his 2 cm automatic on the rim of the hill and squeezing off. The motor whirred, spinning the barrels as rock and vegetation burst in the blue-green sleet. Spent cases, gray and porous, spun out of the mechanism in a jet of coolant gas. They bounced on the turret slope, some clinging to the iridium to cool there, ugly dark excrescences on the metal.

"Outgoing."

Simultaneously with Central's laconic warning, giants tore a strip off the sky. The rebel shells dropped but their bursts were smothered in the roar of the Regiment's own rocket howitzers boosting charges to titanic velocity for the several seconds before their motors burned out. Ten meters from the muzzles the rockets went supersonic, punctuating the ripping sound with thunderous slaps. Danny swung his hose toward the grove of trees, the only landmark visible on the hilltop. His burst laced it cyan. Water, flash-heated within the boles by the gunfire, blew the dense wood apart in blasts of steam and splinters. A dozen other guns joined Pritchard's, clawing at rock, air, and the remaining scraps of vegetation.

"Dead on," Central snapped to the artillery. "Now give it battery five and we'll show those freaks how they should've done it."

Kowie hadn't buttoned up. His head stuck up from the driver's hatch, trusting his eyes rather than the vision blocks built into his compartment. The tanks themselves were creations of the highest technical competence, built on Terra itself; but the crews were generally from frontier worlds, claustrophobic in an armored coffin no matter how good its electronic receptors were. Danny knew the feeling. His hatch, too, was open, and his hand gripped the rounded metal of the powergun itself rather than the selsyn unit inside. They were climbing sharply now, the back end hopping and skittering as the driver fed more juice to the rear fans in trying to level the vehicle. The bow skirts grounded briefly, the blades spitting out a section of hillside as pebbles.

For nearly a minute the sky slammed and raved. Slender, clipped-off vapor trails of counter-battery fire streamed from the defiladed artillery. Half a minute after they ceased fire, the drumbeat of shells bursting on the rebels continued. No further incoming rounds fell.

Two Star lurched over the rim of the hill. Seconds later the lead blowers of K and M bucked in turn onto the flatter area. Smoke and ash from the gun-lit brushfire shoomped out in their downdrafts. There was no sign of the enemy, either Densonite rebels or Foster's crew—though if the mercenaries were involved, they would be bunkered beyond probable notice until they popped the cork themselves.

"Tank Section, ground! Ground in place and prepare for director control."

Danny hunched, bracing his palms against the hatch coaming. Inside the turret the movement and firing controls of the main gun glowed red, indicating that they had been locked out of Pritchard's command. Kowie lifted the bow to kill the tank's immense inertia. There was always something spooky about feeling the turret purr beneath you, watching the big gun snuffle the air with deadly precision on its own. Danny gripped his tribarrel, scanning the horizon nervously. It was worst when you didn't know what Central had on its mind . . . and you did know that the primary fire control computer was on the fritz— they always picked the damnedest times!

"Six aircraft approaching from two-eight-three degrees," Central mumbled. "Distance seven point ought four kays, closing at one one ought ought."

Pritchard risked a quick look away from where the gun pointed toward a ridgeline northwest of them, an undistinguished swelling half-obscured by the heat-wavering pall of smoke. Thirteen other tanks had crested the hill before Central froze them, all aiming in the same direction. Danny dropped below his hatch rim, counting seconds.

The sky roared cyan. The tank's vision blocks blanked momentarily, but the dazzle reflected through the open hatch was enough to make Pritchard's skin tingle. The smoke waved and rippled about the superheated tracks of gunfire. The horizon to the northwest was an expanding orange dome that silently dominated the sky.

"Resume advance." Then, "Spectroanalysis indicates five hostiles were loaded with chemical explosives, one was carrying fissionables."

Danny was trembling worse than before the botched attack. The briefing cubes had said the Densonites were religious nuts, sure. But to use unsupported artillery against a force whose satellite spotters would finger the guns before the first salvo landed; aircraft— probably converted cargo haulers—thrown against director-controlled powerguns that shot light swift and line straight; and then nukes, against a regiment more likely to advance stark naked than without a nucleardamper up! They weren't just nuts—Thrush central government was that, unwilling to have any of its own people join the fighting—they were as crazy as if they thought they could breathe vacuum and live. You didn't play that sort of game with the Regiment.

They'd laager for the night on the hilltop, the rest of the outfit rumbling in through the afternoon and early evening hours. At daybreak they'd leapfrog forward again, deeper into the Star Plain, closer to whatever it was the Densonites wanted to hold. Sooner or later, the rebels and Foster's Infantry—a good outfit but not good enough for this job—were going to have to make a stand. And then the Regiment would go out for contact again, because they'd have run out of work on Thrush.

"She'll be in looking for you pretty soon, won't she, handsome?"

"Two bits to stay."

"Check. Sure, Danny-boy, you Romeos from Dunstan, you can pick up a slot anywhere, huh?"

A troop of combat cars whined past, headed for their position in the laager. Pritchard's hole card, a jack, flipped over. He swore, pushed in his hand. "I was folding anyway. And cut it out, will you? I didn't go looking for her. I didn't tell her to come back. And she may as well be the colonel for all my chance of putting her flat."

Wanatamba, the lean, black Terran who drove Fourteen, laughed and pointed. A gold-spangled skimmer was dropping from the east, tracked by the guns of two of the blowers on that side. Everybody knew what it was, though. Pritchard grimaced and stood. "Seems that's the game for me," he said.

"Hey, Danny," one of the men behind him called as he walked away. "Get a little extra for us, hey?"

The skimmer had landed in front of Command Central, at rest an earth-blended geodesic housing the staff and much of the commo hardware. Wearing a wrist-to-ankle sunsuit, yellow where it had tone, she was leaning on the plex windscreen. An officer in fatigues with unlatched body armor stepped out of the dome and did a double take. He must have recollected, though, because he trotted off toward a bunker before Danny reached the skimmer.

"Hey!" the girl called brightly. She looked about seventeen, her hair an unreal cascade of beryl copper over one shoulder. "We're going on a trip."

"Uh?"

The dome section flipped open again. Pritchard stiffened to attention when he saw the short, mustached figure who exited. "Peace, Colonel," the girl said.

"Peace, Sonna. You're such an ornament to a firebase that I'm thinking of putting you on requisition for our next contract."

Laughing cheerfully, the girl gestured toward the

rigid sergeant. "I'm taking Danny to the Hamper Shrine this afternoon."

Pritchard reddened. "Sir, Sergeant-Commander Daniel Pritchard—"

"I know you, trooper," the colonel said with a friendly smile. "I've watched Two Star in action often enough, you know." His eyes were blue.

"Sir, I didn't request—that is . . ."

"And I also know there's small point in arguing with our girl here, hey, Sonna? Go see your shrine, soldier, and worse comes to worst, just throw your hands up and yell 'Exchange.' You can try Colonel Foster's rations for a week or two until we get this little business straightened out." The colonel winked, bowed low to Sonna, and reentered the dome.

"I don't figure it," Danny said as he settled into the passenger seat. The skimmer was built low and sleek as if a racer, though its top speed was probably under a hundred kays. Any more would have put too rapid a drain of the rechargables packed into the decimeter-thick floor—a fusion unit would have doubled the flyer's bulk and added four hundred kilos right off the bat. At that, the speed and an operating altitude of thirty meters were more than enough for the tanker. You judge things by what you're used to, and the blower chief who found himself that far above the cold, hard ground—it could happen on a narrow switchback—had seen his last action.

While the wind whipped noisily about the open cockpit, the girl tended to her flying and ignored Danny's curiosity. It was a hop rather than a real flight, keeping over the same hill at all times and circling down to land scarcely a minute after takeoff. On a field of grass untouched by the recent fire rose the multi-tented crystalline structure Pritchard had glimpsed during the assault. With a neat spin and a brief whine from the fans, the skimmer settled down.

Sonna grinned. Her sunsuit, opaquing completely in the direct light, blurred her outline in a dazzle of fluorescent saffron. "What don't you figure?"

"Well, ah . . ." Danny stumbled, his curiosity drawn between the girl and the building. "Well, the colonel isn't that, ah, easy to deal with usually. I mean . . ."

Her laugh bubbled in the sunshine. "Oh, it's because I'm an Advisor, I'm sure."

"Excuse?"

"An Advisor. You know, the . . . well, a representative. Of the government, if you want to put it that way."

"My Lord!" the soldier gasped. "But you're so young."

She frowned. "You really don't know much about us, do you?" she reflected.

"Umm, well, the briefing cubes mostly didn't deal with the friendlies this time because we'd be operating without support. . . . Anything was going to look good after Emporion, that was for sure. All desert there—you should've heard the cheers when the colonel said that we'd lift."

She combed a hand back absently through her hair. It flowed like molten bronze. "You won on Emporion?" she asked.

"We could've," Danny explained, "even though it was really a Lord-stricken place, dust and fortified plateaus and lousy recce besides because the government had two operating spacers. But the Monarchists ran out of money after six months and that's one sure rule for Hammer's Slammers—no pay, no play. Colonel yanked their bond so fast their ears rang. And we hadn't orbited before offers started coming in."

"And you took ours and came to a place you didn't know much about," the girl mused. "Well, we didn't know much about you either."

"What do you need to know except we can bust anybody else in this business?" the soldier said with amusement. "Anybody, public or planet-tied. If you're worried about Foster, don't; he wouldn't back the freaks today, but when he has to, we'll eat him for breakfast."

"Has to?" the girl repeated in puzzlement. "But he always has to—the Densonites hired him, didn't they?"

Strategy was a long way from Danny's training, but the girl seemed not to know that. And besides, you couldn't spend seven years with the Slammers and not pick up some basics. "OK," he began, "Foster's boys'll fight, but they're not crazy. Trying to block our advance in open land like this'd be pure suicide—as those coppy freaks—pardon, didn't mean that—must've found out today. Foster likely got orders to support the civvies but refused. I know for a fact that his arty's better'n what we wiped up today, and those *planes* . . ."

"But his contract . . . ?" Sonna queried.

"Sets out the objectives and says the outfit'll obey civvie orders where it won't screw things up too bad," Danny said. "Standard form. The legal of it's different, but that's what it means."

The girl was nodding, eyes slitted, and in a low voice she quoted, ". . . 'except in circumstances where such directions would significantly increase the risks to be undergone by the party of the second part without corresponding military advantage.'" She looked full at Danny. "Very . . . interesting. When we hired your colonel, I don't think any of us understood that clause."

Danny blinked, out of his depth and aware of it. "Well, it doesn't matter really. I mean, the colonel didn't get his rep from ducking fights. It's just, well . . . say we're supposed to clear the Densonites off the, the Star Plain? Right?"

The girl shrugged.

"So that's what we'll do." Danny wiped his palms before gesturing with both hands. "But if your Advisors—"

"We Advisors," the girl corrected, smiling.

"Anyway," the tanker concluded, his enthusiasm chilled, "if you tell the colonel to fly the whole Regiment up to ten thousand and jump it out, he'll tell you to go piss up a rope. Sorry, he wouldn't say that. But you know what I mean. We know our job, don't worry."

"Yes, that's true," she said agreeably. "And we don't, and we can't understand it. We thought that— one to one, you know?—perhaps if I got to know you, one of you . . . They thought we might understand all of you a little."

The soldier frowned uncertainly.

"What we don't see," she finally said, "is how you—"

She caught herself. Touching her cold fingertips to the backs of the tanker's wrists, the girl continued, "Danny, you're a nice . . . you're not a, a sort of monster like we thought you all must be. If you'd been born of Thrush you'd have had a—different— education, you'd be more, forgive me, I don't mean it as an insult, sophisticated in some ways. That's all.

"But how can a nice person like you go out and kill?"

He rubbed his eyes, then laced together his long,

brown fingers. "You . . . well, it's not like that. What I said the other night—look, the Slammers're a good outfit, the best, and I'm damned lucky to be with them. I do my job the best way I know. I'll keep on doing that. And if somebody gets killed, OK. My brother Jig stayed home and he's two years dead now. Tractor rolled on a wet field but Via, coulda been a tow-chain snapped or old age; doesn't matter. He wasn't going to live forever and neither is anybody else. And I haven't got any friends on the far end of the muzzle."

Her voice was very soft as she said, "Perhaps if I keep trying . . ."

Danny smiled. "Well, I don't mind," he lied, looking at the structure. "What is this place, anyhow?"

Close up, it had unsuspected detail. The sides were a hedge of glassy rods curving together to a series of peaks ten meters high. No finger-slim member was quite the thickness or color of any other, although the delicacy was subliminal in impact. In ground plan it was a complex oval thirty meters by ten, pierced by scores of doorways which were not closed off but were foggy to look at.

"What do you think of it?" the girl asked.

"Well, it's . . ." Danny temporized. A fragment of the briefing cubes returned to him. "It's one of the alien, the Gedel, artifacts, isn't it?"

"Of course," the girl agreed. "Seven hundred thousand years old, as far as we can judge. Only a world in stasis, like Thrush, would have let it survive the way it has. The walls are far tougher than they look, but seven hundred millennia of earthquakes and volcanoes . . ."

Danny stepped out of the skimmer and let his hand run across the building's cool surface. "Yeah, if they'd picked some place with a hotter core there wouldn't be much left but sand by now, would there?"

"Pick it? Thrush was their home," Sonna's voice rang smoothly behind him. "The Gedel chilled it themselves to make it suitable, to leave a signpost for the next races following the Way. We can't even imagine how they did it, but there's no question but that Thrush was normally tectonic up until the last million years or so."

"Via!" Danny breathed, turning his shocked face toward the girl. "No wonder those coppy fanatics wanted to control this place. Why, if they could figure out just a few of the Gedel tricks they'd . . . Lord, they wouldn't stop with Thrush, that's for sure."

"You still don't understand," the girl said. She took Danny by the hand and drew him toward the nearest of the misty doorways. "The Densonites have, well, quirks that make them hard for the rest of us on Thrush to understand. But they would no more pervert Gedel wisdom to warfare than you would, oh, spit on your colonel. Come here."

She stepped into the fuzziness and disappeared. The tanker had no choice but to follow or break her grip; though, oddly, she was no longer clinging to him on the other side of the barrier. She was not even beside him in the large room. He was alone at the first of a line of tableaux, staring at a group of horribly inhuman creatures at play. Their sharp-edged faces, scale-dusted but more avian than reptile, stared enraptured at one of their number who hung in the air. The acrobat's bare, claw-tipped legs pointed 180 degrees apart, straight toward ground and sky.

Pritchard blinked and moved on. The next scene was only a dazzle of sunlight in a glade whose foliage was redder than that of Thrush or Dunstan. There was something else, something wrong or strange about the tableau. Danny felt it, but his eyes could not explain.

Step by step, cautiously, Pritchard worked his way down the line of exhibits. Each was different, centered on a group of the alien bipeds or a ruddy, seemingly empty landscape that hinted unintelligibly. At first, Danny had noticed the eerie silence inside the hall. As he approached the far end he realized he was conscious of music of some sort, very crisp and distant. He laid his bare palm on the floor and found, as he had feared, that it did not vibrate in the least. He ran the last twenty steps to plunge out into the sunlight. Sonna still gripped his hand, and they stood outside the doorway they had entered.

The girl released him. "Isn't it incredible?" she asked, her expression bright. "And every one of the doorways leads to a different corridor—recreation there, agriculture in another, history—everything. A whole planet in that little building."

"That's what the Gedel looked like, huh?" Danny said. He shook his head to clear the strangeness from it.

"The Gedel? Oh, no," the girl replied, surprised again at his ignorance. "These were the folk we call the Hampers. No way to pronounce their own language, a man named Hamper found this site is all. But their homeworld was Kalinga IV, almost three days transit from Thrush. The shrine is here, we think, in the same relation to Starhome as Kalinga was to Thrush.

"You still don't understand," she concluded aloud, watching Danny's expression. She sat on the edge of the flyer, crossing her hands on the lap of her sunsuit. In the glitter thrown by the structure the fabric patterned oddly across her lithe torso. "The Gedel association—it wasn't an empire, couldn't have been.

But to merge, a group ultimately needs a center, physical and intellectual. And Thrush and the Gedel were that for twenty races.

"And they achieved genuine unity, not just within one race but among all of them, each as strange to the others as any one of them would have been to man, to us. The . . . power that gave them, over themselves as well as the universe, was incredible. This—even Starhome itself—is such a tiny part of what could be achieved by perfect peace and empathy."

Danny looked at the crystal dome and shivered at what it had done to him. "Look," he said, "peace is just great if the universe cooperates. I don't mean just my line of work, but it doesn't happen that way in the real world. There's no peace spending your life beating wheat out of Dunstan, not like I'd call peace. And what's happened to the Gedel and their buddies for the last half million years or so if things were so great?"

"We can't even imagine what happened to them," Sonna explained gently, "but it wasn't the disaster you imagine. When they reached what they wanted, they set up this, Starhome, the other eighteen shrines as . . . monuments. And then they went away, all together. But they're not wholly gone, even from here, you know. Didn't you feel them in the background inside, laughing with you?"

"I . . ." Danny attempted. He moved, less toward the skimmer than away from the massive crystal behind him. "Yeah, there was something. That's what you're fighting for?"

You couldn't see the laager from where the skimmer rested, but Danny could imagine the silvery glitter of tanks and combat cars between the sky and the raw yellow grass. Her eyes fixed on the same stretch of horizon, the girl said, "Someday men will be able to walk through Starhome and understand. You can't live on Thrush without feeling the impact of the Gedel. That impact has . . . warped, perhaps, the Densonites. They have some beliefs about the Gedel that most of us don't agree with. And they're actually willing to use force to prevent the artifacts from being defiled by anyone who doesn't believe as they do."

"Well, you people do a better job of using force," Danny said. His mind braced itself on its memory of the Regiment's prickly hedgehog.

"Oh, not us!" the girl gasped.

Suddenly angry, the tanker gestured toward the unseen firebase. "Not you? The Densonites don't pay us. And if force isn't what happened to those silly bastards today when our counter-battery hit them, I'd like to know what is."

She looked at him in a way that, despite her previous curiosity, was new to him. "There's much that I'll have to discuss with the other Advisors," she said after a long pause. "And I don't know that it will stop with us, we'll have to put out the call to everyone, the Densonites as well if they will come." Her eyes caught Danny's squarely again. "We acted with little time for deliberation when the Densonites hired Colonel Foster and turned all the other pilgrims out of the Star Plain. And we acted in an area beyond our practice—thank the Lord! The key to understanding the Gedel and joining them, Lord willing and the Way being short, is Starhome. And nothing that blocks any man, all men, from Starhome can be . . . tolerated. But with what we've learned since . . . well, we have other things to take into account."

She broke off, tossed her stunning hair. In the flat evening sunlight her garment had paled to translu-

cence. The late rays licked her body red and orange.
"But now I'd better get you back to your colonel."
She slipped into the skimmer.

Danny boarded without hesitation. After the Gedel
building, the transparent skimmer felt almost comfortable. "Back to my tank," he corrected lightly.
"Colonel may not care where I am, but he damn well
cares if Two Star is combat ready." The sudden rush
of air cut off thought of further conversation, and
though Sonna smiled as she landed Danny beside his
blower, there was a blankness in her expression that
indicated her thoughts were far away.

Hell with her, Danny thought. His last night in
the Rec Center on Emporion seemed a long time in
the past.

At three in the morning the Regiment was almost
two hundred kilometers from the camp they had abandoned at midnight. There had been no warning, only
the low hoot of the siren followed by the colonel's voice
rasping from every man's lapel speaker, "Mount up
and move, boys. Order seven, and your guides are
set." It might have loomed before another outfit as a
sudden catastrophe. After docking one trip with the
Slammers, though, a greenie learned that everything
not secured to his blower had better be secured to
him. Colonel Hammer thought an armored regiment's
firepower was less of an asset than its mobility. He
used the latter to the full with ten preset orders of
march and in-motion recharging for the infantry skimmers, juicing from the tanks and combat cars.

Four pongoes were jumpered to Two Star when
Foster's outpost sprang its ambush.

The lead combat car, half a kay ahead, bloomed in
a huge white ball that flooded the photon amplifiers

of Danny's goggles. The buzzbomb's hollow detona-
tion followed a moment later while the tanker, cursing, simultaneously switched to infra-red and swung
his turret left at max advance. He ignored the head
of the column, where the heated-air thump of powerguns merged with the crackle of mines blasted to
either side by the combat cars; that was somebody
else's responsibility. He ignored the two infantrymen
wired to his tank's port side as well. If they knew
their business, they'd drop the jumpers and flit for
Two Star's blind side as swiftly as Danny could spin
his heavy turret. If not, well, you don't have time for
niceness when somebody's firing shaped charges at
you.

"Damp that ground-sender!" Central snapped to
the lead elements. Too quickly to be a response to
the command, the grass trembled under the impact
of a delay-fused rocket punching down toward the
computed location of the enemy's subsurface signal-
ing. The Regiment must have rolled directly over an
outpost, either through horrendously bad luck or
because Foster had sewn his vedettes very thickly.

The firing stopped. The column had never slowed
and Michael, first of the heavy companies behind the
screen of combat cars, fanned the grass fires set by
the hoses. Pritchard scanned the area of the firefight
as Two Star rumbled through it in turn. The antipersonnel charges had dimpled the ground with shrapnel, easily identifiable among the glassy scars left by
the powerguns. In the center of a great vitrified
blotch lay a left arm and a few scraps of gray coverall.
Nearby was the plastic hilt of a buzzbomb launcher.
The other vedette had presumably stayed on the
commo in his covered foxhole until the penetrator
had scattered it and him over the landscape. If there

had been a third bunker, it escaped notice by Two Star's echo sounders.

"Move it out, up front," Central demanded. "This cuts our margin."

The burned-out combat car swept back into obscurity as Kowie put on speed. The frontal surfaces had collapsed inward from the heat, leaving the driver and blower chief as husks of carbon. There was no sign of the wing gunners. Perhaps they had been far enough back and clear of the spurt of directed radiance to escape. The ammo canister of the port tri-barrel had flash-ignited, though, and it was more likely that the men were wasted on the floor of the vehicle.

Another hundred and fifty kays to go, and now Foster and the Densonites knew they were coming.

There were no further ambushes to break the lightless monotony of gently rolling grassland. Pritchard took occasional sips of water and ate half a tube of protein ration. He started to fling the tube aside, then thought of the metal detectors on following units. He dropped it between his feet instead.

The metal-pale sun was thrusting the Regiment's shadow in long fingers up the final hillside when Central spoke again. You could tell it was the colonel himself sending. "Everybody freeze but Beta-First, Beta-First proceed in column up the rise and in. Keep your intervals, boys, and don't try to bite off too much. Last data we got was Foster had his anti-aircraft company with infantry support holding the target. Maybe they pulled out when we knocked on the door tonight, maybe they got reinforced. So take it easy—and don't bust up anything you don't have to."

Pritchard dropped his seat back inside the turret. There was nothing to be seen from the hatch but the monochrome sunrise and armored vehicles grounded on the yellow background. Inside, the three vision blocks gave greater variety. One was the constant 360 degrees display, better than normal eyesight according to the designers because the blower chief could see all around the tank without turning his head. Danny didn't care for it. Images were squeezed a good deal horizontally. Shapes weren't quite what you expected, so you didn't react quite as fast; and that was a good recipe for a dead trooper. The screen above the three-sixty was variable in light sensitivity and in magnification, useful for special illumination and first-shot hits.

The bottom screen was the remote rig; Pritchard dialed it for the forward receptors of Beta-First-Three. It was strange to watch the images of the two leading combat cars trembling as they crested the hill, yet feel Two Star as stable as 170 tonnes can be when grounded.

"Nothing moving," the platoon leader reported unnecessarily. Central had remote circuits too, as well as the satellite net to depend on.

The screen lurched as the blower Danny was slaved to boosted its fans to level the downgrade. Dust plumed from the leading cars, weaving across a sky that was almost fully light. At an unheard command, the platoon turned up the wick in unison and let the cars hurtle straight toward the target's central corridor. It must have helped, because Foster's gunners caught only one car when they loosed the first blast through their camouflage.

The second car blurred in a mist of vaporized armor plate. Incredibly, the right wing gunner shot back. The deadly flame-lash of his hose was pale against the richer color of the hostile fire. Foster had sited his calliopes, massive 3 cm guns whose nine fixed barrels fired extra-length charges. Danny had never seen a combat car turned into swiss cheese faster than the one now spiked on the muzzles of a pair of the heavy guns.

Gray-suited figures were darting from cover as if the cars' automatics were harmless for being out-classed. The damaged blower nosed into the ground. Its driver leaped out, running for the lead car which had spun on its axis and was hosing blue-green fire in three directions. One of Foster's troops raised up-right, loosing a buzzbomb at the wreckage of the grounded car. The left side of the vehicle flapped like a batwing as it sailed across Danny's field of view. The concussion knocked down the running man. He rose to his knees, jumped for a handhold as the lead car accelerated past him. As he swung him-self aboard, two buzzbombs hit the blower simulta-neously. It bloomed with joined skullcaps of pearl and bone.

Pritchard was swearing softly. He had switched to a stern pickup already, and the tumbled wreckage in it was bouncing, fading swiftly. Shots twinkled briefly as the four escaping blowers dropped over the ridge.

"In column ahead," said the colonel grimly, "Ho-tel, Kitchen, Michael. Button up and hose 'em out, you know the drill."

And then something went wrong. "Are you in-sane?" the radio marveled, and Danny recognized that voice too. "I forbid you!"

"You can't. Somebody get her out of here."

"Your contract is over, finished, do you hear? Heav-enly Way, we'll all become Densonites if we must. This horror must end!"

"Not yet. You don't see—"

"I've seen too—" The shouted words cut off.

"So we let Foster give us a bloody nose and back off? That's what you want? But it's bigger than what you want now, sister, it's the whole Regiment. It's never bidding another contract without somebody saying, 'Hey, they got sandbagged on Thrush, didn't they?' And nobody remembering that Foster figured the civvies would chill us—and he was right. Don't you see? They killed my boys, and now they're going to pay the bill.

"Tank Section, execute! Dig 'em out, panzers!"

Danny palmed the panic bar, dropping the seal and locking the hatch over it. The rushing-air snarl of the fans was deadened by the armor, but a hot bearing somewhere filled the compartment with its high keening. Two Star hurdled the ridge. Its whole horizon flared with crystal dancing and scattering in sunlight and the reflected glory of automatic weapons firing from its shelter. Starhome was immensely larger than Danny had expected.

A boulevard twenty meters wide divided two ranks of glassy buildings, any one of which, towers and pavillions, stood larger than the shrine Danny had seen the previous day. At a kilometer's distance it was a coruscating unity of parts as similar as the strands of a silken rope. Danny rapped up the magnification and saw the details spring out; rods woven into columns that streaked skyward a hundred meters; translucent sheets formed of myriads of pinhead beads, each one glowing a color as different from the rest as one star is from the remainder of those seen on a moonless night; a spiral column, free-standing and the thickness of a woman's wrist, that pulsed slowly through the spectrum as it climbed almost out of sight. All the structures seemed to front on the central corridor, with the buildings on either side welded together by tracery mazes, porticoes, arcades —a thousand different plates and poles of glass.

A dashed cyan line joined the base of an upswept web of color to the tank. Two Star's hull thudded to the shock of vaporizing metal. The stabilizer locked the blower's pitching out of Danny's sight picture. He swung the glowing orange bead onto the source of fire and kicked the pedal. The air rang like a carillon as the whole glassy facade sagged, then avalanched into the street. There was a shock of heat in the closed battle compartment as the breech flicked open and belched out the spent case. The plastic hissed on the floor, outgassing horribly while the air-conditioning strained to clear the chamber. Danny ignored the stench, nudged his sights onto the on-rushing splendor of the second structure on the right of the corridor. The breech of the big powergun slapped again and again, recharging instantly as the tanker worked the foot trip.

Blue-green lightning scattered between the walls as if the full power of each bolt was flashing the length of the corridor. Two Star bellowed in on the wake of its fire, and crystal flurried under the fans. Kowie leveled their stroke slightly, cutting speed by a fraction but lifting the tank higher above the abrasive litter. The draft hurled glittering shards across the corridor, arcs of cold fire in the light of Two Star's gun and those of the blowers following. Men in gray were running from their hiding places to avoid the sliding crystal masses, the iridescent rain that pattered on the upper surfaces of the tanks but smashed jaggedly through the infantry's body armor.

Danny set his left thumb to rotate the turret

counter-clockwise, held the gun-switch down with his foot. The remaining sixteen rounds of his basic load blasted down the right half of Starhome, spread by the blower's forward motion and the turret swing. The compartment was gray with fumes. Danny slammed the hatch open and leaned out. His hands went to the 2 cm as naturally as a calf turns to milk. The wind was cold on his face. Kowie slewed the blower left to avoid the glassy wave that slashed into the corridor from one of the blasted structures. The scintillance halted, then ground a little further as something gave way inside the pile.

A soldier in gray stepped from an untouched archway to the left. The buzzbomb on his shoulder was the size of a landing vessel as it swung directly at Danny. The tribarrel seemed to traverse with glacial slowness. It was too slow. Danny saw the brief flash as the rocket leaped from the shoulder of the other mercenary. It whirred over Two Star and the sergeant, exploded cataclysmically against a spike of Starhome still rising on the other side.

The infantryman tossed the launcher tube aside. He froze, his arms spread wide, and shouted, "Exchange!"

"Exchange yourself, mother!" Danny screamed back white-faced. He triggered his hose. The gray torso exploded. The body fell backward in a mist of blood, chest and body armor torn open by four hits that shriveled bones and turned fluids to steam.

"Hard left and goose it, Kowie," the sergeant demanded. He slapped the panic bar again. As the hatch clanged shut over his head, Danny caught a momentary glimpse of the vision blocks, three soldiers with powerguns leaping out of the same towering structure from which the rocketeer had come.

Their faces were blankly incredulous as they saw the huge blower swinging toward them at full power. The walls flexed briefly under the impact of the tank's frontal slope, but the filigree was eggshell thin. The structure disintegrated, lurching toward the corridor while Two Star plowed forward within it. A thousand images kaleidoscoped in Danny's skull, sparkling within the windchime dissonance of the falling tower.

The fans screamed as part of the structure's mass collapsed onto Two Star. Kowie rocked the tank, raising it like a submarine through a sea of ravaged glass. The gentle, green-furred humanoids faded from Danny's mind. He threw the hatch open. Kowie gunned the fans, reversing the blower in a polychrome shower. Several tanks had moved ahead of Two Star, nearing the far end of the corridor. Gray-uniformed soldiers straggled from the remaining structures, hands empty, eyes fixed on the ground. There was very little firing. Kowie edged into the column and followed the third tank into the laager forming on the other side of Starhome. Pritchard was drained. His throat was dry, but he knew from past experience that he would vomit if he swallowed even a mouthful of water before his muscles stopped trembling. The blower rested with its skirts on the ground, its fans purring gently as they idled to a halt.

Kowie climbed out of the driver's hatch, moving stiffly. He had a powergun in his hand, a pistol he always carried for moral support. Two Star's bow compartment was frequently nearer the enemy than anything else in Hammer's Slammers.

Several towers still stood in the wreckage of Starhome. The nearest one wavered from orange to red and back in the full blaze of sunlight. Danny watched it in the iridium mirror of his tank's deck, the outline muted by the hatchwork of crystal etching on the metal.

Kowie shot off-hand. Danny looked up in irritation. The driver shot again, his light charge having no discernible effect on the structure.

"Shut it off," Danny croaked. "These're shrines."

The ground where Starhome had stood blazed like the floor of Hell.

Interlude: The Church of the Lord's Universe

PERHAPS THE MOST surprising thing about the faith that men took to the stars—and vice versa—was that it appeared to differ so little from the liturgical protestantism of the Nineteenth and Twentieth Centuries. Indeed, services of the Church of the Lord's Universe—almost always, except by Unitarians, corrupted to "Universal Church"—so resembled those of a high-flying Anglican parish of 1920 that a visitor from the past would have been hard put to believe that he was watching a sect as extreme in its own way as the Society for Krishna Consciousness was in its.

The Church of the Lord's Universe was officially launched in 1985 in Minneapolis, Minnesota, by the merger of 230 existing protestant congregations—Methodist, Presbyterian, Episcopalian, and Lutheran. In part the new church was a revolt against the extreme fundamentalism peaking at that time. The

Universalists sought converts vigorously from the start. Their liturgy obviously attempted to recapture the traditional beauty of Christianity's greatest age, but there is reason to believe that the extensive use of Latin in the service was part of a design to avoid giving doctrinal offense as well. Anyone who has attended both Presbyterian and Methodist services has felt uneasiness at the line, "Forgive us our debts/ trespasses . . ." St. Jerome's Latin version of the Lord's Prayer flows smoothly and unnoticed from the tongue of one raised in either sect.

But the Church of the Lord's Universe had a mission beyond the entertainment of its congregations for an hour every Sunday. The priests and laity alike preached the salvation of Mankind through His works. To Universalists, however, the means and the end were both secular. The Church taught that Man must reach the stars and there, among infinite expanses, find room to live in peace. This temporal paradise was one which could be grasped by all men. It did not detract from spiritual hopes; but heaven is in the hands of the Lord, while the stars were not beyond Man's own strivings.

The Doctrine of Salvation through the Stars—it was never labeled so bluntly in Universalist writings, but the peevish epithet bestowed by a Baptist theologian was not inaccurate—gave the Church of the Lord's Universe a dynamism unknown to the Christian center since the days of Archbishop Laud. It was a naive doctrine, of course. Neither the stars nor anything else brought peace to Man; but realists did not bring men to the stars, either, while the hopeful romantics of the Universal Church certainly helped.

The Universalist credo was expressed most clearly in the BOOK OF THE WAY, a slim volume commissioned at the First Consensus and adopted after numerous emendations by the Tenth. The BOOK OF THE WAY never officially replaced the Bible, but the committee of laymen which framed it struck a chord in the hearts of all Universalists. Despite its heavily Eastern leanings (including suggestions of reincarnation), the BOOK spoke in an idiom intelligible and profoundly moving to men and women who in another milieu would have been Technocrats.

While the new faith appealed to men and women everywhere, it by no means appealed to every man and woman. By their uncompromising refusal to abandon future dreams to cope with present disasters—the famines, pollution, and pogroms of every day—the Universalists faced frequent hatred. During the Food Riots of 2039, three hundred Universalists were ceremonially murdered and eaten in a packed amphitheatre in Dakkah, and there were other martyrs as well. But the survivors and their faith drove on. Their ranks swelled every time catastrophe proved Man was incapable of solving his problems on Earth alone.

Thus, when Man did reach the stars, the ships were crewed in large measure by Universalists. Those who had prayed for, worked for, and even sworn by the Way of the Stars, *Via Stellarum*, were certain to be among the first treading it. On Earth, the Church of the Lord's Universe had been a vocal minority; in the colonies spreading like a bacterial culture through the galaxy, Universalists were frequently in the majority.

There were changes. Inevitably, fragmentation followed success as centuries and the high cost of interstellar communication made each congregation a separate entity. But the basic thrust of the Church, present peace and safety for Mankind, remained even when reality diluted it to lip service or less. Mercenaries were recruited mostly from rural cultures which were used to privation—and steeped in religion as well. Occastonally a trooper might feel uneasy as he swore, "Via!," for the Way had been a way of peace.

But mercs swore by blood and the martyrs as well; and few had better knowledge of either blood or innocent victims than the gunmen of the mercenary companies.

Under the Hammer

"THINK you're going to like killing, boy?" asked the old man on double crutches.

Rob Jenne turned from the streams of moving cargo to his unnoticed companion in the shade of the starship's hull. His own eyes were pale gray, suited like his dead-white skin to Burlage, whose ruddy sun could raise a blush but not a tan. When they adjusted, they took in the clerical collar which completed the other's costume. The smooth, black synthetic contrasted oddly with the coveralls and shirt of local weave. At that, the Curwinite's outfit was a cut above Rob's own, the same worksuit of Burlage sisal that he had worn as a quarryhand at home. Uniform issue would come soon.

At least, he hoped and prayed it would.

When the youth looked away after an embarrassed grin, the priest chuckled. "Another damned old fool, hey, boy? There were a few in your family, weren't

there . . . the ones who'd quote the Book of the Way
saying not to kill—and here you go off for a hired
murderer. Right?" He laughed again, seeing he had
the younger man's attention. "But that by itself
wouldn't be so hard to take—you were leaving your
family anyway, weren't you, nobody really believes
they'll keep close to their people after five years, ten
years of star hopping. But your mates, though, the
team you worked with . . . how did you explain to
them why you were leaving a good job to go on
contract? 'Via!'" the priest mimicked, his tones so
close to those of Barney Larsen, the gang boss, that
Rob started in surprise, "you get your coppy ass shot
off, lad, and it'll serve you right for being a fool!"

"How do you know I signed for a mercenary?"
Jenne asked, clenching his great, callused hands on
the handle of his carry-all. It was everything he
owned in the universe in which he no longer had a
home. "And how'd you know about my Aunt Gudrun?"

"Haven't I seen a thousand of you?" the priest
blazed back, his eyes like sparks glinting from the
drill shaft as the sledge drove it deeper into the rock.
"You're young and strong and bright enough to pass
Alois Hammer's tests—you be proud of that, boy,
few enough are fit for Hammer's Slammers. There
you were, a man grown who'd read all the cop about
mercenaries, believed most of it . . . more'n ever
you did the Book of the Way, anyhow. Sure, I know.
So you got some off-planet factor to send your papers
in for you, for the sake of the bounty he'll get from
the colonel if you make the grade—"

The priest caught Rob's blink of surprise. He chuckled again, a cruel, unpriestly sound, and said, "He
told you it was for friendship? One a these days
you'll learn what friendship counts, when you get an

order that means the death of a friend—and you carry it out."

Rob stared at the priest in repulsion, the grizzled chin resting on interlaced fingers and the crutches under either armpit supporting most of his weight. "It's my life," the recruit said with sulky defiance. "Soon as they pick me up here, you can go back to living your own. 'Less you'd be willing to do that right now?"

"They'll come soon enough, boy," the older man said in a milder voice. "Sure, you've been ridden by everybody you know . . . now that you're alone, here's a stranger riding you too. I don't mean it like I sound . . . wasn't born to the work, I guess. There's priests—and maybe the better ones—who'd say that signing on with mercenaries means so long a spiral down that maybe your soul won't come out of it in another life or another hundred. But I don't see it like that.

"Life's a forge, boy, and the purest metal comes from the hottest fire. When you've been under the hammer a few times, you'll find you've been beaten down to the real, no lies, no excuses. There'll be a time, then, when you got to look over the product . . . and if you don't like what you see, well, maybe there's time for change, too."

The priest turned his head to scan the half of the horizon not blocked by the bellied-down bulk of the starship. Ant columns of stevedores manhandled cargo from the ship's rollerway into horse and oxdrawn wagons in the foreground: like most frontier worlds, Burlage included, self-powered machinery was rare in the backcountry. Beyond the men and draft animals stretched the fields, studded frequently by orange-golden clumps of native vegetation.

"Nobody knows how little his life's worth till he's put it on the line a couple times," the old man said. "For nothing. Look at it here on Curwin—the seaboard taxed these uplands into revolt, then had to spend what they'd robbed and more to hire an armored regiment. So boys like you from—Scania? Felsen?—"

"Burlage, sir."

"Sure, a quarryman, should have known from your shoulders. You come in to shoot farmers for a gang of coastal moneymen you don't know and wouldn't like, if you did." The priest paused, less for effect than to heave in a quick, angry breath that threatened his shirt buttons. "And maybe you'll die, too; if the Slammers were immortal, they wouldn't need recruits. But some that die will die like saints, boy, die martyrs of the Way, for no reason, for no reason . . .

"Your ride's here, boy."

The suddenly emotionless words surprised Rob as much as a scream in a silent prayer would have. Hissing like a gun-studded dragon, a gray-metal combat car slid onto the landing field from the west. Light dust puffed from beneath it: although the flat-bed trailer behind was supported on standard wheels, the armored vehicle itself hovered a hand's-breadth above the surface at all points. A dozen powerful fans on the underside of the car kept it floating on an invisible bubble of air, despite the weight of the fusion power unit and the iridium-ceramic armor. Rob had seen combat cars on the entertainment cube occasionally, but those skittering miniatures gave no hint of the awesome power that emanated in reality from the machines. This one was seven meters long and three wide at the base, the armored sides curving up like a turtle's back to the open fighting compartment in the rear.

From the hatch in front of the powerplant stuck the driver's head, a blank-mirrored ball in a helmet with full face shield down. Road dust drifted away from the man in a barely-visible haze, cleaned from the helmet's optics by a static charge. Faceless and terrible to the unfamiliar Burlager, the driver guided toward the starship a machine that appeared no more inhuman than did the man himself.

"Undercrewed," the priest murmured. "Two men on the back deck aren't enough for a car running single."

The older man's jargon was unfamiliar but Rob could follow his gist by looking at the vehicle. The two men standing above the waist-high armor of the rear compartment were clearly fewer than had been contemplated when the combat car was designed. Its visible armament comprised a heavy powergun forward to fire over the head of the driver, and similar weapons, also swivel-mounted, on either side to command the flanks and rear of the vehicle. But with only two men in the compartment there was a dangerous gap in the circle of fire the car could lay down if ambushed. Another vehicle for escort would have eased the danger, but this one was alone save for the trailer it pulled.

Though as the combat car drew closer, Rob began to wonder if the two soldiers present couldn't handle anything that occurred. Both were in full battle dress, wearing helmets and laminated back and breast armor over their khaki. Their faceplates were clipped open. The one at the forward gun, his eyes as deep-sunken and deadly as the three revolving barrels of his weapon, was in his forties and further aged by the dust sweated into black grime in the creases of his face. His head rotated in tiny jerks, taking in every nuance of the sullen crowd parting for his war-car. The other soldier was huge by comparison with the first and lounged across the back in feigned leisure: feigned, because either hand was within its breadth of a powergun's trigger, and his limbs were as controlled as spring steel.

With careless expertise, the driver backed his trailer up to the conveyor line. A delicate hand with the fans allowed him to angle them slightly, drifting the rear of the combat car to edge the trailer in the opposite direction. The larger soldier contemptuously thumbed a waiting horse and wagon out of its slot. The teamster's curse brought only a grin and a big hand rested on a powergun's receiver, less a threat than a promise. The combat car eased into the space.

"Wait for an old man," the priest said as Rob lifted his carry-all, "and I'll go with you." Glad even for that company, the recruit smiled nervously, fitting his stride to the other's surprisingly nimble swing-and-pause, swing-and-pause.

The driver dialed back minusculy on the power and allowed the big vehicle to settle to the ground without a skip or a tremor. One hand slid back the face shield to a high, narrow nose and eyes that alertly focused on the two men approaching. "The Lord and his martyrs!" the driver cried in amazement. "It's Blacky himself come in with our newbie!"

Both soldiers on the back deck slewed their eyes around at the cry. The smaller one took one glance, then leaped the two meters to the ground to clasp Rob's companion. "Hey!" he shouted, oblivious to the recruit shifting his weight uncertainly. "Via, it's good to see you! But what're you doing on Curwin?"

"I came back here afterwards," the older man answered with a smile. "Born here, I must've told you . . . though we didn't talk a lot. I'm a priest now, see?"

"And I'm a flirt like the load we're supposed to pick up," the driver said, dismounting with more care than his companion. Abreast of the first soldier, he too took in the round collar and halted gapemouthed. "Lord, I'll be a coppy rag if you ain't," he breathed. "Whoever heard of a blower chief taking the Way?"

"Shut up, Jake," the first soldier said without rancor. He stepped back from the priest to take a better look, then seemed to notice Rob. "Umm," he said, "you the recruit from Burlage?"

"Yessir. M-my name's Rob Jenne, sir."

"Not 'sir,' there's enough sirs around already," the veteran said. "I'm Chero, except if there's lots of brass around, then make it Sergeant-Commander Worzer. Look, take your gear back to the trailer and give Leon a hand with the load.

"Hey, Blacky," he continued with concern, ignoring Rob again, "what's wrong with your legs? We got the best there was."

"Oh, they're fine," Rob heard the old man reply, "but they need a weekly tuning. Out here we don't have the computers, you know; so I get the astrogation boys to sync me up on the ships' hardware whenever one docks in—just waiting for a chance now. But in six months the servos are far enough out of line that I have to shut off the power till the next ship arrives. You'd be surprised how well I get around on these pegs, though. . . ."

Leon, the huge third crew member, had loosed the top catches of his body armor for ventilation. From the look of it, the laminated casing should have been a size larger; but Rob wasn't sure anything larger was made. The gunner's skin where exposed was the dense black of a basalt outcropping. "They'll be a big crate to go on, so just set your gear down till we get it loaded," he said. Then he grinned at Rob, teeth square and slightly yellow against his face. "Think you can take me?"

That was a challenge the recruit could understand, the first he could meet fairly since boarding the starship with a one-way ticket to a planet he had never heard of. He took in the waiting veteran quickly but carefully, proud of his own rock-hardened muscles but certain the other man had been raised just as hard. "I give you best," the blond said. "Unless you feel you got to prove it?"

The grin broadened and a great black hand reached out to clasp Rob's. "Naw," the soldier said, "just like to clear the air at the start. Some of the big ones; Lord, testy ain't the word. All they can think about's what they want to prove with me . . . so they don't watch their side of the car, and then there's trouble for everybody."

"Hammer's Regiment?" called an unfamiliar voice. Both men looked up. Down the conveyor rode a blue-tunicked ship's man in front of what first appeared to be a huge crate. At second glance Rob saw that it was a cage of light alloy holding four . . . "Dear Lord!" the recruit gasped.

"Roger, Hammer's," Leon agreed, handing the crewman a plastic chit while the latter cut power to the rollers to halt the cage. The chit slipped into the computer linkage on the crewman's left wrist, lighting a green indicator when it proved itself a genuine bill of lading.

There were four female humanoids in the cage— stark naked except for a dusting of fine blue scales. Rob blinked. One of the near-women stood with a smile—Lord, she had no teeth!—and rubbed her groin deliberately against one of the vertical bars.

"First quality Genefran flirts," Leon chuckled. "Ain't human, boy, but the next best thing."

"Better," threw in Jake, who had swung himself into the fighting compartment as soon as the cage arrived. "I tell you, kid, you never had it till you had a flirt. Surgically modified and psychologically prepared. Rowf!"

"N-not human?" Rob stumbled, unable to take his eyes off the cage, "you mean like *monkeys?*"

Leon's grin lit his face again, and the driver cackled, "Well, don't know about monkeys, but they're a whole lot like sheep."

"You take the left side and we'll get this aboard," Leon directed. The trailer's bed was half a meter below the rollerway so that the cage, though heavy and awkward, could be slid without much lifting.

Rob gripped the bars numbly, turning his face down from the tittering beside him. "Amazing what they can do with implants and a wig," Jake was going on, "though a course there's a lot of cutting to do first, but those ain't the differences you see, if you follow. The scales, now—they have a way—"

"Lift!" Leon ordered, and Rob straightened at the knees. They took two steps backward with the cage wobbling above them as the girls—the flirts!—squealed and hopped about. "Down!" and cage clashed on trailer as the two big men moved in unison.

Rob stepped back, his mouth working in distaste, unaware of the black soldier's new look of respect. Quarry work left a man used to awkward weights. "This is foul," the recruit marveled. "Are those really going back with us for, for . . ."

"Rest'n relaxation," Leon agreed, snapping tie-downs around the bars.

"But how . . ." Rob began, looking again at the cage. When the red-wigged flirt fondled her left breast upward, he could see the implant scars pale against the blue. The scales were more thinly spread where the skin had been stretched in molding it. "I'll *never* touch something like that. Look, maybe Burlage is pretty backward about . . . things, about sex, I don't know. But I don't see how anybody could . . . I mean—"

"Via, wait till you been here as long as we have," Jake gibed. He clenched his right hand and pumped it suggestively. "Field expedients, that's all."

"On this kinda contract," Leon explained, stepping around to get at the remaining tiedowns, "you can't trust the local girls. Least not in the field, like we are. The colonel likes to keep us patrol sections pretty much self-contained."

"Yeah," Jake broke in—would his cracked tenor never cease? "Why, some of these whores, they take a razor blade, see—in a cork you know?—and, well, never mind." He laughed, seeing Rob's face.

"Jake," Sergeant Worzer called, "Shut up and hop in."

The driver slipped instantly into his hatch. Disgusting as Rob found the little man, he recognized his ability. Jake moved with lethal certainty and a speed that belied the weight of his body armor.

"Ready to lift, Chero?" he asked.

The priest was levering himself toward the starship again. Worzer watched him go for a moment, shook his head. "Just run us out to the edge of the field," he directed. "I got a few things to show our recruit before we head back; nobody rides in my car without knowing how to work the guns." With a sigh he hopped into the fighting compartment. Leon motioned Rob in front of him. Gingerly, the recruit stepped onto the trailer hitch, gripped the armored rim with both hands, lifted himself aboard. Leon followed. The trailer bonged as he pushed off from it, and his bulk cramped the littered compartment as soon as he grunted over the side.

"Put this on," Worzer ordered, handing Rob a dusty, bulbous helmet like the others wore. "Brought a battle suit for you, too," he said, kicking the jointed armor leaning against the back of the compartment, "but it'd no more fit you than it would Leon there."

The black laughed. "Gonna be tight back here till the kid or me gets zapped."

"Move 'er out," Worzer ordered. The words came through unsuspected earphones in Rob's helmet, although the sergeant had simply spoken, without visibly activating a pick up.

The car vibrated as the fans revved, then lifted with scarcely a jerk. From behind came the squeals and chirrups of the flirts as the trailer rocked over the irregularities in the field.

Worzer looked hard at the starship's open crew portal as they hissed past it. "Funny what folks go an' do," he said to no one in particular. "Via, wonder what I'll be in another ten years."

"Pet food, likely," joked the driver, taking part in the conversation although physically separated from the other crewmen.

"Shut up, Jake," repeated the blower captain. "And you can hold it up here, we're out far enough."

The combat car obediently settled on the edge of the stabilized area. The port itself had capacity for two ships at a time; the region it served did not. Though with the high cost of animal transport many manufactures could be star-hopped to Curwin's back country more cheaply than they could be carried from the planet's own more urbanized areas, the only available exchange was raw agricultural produce—again limited to the immediate locality by the archaic transport. Its fans purring below audibility, the armored vehicle rested on an empty area of no significance to the region—unless the central government should choose to land another regiment of mercenaries on it.

"Look," the sergeant said, his deep-set eyes catching Rob's, "we'll pass you on to the firebase when we take the other three flirts in next week. They got a training section there. We got six cars in this patrol, that's not enough margin to fool with training a newbie. But neither's it enough to keep somebody useless underfoot for a week, so we'll give you some basics. Not so you can wise-ass when you get to training section, just so you don't get somebody killed if it drops in the pot. Clear?"

"Yessir." Rob broke his eyes away, then realized how foolish he must look staring at his own clasped hands. He looked back at Worzer.

"Just so it's understood," the sergeant said with a nod. "Leon, show him how the gun works."

The big black rotated his weapon so that the muzzles faced forward and the right side was toward Rob and the interior of the car. The mechanism itself was encased in dull-enameled steel ornamented with knobs and levers of unguessable intent. The barrels were stubby iridium cylinders with smooth, 2 cm. bores. Leon touched one of the buttons, then threw a lever back. The plate to which the barrels were attached rotated 120 degrees around their common axis, and a thick disk of plastic popped out into the gunner's hand.

"When the bottom barrel's ready to fire, the next one clockwise is loading one a these"—Leon held up the 2 cm disk—"and the other barrel, the one that's just fired, blows out the empty."

"There's a liquid nitrogen ejector," Worzer put in. "Cools the bore same time it kicks out the empty."

"She feeds up through the mount," the big soldier went on, his index finger tracing the path of the energized disks from the closed hopper bulging in the sidewall, through the ball joint and into the weapon's receiver. "If you try to fire and she don't, check this." The columnar finger indicated but did not move the stud it had first pressed on the side of the gun. "That's the safety. She still doesn't fire, pull this"—he clacked the lever, rotating the barrel cluster another one-third turn and catching the loaded round that flew out. "Maybe there was a dud round. She still don't go, just get down outa the way. We start telling you about second-order malfunctions and you won't remember where the trigger is."

"Ah, where is the trigger?" Rob asked diffidently.

Jake's laughter rang through the earphones and Worzer himself smiled for the first time. The sergeant reached out and rotated the gun. "See the grips?" he asked, pointing to the double handles at the back of the receiver. Rob nodded.

"OK," Worzer continued, "you hold it there"—he demonstrated—"and to fire, you just press your thumbs against the trigger plate between 'em. Let up and it quits. Simple."

"You can clear this field as quick as you can spin this little honey," Leon said, patting the gun with affection. "The hicks out there"—his arm swept the woods and cultivated fields promiscuously—"got some rifles, they hunted before the trouble started, but no powerguns to mention. About all they do since we moved in is maybe pop a shot or two off, and hide in their holes."

"They've got some underground stockpiles," Worzer said, amplifying Leon's words, "explosives, maybe some factories to make rifle ammo. But the colonel set up a recce net—spy satellites, you know—as part a the contract. Any funny movement day or night, a signal goes down to whoever's patrolling there. A couple calls and we check out the area with ground sensors . . . anything funny then—vibration, hollows showing up on the echo sounder, magnetics—anything! —and bam! we call in the artillery."

"Won't take much of a jog on the way back," Leon suggested, "and we can check out that report from last night."

"Via, that was just a couple dogs," Jake objected.

"OK, so we prove it was a couple dogs," rumbled the gunner. "Or maybe the hicks got smart and they're shielding their infra-red now. Been too damn long since anything popped in this sector."

"Thing to remember, kid," Worzer summed up, "is never get buzzed at this job. Stay cool, you're fine. This car's got more firepower'n everything hostile in fifty klicks. One call to the firebase brings in our arty, anything from smoke shells to a nuke. The rest of our section can be here in twenty minutes, or a tank platoon from the firebase in two hours. Just stay cool."

Turning forward, the sergeant said, "OK, take her home. Jake. We'll try that movement report on the way."

The combat car shuddered off the ground, the flirts shrieking. Rob eyed them, blushed, and turned back to his powergun, feeling conspicuous. He took the grips, liking the deliberate way the weapon swung. The safety button was glowing green, but he suddenly realized that he didn't know the color code. Green for safe? Or green for ready? He extended his index finger to the switch.

"Whoa, careful, kid!" Leon warned. "You cut fifty civvies in half your first day and the colonel won't like it one bit."

Sheepishly, Rob drew back his finger. His ears burned, mercifully hidden beneath the helmet.

They slid over the dusty road in a flat, white cloud at about forty kph. It seemed shockingly fast to the recruit, but he realized that the car could probably move much faster were it not for the live cargo behind. Even as it was, the trailer bounced dangerously from side to side.

The road led through a gullied scattering of grain plots, generally fenced with withes rather than imported metal. Houses were relatively uncommon. Apparently each farmer plowed several separate locations rather than trying to work the rugged or less productive areas. Occasionally they passed a rough-garbed local at work. The scowls thrown up at the smoothly-running war-car were hostile, but there was nothing more overt.

"OK," Jake warned, "here's where it gets interesting. Sure you still want this half-assed check while we got the trailer hitched?"

"It won't be far," Worzer answered. "Go ahead." He turned to Rob, touching the recruit's shoulder and pointing to the lighted map panel beside the forward gun. "Look, Jenne," he said, keeping one eye on the countryside as Jake took the car off the road in a sweeping turn, "if you need to call in a location to the firebase, here's the trick. The red dot"—it was in the center of the display and remained there although the map itself seemed to be flowing kitty-corner across the screen as the combat car moved—"that's us. The black dot"—the veteran thumbed a small wheel beside the display and the map, red dot and all, shifted to the right on the panel, leaving a black dot in the center—"that's your pointer. The computer feeds out the grid coordinates here"—his finger touched the window above the map display. Six digits, changing as the map moved under the centered black dot, winked brightly. "You just put the black dot on a bunker site, say, and read off the figures to Fire Central. The arty'll do all the rest."

"Ah," Rob murmured, "ah . . . Sergeant, how do you get the little dot off that and onto a bunker like you said?"

There was a moment's silence. "You know how to read a map, don't you, kid?" Worzer finally asked.

"What's that, sir?"

The earphones boomed and cackled with raucous laughter. "Oh my coppy ass!" the sergeant snarled. He snapped the little wheel back, re-centering the red dot. "Lord, I don't know how the training cadre takes it!"

Rob hid his flaming embarrassment by staring over his gunsights. He didn't really know how to use them, either. He didn't know why he'd left Conner's Stoneworks, where he was the cleanest, fastest driller on the whole coppy crew. His powerful hands squeezed at the grips as if they were the driver's throat through which bubbles of laughter still burst.

"Shut up, Jake," the sergeant finally ordered. "Most of us had to learn something new when we joined. Remember how the ol' man found you your first day, pissing up against the barracks?"

Jake quieted.

They had skirted a fence of cane palings, brushing it once without serious effect. Russet grass flanking the fence flattened under the combat car's downdraft, then sprang up unharmed as the vehicle moved past. Jake seemed to be following a farm track leading from the field to a rambling, substantially-constructed building on the near hilltop. Instead of running with the ground's rise, however, the car cut through brush and down a half-meter bank into a broad-based arroyo. The bushes were too stiff to lie down under the fans. They crunched and howled in the blades, making the car buck, and ricocheted wildly from under the skirts. The bottom of the arroyo was sand, clean-swept by recent run-off. It boiled fiercely as the car first shoomped into it, then ignored the fans entirely. Somehow Jake had managed not to overturn the trailer, although its cargo had been screaming with fear for several minutes.

"Hold up," Worzer ordered suddenly as he swung his weapon toward the left-hand bank. The wash was about thirty meters wide at that point, sides sheer and a meter high. Rob glanced forward to see that a small screen to Worzer's left on the bulkhead, previously dark, was now crossed by three vari-colored lines. The red one was bouncing frantically.

"They got an entrance, sure 'nough," Leon said. He aimed his powergun at the same point, then snapped his face shield down. "Watch it, kid," he said. The black's right hand fumbled in a metal can welded to the blower's side. Most of the paint had chipped from the stencilled legend: GRENADES. What appeared to be a lazy overarm toss snapped a knobby ball the size of a child's fist straight and hard against the bank.

Dirt and rock fragments shotgunned in all directions. The gully side burst in a globe of black streaked with garnet fire, followed by a shock wave that was a physical blow.

"Watch your side, kid!" somebody shouted through the din, but Rob's bulging eyes were focused on the collapsing bank, the empty triangle of black gaping suddenly through the dust—the two ravening whip-lashes of directed lightning ripping into it to blast and scatter.

The barrel clusters of the two veterans' powerguns spun whining, kicking gray, eroded disks out of their mechanisms in nervous arcs. The bolts they shot were blue-green flashes barely visible until they struck a target and exploded it with transferred energy. The very rocks burst in droplets of glassy slag splashing high in the air and even back into the war-car to pop against the metal.

Leon's gun paused as his fingers hooked another grenade. "Hold it!" he warned. The sergeant, too, came off the trigger, and the bomb arrowed into the now-vitrified gap in the tunnel mouth. Dirt and glass shards blew straight back at the bang. A stretch of ground sagged for twenty meters beyond the gully wall, closing the tunnel the first explosion had opened.

Then there was silence. Even the flirts, huddled in a terrified heap on the floor of their cage, were soundless.

Glowing orange specks vibrated on Rob's retinas; the cyan bolts had been more intense than he had realized. "Via," he said in awe, "how do they dare . . . ?"

"Bullet kills you just as dead," Worzer grunted. "Jake, think you can climb that wall?"

"Sure. She'll buck a mite in the loose stuff." The gully side was a gentle declivity, now, where the grenades had blown it in. "Wanna unhitch the trailer first?"

"Negative, nobody gets off the blower till we cleaned this up."

"Umm, don't want to let somebody else in on the fun, maybe?" the driver queried. If he was tense, his voice did not indicate it. Rob's palms were sweaty.

His glands had understood before his mind had that his companions were considering smashing up, un-aided, a guerrilla stronghold.

"Cop," Leon objected determinedly. "We found it, didn't we?"

"Let's go," Worzer ordered. "Kid, watch your side. They sure got another entrance, maybe a couple."

The car nosed gently toward the subsided bank, wallowed briefly as the driver fed more power to the forward fans to lift the bow. With a surge and a roar, the big vehicle climbed. Its fans caught a few pebbles and whanged them around inside the plenum chamber like a rattle of sudden gunfire. At half speed, the car glided toward another fenced grainplot, leaving behind it a rising pall of dust.

"Straight as a plumb line," Worzer commented, his eyes flicking his sensor screen. "Bastards'll be waiting for us."

Rob glanced at him—a mistake. The slam-spang! of shot and ricochet were nearly simultaneous. The recruit whirled back, bawling in surprise. The rifle pit had opened within five meters of him, and only the haste of the dark-featured guerrilla had saved Rob from his first shot. Rob pivoted his powergun like a hammer, both thumbs mashing down the trigger. Nothing happened. The guerrilla ducked anyway, the black circle of his foxhole shaped into a thick crescent by the lid lying askew.

Safety, *safety!* Rob's mind screamed and he punched the button fat-fingered. The rifleman raised his head just in time to meet the hose of fire that darted from the recruit's gun. The guerrilla's head exploded. His brains, flash-cooked by the first shot, changed instantly from a colloid to a blast of steam that scattered itself over a three-meter circle. The smoldering fragments of the rifle followed the torso as it slid downward.

The combat car roared into the field of waist-high grain, ripping down twenty meters of woven fencing to make its passage. Rob, vaguely aware of other shots and cries forward, vomited onto the floor of the compartment. A colossal explosion nearby slewed the car sideways. As Rob raised his eyes, he noticed three more swarthy riflemen darting through the grain from the right rear of the vehicle.

"Here!" he cried. He swiveled his weapon blindly, his hips colliding with Worzer in the cramped space. A rifle bullet cracked past his helmet. He screamed something again but his own fire was too high, blue-green droplets against the clear sky, and the guerrillas had grabbed the bars while the flirts jumped and blatted.

The rifles were slamming but the flirts were in the way of Rob's gun. "Down! Down!" he shouted uselessly, and the red-haired flirt pitched across the cage with one synthetic breast torn away by the bullet she had leaped in front of. Leon cursed and slumped against Rob's feet, and then it was Chero Worzer shouting, "Hard left, Jake," and leaning across the fallen gunner to rotate his weapon. The combat car tilted left as the bow came around, pinching the trailer against the left rear of the vehicle—in the path of Worzer's powergun. The cage's light alloy bloomed in superheated fireballs as the cyan bolts ripped through it. Both tires exploded together, and there was a red mist of blood in the air. The one guerrilla who had ducked under the burst dropped his rifle and ran.

Worzer cut him in half as he took his third step.

The sergeant gave the wreckage only a glance, then knelt beside Leon. "Cop, he's gone," he said.

The bullet had struck the big man in the neck between helmet and body armor, and there was almost
a gallon of blood on the floor of the compartment.

"Leon?" Jake asked.

"Yeah. Lord, there musta been twenty kilos of
explosive in that satchel charge. If he hadn't hit it in
the air . . ." Worzer looked back at the wreck of the
trailer, then at Rob. "Kid, can you unhitch that
yourself?"

"You just *killed* them," Rob blurted. He was half
blinded by tears and the after-image of the gunfire.

"Via, they did their best on us, didn't they?" the
sergeant snarled. His face was tiger striped by dust
and sweat.

"No, not them!" the boy cried. "Not them—the
girls. You just—"

Worzer's iron fingers gripped Rob by the chin and
turned the recruit remorselessly toward the carnage
behind. The flirts had been torn apart by their own
fluids, some pieces flung through gaps in the mangled cage. "Look at 'em, Jenne!" Worzer demanded.
"They ain't human but if they was, if it was *Leon*
back there, I'd a done it."

His fingers uncurled from Rob's chin and slammed
in a fist against the car's armor. "This ain't heroes, it
ain't no coppy game you play when you want to! You
do what you got to do, 'cause if you don't, some poor
bastard gets killed later when he tries to.

"Now get down there and unhitch us."

"Yes, sir." Rob gripped the lip of the car for support.

Worzer's voice, more gentle, came through the
haze of tears: "And watch it, kid. Just because they're
keeping their heads down don't mean they're all
gone." Then, "Wait." Another pause while the sergeant unfastened the belt and holstered handgun
from his waist and handed it to Rob. Leon wore a

similar weapon, but Worzer did not touch the body. Rob wordlessly clipped the belt, loose for not being fitted over armor, and swung down from the combat car.

The hitch had a quick-release handle, but the torqueing it had received in the last seconds of battle had jammed it. Nervously aware that the sergeant's darting-eyed watchfulness was no pretense, that the shot-scythed grainfield could hide still another guerrilla, or a platoon of them, Rob smashed his boot heel against the catch. It held. Wishing for his driller's sledge, he kicked again.

"Sarge!" Jake shouted. Grain rustled on the other side of the combat car, and against the sky beyond the scarred armor loomed a parcel. Rob threw himself flat.

The explosion picked him up from the ground and bounced him twice, despite the shielding bulk of the combat car. Stumbling upright, Rob steadied himself on the armored side.

The metal felt odd. It no longer trembled with the ready power of the fans. The car was dead, lying at rest on the torn-up soil. With three quick strides, the recruit rounded the bow of the vehicle. He had no time to inspect the dished-in metal, because another swarthy guerrilla was approaching from the other side.

Seeing Rob, the ex-farmer shouted something and drew a long knife. Rob took a step back, remembered the pistol. He tugged at its unfamiliar grip and the weapon popped free into his hand. It seemed the most natural thing in the world to finger the safety, placed just as the tribarrel's had been, then trigger two shots into the face of the lunging guerrilla. The snarl of hatred blanked as the body tumbled face-

down at Rob's feet. The knife had flown somewhere
into the grain.

"Ebros?" a man called. Another lid had raised
from the ground ten meters away. Rob fired at the
hole, missed badly. He climbed the caved-in bow,
clumsily one-handed, keeping the pistol raised. There
was nothing but twisted metal where the driver had
been. Sergeant Worzer was still semi-erect, clutched
against his powergun by a length of structural tubing. It had curled around both his thighs, fluid under
the stunning impact of the satchel charge. The map
display was a pearly blank, though the window above
it still read incongruously 614579 and the red line on
the detector screen blipped in nervous solitude.
Worzer's helmet was gone, having flayed a bloody
track across his scalp as it sailed away. His lips moved,
though, and when Rob put his face near the sergeant's he could hear, "The red . . . pull the red
tab . . ."

Over the left breast of each set of armor were a
blue and a red tab. Rob had assumed they were
decorations of some sort. He shifted the sergeant
gently. The tab was locked down by a cotter pin
which he yanked out. Something hissed in the armor
as he pulled the tab, and Sergeant Worzer murmured,
"Oh Lord. Oh Lord." Then, "Now the stimulant, the
blue tab."

After the second injection sped into his system,
the sergeant opened his eyes. Rob was already trying
to straighten the entrapping tube. "Forget it," Worzer
ordered weakly. "It's inside, too . . . damn armor
musta flexed. Oh Lord." He closed his eyes, opened
them in time to see another head peak cautiously
from the tunnel mouth. "Bastard!" he rasped, and
faster than he spoke he triggered his powergun. Its

motor whined spitefully though the burst went wide. The head disappeared.

"I want you to run back to the gully," the sergeant said, resting his eyes again. "You get there, you say 'Fire Central.' That cuts in the arty frequency automatic. Then you say, 'Bunker complex . . . '" Worzer looked down. "'Six-one-four, five-seven-nine.' Stay low and wait for a patrol."

"It won't bend!" Rob snarled in frustration as his fingers slid again from the blood-slick tubing.

"Jenne, get your ass out of here, *now*."

"Sergeant—"

"Lord curse your soul, get out or I'll call it in myself! Do I look like I wanna live?"

"Oh, Via . . ." Rob tried to reholster the pistol he had set on the bloody floor. It slipped back with a clang. He left it, gripping the sidewall again.

"Maybe tell Dad it was good to see him," Worzer whispered. "You lose touch in this business, Lord knows you do."

"Sir?"

"The priest . . . you met him. Sergeant-Major Worzer, he was. Oh Lord, *move it*—"

At the muffled scream, the recruit leaped from the smashed war-car and ran blindly back the way they had come. He did not know he had reached the gully until the ground flew out from under him and he pitched spread-eagled onto the sand. "Fire Central," he sobbed through strangled breaths, "Fire Central."

"Clear," a strange voice snapped crisply. "Data?"

"Wh-what?"

"Lord and martyrs," the voice blasted, "if you're screwing around on firing channels, you'll wish you never saw daylight!"

"S-six . . . oh Lord, yes, six-one-four, five-seven

nine," Rob sing-songed. He was staring at the smooth sand. "Bunkers, the sergeant says it's bunkers."

"Roger," the voice said, businesslike again. "Ranging in fifteen."

Could they really swing those mighty guns so swiftly, those snub-barrelled rocket howitzers whose firing looked so impressive on the entertainment cube?

"On the way," warned the voice.

The big tribarrel whined again from the combat car, the silent lash of its bolts answered this time by a crash of rifle shots. A flattened bullet burred through the air over where Rob lay. It was lost in the eerie, thunderous shriek from the northwest.

"Splash," the helmet said.

The ground bucked. From the grainplot spouted rock, smoke and metal fragments into a black column fifty meters high.

"Are we on?" the voice demanded.

"Oh Lord," Rob prayed, beating his fists against the sand, "Oh Lord."

"Via, what is this?" the helmet wondered aloud. Then, "All guns, battery five."

And the earth began to ripple and gout under the hammer of the guns.

Interlude:
Powerguns

By THE 21st Century, missile-firing small arms appeared to have reached the pinnacle of their development, and there was nothing on hand to replace them. The mass and velocity of projectiles could be juggled, but they could not be increased in sum without a corresponding increase in recoil or backblast. Explosive bullets were very destructive on impact, but they had no penetration beyond the immediate blast radius. An explosive bullet might vaporize a leaf it hit near the muzzle as easily as the intended target down-range, and using explosives in heavy brush was worse than useless because it endangered the shooter.

Lasers, though they had air-defense applications, were not the infantryman's answer either. The problem with lasers was the power source. Guns store energy in the powder charge. A machinegun with one cartridge is just as effective—once—as it is with a thousand round belt, so the ammunition load can be tailored to circumstances. Man-killing lasers required a four hundred-kilo fusion unit to drive them. Hooking a laser on line with any less bulky energy source was of zero military effectiveness rather than lesser effectiveness.

Science lent Death a hand in this impasse—as Science has always done, since the day the first wedge became the first knife. Thirty thousand residents of St. Pierre, Martinique, had been killed on May 8, 1902. The agent of their destruction was a "burning cloud" released during an eruption of Mt. Pelee. Popular myth had attributed the deaths to normal volcanic phenomena, hot gases or ash like that which buried Pompeii; but even the most cursory examination of the evidence indicated that direct energy release had done the lethal damage. In 2073, Dr. Marie Weygand, heading a team under contract to Olin-America, managed to duplicate the phenomenon.

The key had come from spectroscopic examination of pre-1902 lavas from Pelee's crater. The older rocks had showed inexplicable gaps among the metallic elements expected there. A year and a half of empirical research followed, guided more by Dr. Weygand's intuition than by the battery of scientific instrumentation her employers had rushed out at the first signs of success. The principle ultimately discovered was of little utility as a general power source—but then, Olin-America had not been looking for a way to heat homes.

Weygand determined that metallic atoms of a fixed magnetic orientation could be converted directly into energy by the proper combination of heat, pressure, and intersecting magnetic fields. Old lava locks its rich metallic burden in a pattern dictated by the magnetic ambiance at the time the flow cools. At Pelee in 1902, the heavy Gauss loads of the new eruption made a chance alignment with the restressed lava of the crater's rim. Matter flashed into energy in a line dictated by the intersection, ripping other atoms free of the basalt matrix and converting them in turn. Below in St. Pierre, humans burned.

When the principle had been discovered, it remained only to refine its destructiveness. Experiments were held with different fuel elements and matrix materials. A copper-cobalt charge in a wafer of microporous polyurethane became the standard, since it appeared to give maximum energy release with the least tendency to scatter. Because the discharge was linear, there was no need of a tube to channel the force as a rifle's barrel does; but some immediate protection from air-induced scatter was necessary for a hand-held weapon. The best barrel material was iridium. Tungsten and osmium were even more refractory, but those elements absorbed a large component of the discharge instead of reflecting it as the iridium did.

To function in service, the new weapons needed to be cooled. Even if a white-hot barrel did not melt, the next charge certainly would vaporize before it could be fired. Liquified gas, generally nitrogen or one of the noble gases which would not themselves erode the metal, was therefore released into the bore after every shot. Multiple barrels, either rotating like those of a Gatling gun or fixed like those of the mitrailleuse, the Gatling's French contemporary, were used to achieve high rates of fire or to fire very high intensity charges. Personal weapons were generally semi-automatic to keep weight and bulk within manageable limits. Submachineguns with large gas reservoirs to fire pistol charges had their uses and advocates, as their bullet-firing predecessors had.

Powerguns—the first usage of the term is as uncertain as that of "gun" itself, though the derivation is obvious—greatly increased the range and destructiveness of the individual soldier. The weapons were so destructive, in fact, that even on most frontier planets their use was limited to homicide. Despite that limited usefulness, factories for the manufacture of powerguns and their ammunition would probably have been early priority items on most worlds—had not that manufacture been utterly beyond the capacity of all but the most highly industrialized planets.

Precision forming of metal as hard as iridium is an incredible task. Gas reservoirs required a nulconductive sheath if they were not to bleed empty before they even reached the field. If ammunition wafers were rolled out in a fluctuating electrical field, they were as likely to blow out the breech of a weapon or gang-fire in the loading tube as they were to injure a foe. All the planetary pride in the cosmos would not change laws of physics.

Of course, some human cultures preferred alternate weaponry. The seven worlds of the Gorgon Cluster equipped their armies—and a number of mercenary units—with flechette guns for instance. Their hypervelocity osmium projectiles had better short-range penetration than 2 cm powerguns, and they cycled at a very high rate. But the barrels of flechette guns were of synthetic diamond, making them at least as difficult to manufacture as the more common energy weapons.

Because of the expense of modern weapons, would-be combatants on rural worlds often delayed purchasing guns until fighting was inevitable. Then it became natural to consider buying not only the guns but men who were used to them—for powerguns were no luxury to the mercenaries whose lives and pay depended on their skill with the best possible equipment. The gap between a citizen-soldier holding a powergun he had been issued a week before, and the professional who had trained daily for years with the weapon, was a wide one.

Thus if only one side on a poor world hired mercenaries, its victory was assured—numbers and ideology be damned. That meant, of course, that both sides had to make the investment even if it meant mortgaging the planetary income for a decade. Poverty was preferable to what came with defeat.

All over the galaxy, men with the best gifts of Science and no skills but those of murder looked for patrons who would hire them to bring down civilization. Business was good.

Cultural Conflict

PLATOON SERGEANT HORTHY stood with his right arm—his only arm—akimbo, surveying the rippling treetops beneath him and wishing they really were the waves of a cool, gray ocean. The trees lapped high up the sides of the basalt knob that had become Firebase Bolo three weeks before when a landing boat dropped them secretly onto it. Now, under a black plastic ceiling that mimicked the basalt to the eye of the Federation spy satellite, nestled a command car, a rocket howitzer with an air cushion truck to carry its load of ammunition, and Horthy's three combat cars.

Horthy's cars—except on paper. There Lieutenant Simmons-Brown was listed as platoon leader.

One of the long-limbed native reptiles suddenly began to gesture and screech up at the sergeant. The beasts occasionally appeared on the treetops, scurrying and bounding like fleas in a dog's fur. Recently their bursts of rage had become more common—and more irritating. Horthy was a short, wasp-waisted man who wore a spiky goatee and a drum-magazined powergun slung beneath his shoulder. His hand now moved to its grip . . . but shooting meant giving in to frustration, and instead Horthy only muttered a curse.

"You say something, Top?" asked a voice behind him. He turned without speaking and saw Jenne and Scratchard, his two gunners, with a lanky howitzer crewman whose name escaped him.

"Nothing that matters," Horthy said.

Scratchard's nickname was Ripper Jack because he carried a long knife in preference to a pistol. He fumbled a little nervously with its hilt as he said, "Look, Top, ah . . . we been talking and Bonmarcher here—" he nodded at the artilleryman—"he says we're not supporting the rest of the Regiment, we're stuck out here in the middle of nowhere to shoot up Federation ships when the war starts."

The sergeant looked sharply at Bonmarcher, then said, "*If* the war starts. Yeah, that's pretty much true. We're about the only humans on South Continent, but if the government decides it still wants to be independent and the Federation decides it's gotta have Squire's World as a colony—well, Fed supply routes pass through two straits within hog shot of this rock." Simmons-Brown would cop a screaming worm if he heard Horthy tell the men a truth supposed to be secret, but one way or another it wasn't going to matter very long.

"But Lord and *Martyrs*, Top," Bonmarcher burst out, "how long after we start shooting is it gonna be before the Feds figure out where the shells're coming from? Sure, this cap—" he thumbed toward the plastic supported four meters over the rock by thin pillars—"hides us now. But sure as death, we'll loose one off while the satellite's still over us, or the Feds'll triangulate radar tracks as the shells come over the horizon at them. Then what'll happen?"

"That's what our combat cars are for," Horthy said wearily, knowing that the Federation would send not troops but a salvo of their own shells to deal with the thorn in their side. "We'll worry about that when it happens. Right now—" He broke off. Another of those damned, fluffy reptiles was shrieking like a cheated whore not twenty meters from him.

"Bonmarcher," the sergeant said in sudden inspiration, "you want to go down there and do something about that noisemaker for me?" Two noisemakers, actually—the beast and the artilleryman himself for as long as the hunt kept him out of the way.

"Gee, Top, I'd sure love to get outa this oven, but I heard the lieutenant order . . ." Bonmarcher began, looking sidelong at the command car fifty meters away in the center of the knob. Its air conditioner whined, cooling Simmons-Brown and the radioman on watch within its closed compartment.

"Look, you just climb down below the leaf cover and don't loose off unless you've really got a target," said Horthy. "I'll handle the lieutenant."

Beaming with pleasure, Bonmarcher patted his sidearm to make sure it was snapped securely in its holster. "Thanks, Top," he said and began to descend by the cracks and shelvings that eternity had forged even into basalt.

Horthy ignored him, turning instead to the pair of his own men who had waited in silent concern during the exchange. "Look, boys," the one-armed sergeant said quietly, "I won't give you a load of cop about this being a great vacation for us. But you keep your mouths shut and do your jobs, and I'll do my damnedest to get us all out of here in one piece." He looked away from his listeners for a moment, up at the dull iridium vehicles and the stripped or khaki crewmen lounging over them. "Anyhow, neither the Feds or the twats that hired us have any guts. I'll give you even money that one side or the other backs down before anything drops in the pot."

Scratchard, as lean and dark as Horthy, looked at the huge, blond Jenne. There was no belief on either face. Then the rear hatch of the command car flung open and the communications sergeant stepped out whooping with joy. "They've signed a new treaty!" he shouted. "We're being recalled!"

Horthy grinned, punched each of his gunners lightly in the stomach. "See?" he said. "You listen to Top and he'll bring you home."

All three began to laugh with released tension.

Hilf, Caller of the Moon Sept, followed his sept-brother Seida along the wire-thin filaments of the canopy. Their black footpads flashed a rare primary color as they leaped. The world was slate-gray bark and huge pearly leaves sprouting on flexible tendrils, raised to a sky in which the sun was a sizzling platinum bead. Both runners were lightly dusted with the pollen they had shaken from fruiting bodies in their course. The Tree, though an entity, required cross-fertilization among its segments for healthy growth. The mottled gray-tones of Seida's feathery scales blended perfectly with his surroundings, and his strength was as smooth as the Tree's. Hilf knew the young male hoped to become Caller himself in a few years, knew also that Seida lacked the necessary empathy with the Tree and the sept to hold the position. Besides, his recklessness was no substitute for intelligence.

But Seida was forcing Hilf to act against his better judgment. The creatures on the bald, basalt knob were clearly within the sept's territory; but what proper business had any of the Folk with rock-dwellers? Still, knowing that token activity would help calm his brothers, Hilf had let Seida lead him to personally view the situation. At the back of the Caller's mind was the further realization that the Mothers were sometimes swayed by the "maleness" of action as opposed to intelligent lethargy.

Poised for another leap, Hilf noticed the black line of a worm track on the bark beside him. He halted, instinctively damping the springiness of his perch by flexing his hind legs. Seida shrieked but fell into lowering silence when he saw what his Caller was about. Food was an immediate need. As Hilf had known, Seida's unfitness for leadership included his inability to see beyond the immediate.

The branch was a twenty-centimeter latticework of intergrown tendrils, leapfrogging kilometers across the forest. In its career it touched and fused with a dozen trunks, deep-rooted pillars whose tendrils were of massive cross section. Hilf blocked the worm track with a spike-clawed, multi-jointed thumb twice the length of the three fingers on each hand. His other thumb thrust into the end of the track and wriggled. The bark split, baring the hollowed pith and the worm writhing and stretching away from the impaling claw. Hilf's esophagus spasmed once to crush the soft creature. He looked up. Seida stuttered an impoliteness verging on command: he had not forgotten his self-proclaimed mission. The Caller sighed and followed him.

The ancient volcanic intrusion was a hundred-meter thumb raised from the forest floor. The Tree crawled partway up the basalt, but the upper faces of the rock were steep and dense enough to resist attachments by major branches. Three weeks previously a huge ball had howled out of the sky and poised over the rock, discharging other silvery beasts shaped like great sowbugs and guided by creatures not too dissimilar to the Folk. These had quickly raised the black cover which now hung like an optical illusion to the eyes of watchers in the highest nearby branches. The unprecedented event had sparked the hottest debate of the Caller's memory. Despite opposition from Seida and a few other hotheads, Hilf had finally convinced his sept that the rock was not their affair.

Now, on the claim that one of the brown-coated invaders had climbed out onto a limb, Seida was insisting that he should be charged at once with leading a war party. Unfortunately, at least the claim was true.

Seida halted, beginning to hoot and point. Even without such notice the interloper would have been obvious to Hilf. The creature was some fifty meters away—three healthy leaps, the Caller's mind abstracted—and below the observers. It was huddled on a branch which acted as a flying buttress for the high towers of the Tree. At near view it was singularly unattractive: appreciably larger than one of the sept-brothers, it bore stubby arms and a head less regular than the smooth bullets of the Folk.

As he pondered, the Caller absently gouged a feather of edible orange fungus out of the branch. The rest of the aliens remained under their roof, equally oblivious to the Folk and their own sept-brother. The latter was crawling a little closer on his branch, manipulating the object he carried while turning his lumpy face toward Seida.

Hilf, blending silently into the foliage behind his brother, let his subconscious float and merge while his surface mind grappled with the unpalatable alternatives. The creature below was technically an invader, but it did not seem the point of a thrust against the Moon Sept. Tradition did not really speak to the matter. Hilf could send out a war party, losing a little prestige to Seida since the younger brother had cried for that course from the beginning. Far worse than the loss of prestige was the risk to the sept which war involved. If the interlopers were as strong as they were big, the Folk would face a grim battle. In addition, the huge silver beasts which had whined and snarled as they crawled onto the rock were a dangerous uncertainty, though they had been motionless since their appearance.

But the only way to avoid war seemed to be for Hilf to kill his sept-brother. Easy enough to do—a sudden leap and both thumbs rammed into the brainbox. The fact Seida was not prepared for an attack was further proof of his unfitness to lead. No one would dispute the Caller's tale of a missed leap and a long fall. . . . Hilf poised as Seida leaned out to thunder more abuse at the creature below.

The object in the interloper's hand flashed. The foliage winked cyan and Seida's head blew apart. Spasming muscles threw his body forward, following its fountaining blood in an arc to the branch below. The killer's high cackles of triumph pursued Hilf as he raced back to the Heart.

He had been wrong: the aliens *did* mean war.

Simmons-Brown broke radio contact with a curse. His khakis were sweatstained and one of the shoulder-board chevrons announcing his lieutenancy was missing. "Top," he whined to Sergeant Horthy who stood by the open hatch of the command car, "Command Central won't send a space boat to pick us up, they

want us to *drive* all the way to the north coast for
surface pick-up to Johnstown. That's twelve hundred
kilometers and anyhow, we can't even get the cars
down off this Lord-stricken rock!"

"Sure we can," Horthy said, planning aloud rather
than deigning to contradict the wispy lieutenant.
Simmons-Brown was a well-connected incompetent
whose approach to problem solving was to throw a
tantrum while other people tried to work around
him. "We'll link tow cables and . . . no, a winch
won't hold but we can blast-set an eyebolt, then
rappel the cars down one at a time. How long they
give us till pick-up?"

"Fifteen days, but—"

A shot bumped the air behind the men. Both
whipped around. Horthy's hand brushed his submachinegun's grip momentarily before he relaxed.
He said, "It's all plus, just Bonmarcher. I told him
he could shut up a couple of the local noisemakers if
he stayed below the curve of the rock and didn't put
a hole in our camouflage. The fed satellite isn't good
enough to pick up small arms fire in this jungle."

"I distinctly ordered that no shots be fired while
we're on detached duty!" snapped Simmons-Brown,
his full moustache trembling like an enraged caterpillar. "Distinctly!"

Sergeant Horthy looked around the six blowers
and twenty-three men that made up Firebase Bolo.
He sighed. Waiting under commo security, between
bare rock and hot plastic, would have been rough at
the best of times. With Simmons-Brown added . . .
"Sorry, sir," the sergeant lied straight-faced, "I must
have forgotten."

"Well, get the men moving," Simmons-Brown ordered, already closing the hatch on his air con-

ditioning. "Those bastards at Central might just leave us if we missed pick-up. They'd like that."

"Oh, we'll make it fine," Horthy said to himself, his eyes already searching for a good place to sink the eyebolt. "Once we get off the rock there won't be any problem. The ground's flat, and with all the leaves up here cutting off light we won't have undergrowth to bother about. Just set the compasses on north and follow our noses."

"Hey, Top," someone called. "Look what I got!" Bonmarcher had clambered back onto the rock. Behind him, dragged by its lashed ankles, was a deep-chested reptile that had weighed about forty kilos before being decapitated. "Blew this monkey away my first shot," the artilleryman bragged.

"Nice work," Horthy replied absently. His mind was on more important things.

The world of the Moon Sept was not a sphere but a triangular section of forest. That wedge, like those of each of the twenty-eight other septs, was dominated by the main root of a Tree. The ground at the center was thin loam over not subsoil but almost a hectare of ancient root. The trunks sprouting from the edge of this mass were old, too, but not appreciably thicker than the other pillars supporting the Tree for hundreds of kilometers in every direction. Interwoven stems and branches joined eighty meters in the air, roofing the Heart in a quivering blanket of leaves indistinguishable from that of the rest of the forest. The hollow dome within was an awesome thing even without its implications, and few of the Folk cared to enter it.

Hilf himself feared the vast emptiness and the power it focused, but he had made his decision three years before when the Mothers summoned the previous Caller to the Nest and a breeder's diet. Hilf had thrust forward and used the flowing consciousness of the whole sept to face down his rivals for the Callership. Now he thumped to the hard floor without hesitation and walked quickly on feet and knuckles to the pit worn in the center of the root by millennia of Callers. His body prone below the lips of the blond rootwood, Hilf's right claw gashed sap from the Tree and then nicked his own left wrist. Sap and pale blood oozed together, fusing Caller and Tree physically in a fashion dictated by urgency. The intense wood grain rippled from in front of Hilf's eyes and his mind began to fill with shattered, spreading images of the forest. Each heartbeat sent Hilf out in a further surge and blending until every trunk and branch-bundle had become the Tree, each member of the Moon Sept had blurred into the Folk. A black warmth beneath the threshold of awareness indicated that even the Mothers had joined.

The incident trembled through the sept, a kaleidoscope more of emotion than pictures. Seida capered again, gouted and died in the invader's raucous laughter. Reflex stropped claws on the bark of a thousand branches. Response was the Caller's to suggest and guide, not to determine. The first blood-maddened reply by the sept almost overwhelmed Hilf. But his response had been planned, stamped out on the template of experience older than that of any living sept-brother—as old, perhaps, as the joinder of Folk and Tree. The alien nature of the invaders would not be allowed to pervert the traditional response: the remainder of Seida's hatching would go out to punish the death of their brother.

The pattern of the root began to reimpose itself on Hilf's eyes. He continued to lie in the hollow, logy with reaction. Most of the sept were returning to

their foraging or play, but there were always eyes
trained on the knob and the activity there. And
scattered throughout the wedge of the Tree were
thirty-seven of the Folk, young and fierce in their
strength, who drifted purposefully together.

At the forest floor the raindrops, scattered by the
triple canopy, were a saturated fog that clung and
made breath a struggle. Horthy ignored it, letting
his feet and sinewed hand mechanically balance him
against the queasy ride of the air-cushion vehicle.
His eyes swept the ground habitually. When reminded by his conscious mind, they took in the
canopies above also.

The rain had slowed the column. The strangely-
woven tree boles were never spaced too closely to
pass the armored vehicles between them, but frequent clumps of spire-pointed fungus thrust several
meters in the air and confused the aisles. Experience
had shown that when struck by a car the saprophytes
would collapse in a cloud of harmless spores, but in
the fog-blurred dimness they sometimes hid an unyielding trunk behind them. The lead car had its
driving lights on though the water dazzle made them
almost useless, and all six vehicles had closed up
more tightly than Horthy cared to see. There was
little chance of a Federation ambush, but even a
sudden halt would bring on a multiple collision.

The brassy trilling that had grown familiar in the
past several hours sounded again from somewhere in
the forest. Just an animal, though. The war on Squire's
World was over for the time, and whether the Regiment's employers had won or lost there was no reason for Horthy to remain as tense as he was.
Simmons-Brown certainly was unconcerned, riding
in the dry cabin of his command car. That was the

second vehicle, just ahead of Horthy's. The sergeant's wing gunners huddled in the fighting compartment to either side of him. They were miserable and bored, their minds as empty as their slack, dripping faces.

Irritated but without any real reason to slash the men to vigilance, Horthy glared back along his course. The stubby 150 mm howitzer, the cause of the whole Lord-accursed operation, was the fourth vehicle. Only its driver, his head a mirroring ball behind its face shield, was visible. The other five men of the crew were within the open-backed turret whose sheathing was poor protection against hostile fire but enough to keep the rain out.

The ammo transporter was next, sandwiched between the hog and the combat car which brought up the rear of the column. Eighty-kilo shells were stacked ten high on its flat bed, their noses color coded with incongruous gaiety. The nearby mass of explosive drew a wince from Horthy, who knew that if it went off together it could pulverize the basalt they had been emplaced on. On top of the front row of shells where its black fuse winked like a Cyclops' eye was the gas round, a thin-walled cylinder of K3 which could kill as surely by touch as by inhalation. Everyone in the Regiment respected K3, but Horthy was one of the few who understood it well enough to prefer the gas to conventional weapons in some situations.

In part, that was a comment on his personality as well.

To Horthy's right, Rob Jenne began to shrug out of his body armor. "Keep it on, trooper," the sergeant said.

"But Top," Jenne complained, "it rubs in this wet." His fingers lifted the segmented porcelain to display the weal chafed over his floating ribs.

"Leave it on," Horthy repeated, gesturing about the fighting compartment crowded with ammunition and personal gear. "There's not enough room here for us, even without three suits of armor standing around empty. Besides—"

The gray creature's leap carried it skimming over Horthy to crash full into Jenne's chest. Man and alien pitched over the bulkhead. Horthy leaned forward and shot by instinct, using his sidearm instead of the powerful, less handy, tribarrel mounted on the car. His light finger pressure clawed three holes in the creature's back as it somersaulted into the ground with Jenne.

The forest rang as the transporter plowed into the stern of the grounded howitzer. The gun vehicle seemed to crawl with scores of the scale-dusted aliens, including the one whose spear-sharp thumbs had just decapitated the driver. Horthy twisted his body to spray the mass with blue-green fire. The hog's bow fulcrummed in the soil as the transporter's impact lifted its stern. The howitzer upended, its gun tube flopping freely in an arc while inertia vomited men from the turret.

"Watch the bloody ammo!" Horthy shouted into his intercom as a tribarrel hosed one of the aliens off the transporter in a cloud of gore and vaporized metal. Ahead, the command car driver had hit his panic bar in time to save himself, but one of the long-armed creatures was hacking at the vision-blocs as though they were the vehicle's eyes. The rear hatch opened and Simmons-Brown flung himself out screaming with fear. Horthy hesitated. The alien gave up its assault on the optical fibers and sprang on the lieutenant's back.

Horthy's burst chopped both of them to death in a welter of blood.

Only body armor saved the sergeant from the attack that sledged his chest forward into the iridium bulkhead. He tried to rise but could not against the weight and the shocks battering both sides of his thorax like paired trip-hammers.

The blows stopped and the weight slid from Horthy's back and down his ankles. He levered himself upright, gasping with pain as intense as that of the night a bullet-firing machinegun had smashed across his armor. Scratchard, the left gunner, grinned at him. The man's pale skin was spattered with the same saffron blood that covered his knife.

"They've gone off, Top," Scratchard said. "Didn't like the tribarrels—even though we didn't hit much but trees. Didn't like this, neither." He stropped his blade clean on the thighs of the beast he had killed with it.

"Bleeding martyrs," Horthy swore under his breath as he surveyed the damage. The platoon's own four blowers were operable, but the overturned hog was a total loss and the transporter's front fan had disintegrated when the steel ground-effect curtain had crumpled into its arc. If there was any equipment yard on Squire's World that could do the repairs, it sure as cop was too far away from this stretch of jungle to matter. Five men were dead and another, his arm ripped from shoulder to wrist, was comatose under the effects of sedatives, clotting agents, antibiotics, and shock.

"All plus," Horthy began briskly. "We leave the bodies, leave the two arty blowers too; and I just hope our scaly friends get real curious about them soon. Before we pull out, I want ten of the high explosive warheads unscrewed and loaded into the command car—yeah, and the gas shell too."

"Via, Top," one of the surviving artillerymen muttered, "why we got to haul that stuff around?"

" 'Cause I said so," Horthy snarled, "and ain't I in charge?" His hand jerked the safety pin from one of the delay-fused shells, then spun the dial to one hour. "Now get moving, because we want to be a long way away in an hour."

The platoon was ten kilometers distant when the shock wave rippled the jungle floor like the head of a drum. The jungle had blown skyward in a gray puree, forming a momentary bubble over a five-hectare crater.

The Moon Sept waited for twilight in a ring about the shattered clearing in which the invaders were halted. The pain that had slashed through every member of the sept at the initial explosion was literally beyond comparison: when agony gouged at the Tree, the brothers had collapsed wherever they stood, spewing waste and the contents of their stomach uncontrollably. Hours later the second blast tore away ten separate trunks and brought down a hectare of canopy. The huge silver beasts had shoved the debris to the side before they settled down in the new clearing. That explosion was bearable on top of the first only because of the black rage of the Mothers now insulating the Moon Sept from full empathy with their Tree; but not even the Mothers could accept further punishment at that level. Hilf moaned in the root-alcove, only dimly aware that he had befouled it in reaction. He was a conduit now, not the Caller in fact, for the eyeless ones had assumed control. The Mothers had made a two-dimensional observation which the males, to whom up and down were more important than horizontal direction, had missed: the invaders were proceeding toward the Nest. They must be stopped.

The full thousand of the Moon Sept blended into

the leaves with a perfection achieved in the days in which there had been carnivores in the forest. When one of the Folk moved it was to ease cramps out of a muscle or to catch the sun-pearl on the delicate edge of a claw. They did not forage; the wracking horror of the explosions had left them beyond desire for food.

The effect on the Tree had been even worse. In multi-kilometer circles from both blast sites the wood sagged sapless and foliage curled around its stems. The powerguns alone had been devastating to the Tree's careful stasis, bolts that shattered the trunks they clipped and left the splinters ablaze in the rain. Only the lightning could compare in destructiveness, and the charges building in the uppermost branches gave warning enough for the Tree to minimize lightning damage.

There would be a further rain of cyan charges, but that could not be helped. The Mothers were willing to sacrifice to necessity, even a Tree or a sept.

The four silvery beasts lay nose to tail among the craters, only fifty meters from the standing trunks in which the Folk waited. Hilf watched from a thousand angles. Only the rotating cones on the foreheads of each of the beasts seemed to be moving. Their riders were restive, however, calling to one another in low voices whose alien nature could not disguise their tension. The sun that had moments before been a spreading blob on the western horizon was now gone; invisible through the clouds but a presence felt by the Folk, the fixed Moon now ruled the sky alone. It was the hour of the Moon Sept, and the command of the Mothers was the loosing of a blood-mad dog to kill.

"Death!" screamed the sept-brothers as they sprang into the clearing.

There was death in plenty awaiting them.

The antipersonnel strips of the cars were live. Hilf was with the first body when it hurtled to within twenty meters of a car and the strips began to fire on radar command. Each of the white flashes that slammed and glared from just above the ground-effect curtains was fanning out a handful of tetrahedral pellets. Where the energy released by the powerguns blasted flesh into mist and jelly, the projectiles ripped like scythes over a wide area. Then the forest blazed as flickering cyan hosed across it.

The last antipersonnel charge went off, leaving screams and the thump of powerguns that were almost silence after the rattling crescendo of explosions.

The sept, the surprising hundreds whom the shock had paralyzed but not slain, surged forward again. The three-limbed Caller of the invaders shouted orders while he fired. The huge silver beasts howled and spun end for end even as Hilf's brothers began to leap aboard—then the port antipersonnel strips cut loose in a point-blank broadside. For those above the plane of the discharges there was a brief flurry of claws aimed at neck joints and gun muzzles tight against flesh as they fired. Then a grenade, dropped or jarred from a container, went off in the blood-slick compartment of number one car. Mingled limbs erupted. The sides blew out and the bins of ready ammunition gang-fired in a fury of light and gobbets of molten iridium.

The attack was over. The Mothers had made the instant assumption that the third explosion would be on the order of the two previous—and blocked their minds off from a Tree-empathy that might have been lethal. Without their inexorable thrusting, the scatter of sept-brothers fled like grubs from the sun. They had fought with the savagery of their remote ancestors eliminating the great Folk-devouring serpents from the forest.

And it had not been enough.

"Cursed right we're staying here," Horthy said in irritation. "This is the only high ground in five hundred kilometers. If we're going to last out another attack like yesterday's, it'll be by letting our K3 roll downhill into those apes. And the Lord help us if a wind comes up."

"Well, I still don't like it, Top," Jenne complained. "It doesn't look natural."

Horthy fully agreed with that, though he did so in silence. Command Central had used satellite coverage to direct them to the hill, warning again that even in their emergency it might be a day before a landing boat could be cleared to pick them up. From above, the half-kilometer dome of laterite must have been as obvious as a baby in the wedding party, a gritty red pustule on the gray hide of the continent. From the forest edge it was even stranger, and strange meant deadly to men in Horthy's position. But only the antipersonnel strips had saved the platoon the night before, and they were fully discharged. They were left with the gas or nothing.

The hill was as smooth as the porous stone allowed it to be and rose at a gentle 1:3 ratio. The curve of its edge was broken by the great humped roots that lurched and knotted out of the surrounding forest, plunging into the hill at angles that must lead them to its center. As Jenne had said, it wasn't natural. Nothing about this cursed forest was.

"Let's go," Horthy ordered. His driver boosted the angle and power of his drive fans and they began to slide up the hill, followed by the other two cars. Strange that the trees hadn't covered the hill with a network of branches, even if their trunks for some reason couldn't seat in the rock. Enough ground was clear for the powerguns alone to mince an attack, despite the awesome quickness of the gray creatures. Except that the powerguns were low on ammo too.

Maybe there wouldn't be a third attack.

An alien appeared at the hillcrest fifty meters ahead. Horthy killed it by reflex, using a single shot from his tribarrel. There was an opening there, a cave or tunnel mouth, and a dozen more of the figures spewed from it. "Watch the sides!" Horthy roared at Jenne and Scratchard, but all three powerguns were ripping the new targets. Bolts that missed darted off into the dull sky like brief, blue-green suns.

Jenne's grenade spun into the meter-broad hole as the car overran it. If anything more had planned to come out, that settled it. Scratchard jiggled the controls of the echo sounder, checked the read-out again, and swore, "Via! I don't see any more surface openings, Top, but this whole mound's like a fencepost in termite country!"

The three blowers were pulled up close around the opening, the crews awaiting orders. Horthy toothed his lower lip but there was no hesitation in his voice after he decided. "Wixom and Chung," he said, "get that gas shell out and bring it over here. The rest of you cover the forest—I'll keep this hole clear."

The two troopers wrestled the cylinder out of the command car and gingerly carried it to the lip of the opening. The hill was reasonably flat on top and the laterite gave good footing, but the recent shooting had left patches glazed by the powerguns and a film of blood over the whole area. The container should not have ruptured if dropped, but no one familiar with K3 wanted to take the chance.

"All plus," Horthy said. "Fuse it for ten seconds and drop it in. As soon as that goes down, we're going to hover over the hole with our fans on max, just to make sure all the gas goes in the right direction. If we can do them enough damage, maybe they'll leave us alone."

The heavy shell clinked against something as it disappeared into the darkness but kept falling in the passage cleared by the grenade. It was well below the surface when the bursting charge tore the casing open. That muted *whoomp* was lost in the shriek of Horthy's fans as his car wobbled on a column of air a meter above the hilltop. K3 sank even in still air, pooling in invisible deathtraps in the low spots of a battlefield. Rammed by the drive fans, it had permeated the deepest tunnels of the mound in less than a minute.

The rioting air blew the bodies and body parts of the latest victims into a windrow beside the opening. Horthy glanced over them with a professional concern for the dead as he marked time. These creatures had the same long limbs and smooth-faced features as the ones which had attacked in the forest, but there was a difference as well. The genitals of the earlier-seen aliens had been tiny, vestigial or immature, but each of the present corpses carried a dong the length and thickness of a forearm. Bet their girlfriends walk bow-legged, Horthy chuckled to himself.

The hill shook with an impact noticeable even through the insulating air. "Top, they're tunneling out!" cried the command car's driver over the intercom.

"Hold your distance!" Horthy commanded as five meters of laterite crumbled away from the base of the hill. The thing that had torn the gap almost filled it. Horthy and every other gunman in the platoon blasted at it in a reaction that went deeper than fear. Even as it gouted fluids under the multiple impacts, the thing managed to squirm completely out. The tiny head and the limbs that waved like broomstraws thrust into a watermelon were the only ornamentation on the slug-white torso. The face was blind, but it was the face of the reptiloids of the forest until a burst of cyan pulped its obscenity. Horthy's tribarrel whipsawed down the twenty-meter belly. A sphincter convulsed in front of the line of shots and spewed a mass of eggs in jelly against the unyielding laterite. The blackening that K3 brought to its victims was already beginning to set in before the platoon stopped firing.

Nothing further attempted to leave the mound.

"Wh-what do we do now, Top?" Jenne asked.

"Wait for the landing boat," answered Horthy. He shook the cramp out of his hand and pretended that it was not caused by his panicky deathgrip on the tribarrel moments before. "And we pray that it comes before too bleeding long."

The cold that made Hilf's body shudder was the residue of the Mothers' death throes deep in the corridors of the Nest. No warmth remained in a universe which had seen the last generation of the Folk. The yellow leaf-tinge of his blast-damaged Tree no longer concerned Hilf. About him, a psychic pressure rather than a message, he could feel the gathering of the other twenty-eight septs—just too late to protect the Mothers who had summoned them. Except for the Moon Sept's, the Trees were still healthy and would continue to be so for years until there were too few of the Folk scampering among the branches to spread their pollen. Then, with only the infrequent wind to stimulate new growth, the Trees as well would begin to die.

Hilf began to walk forward on all fours, his knuckles gripping firmly the rough exterior of the Nest. "Top!" cried one of the invaders, and Hilf knew that their eyes or the quick-darting antennae of their silver beasts had discovered his approach. He looked up. The three-limbed Caller was staring at him, his stick extended to kill. His eyes were as empty as Hilf's own.

The bolt hammered through Hilf's lungs and he pitched backwards. Through the bloodroar in his ears he could hear the far-distant howl that had preceded the invader's appearance in the forest.

As if the landing boat were their signal, the thirty thousand living males of the Folk surged forward from the Trees.

Interlude: Backdrop to Chaos

THE MERCENARY COMPANIES of the late Third Millennium were both a result of and a response to a spurt of empire-building among the new industrial giants of the human galaxy. Earth's first flash of colonization had been explosive. Transit was an expensive proposition for trade or tourism; but on a national scale, a star colony was just as possible as the high-rise Palace of Government which even most of the underdeveloped countries had built for the sake of prestige.

And colonies were very definitely a matter of prestige. The major powers had them. So, just as Third World countries had squandered their resources on jet fighters in the Twentieth Century (and on ironclads in the Nineteenth), they bought or leased or even built starships in the Twenty-first. These colonies were almost invariably mono-national, under-capitalized, and stratified by class even more rigidly

134

than were their mother countries. All of those factors affected later galactic history. There was a plethora of suitable worlds on which to plant colonies, however, so that even the most ineptly-handled groups of settlers generally managed to survive. Theirs was a hand-to-mouth survival of farming and barter, though, not of spaceports shipping vast quanties of minerals and protein back to Earth.

A few of the better-backed colonies did become very successful. Most of them had been spawned by the larger nations, though a few were private ventures (including that of the Dutch consortium which founded Friesland). Success left their backers in the same situation of those whose colonies were barely surviving, however, since the first result of planetary self-sufficiency was invariably to cut ties and find the best prices available for manufactures on the open market.

There followed a spate of secondary colonization from the successful colony worlds. These new colonies were planted with a specific product in mind: a mineral; a drug; sometimes simply agriculture, freeing more valuable real estate on the homeworlds. Even a planet could be filled in a few centuries by the asymtotic population growth which empty spaces seem to engender in human beings. Secondary colonies were frequently joint efforts, combining settlers and capital from several worlds. They were a business proposition, after all, not matters of national honor.

Unfortunately for the concept, the newly-mixed national and racial groups got along just as badly as their ancestors had a few centuries earlier on Earth. The planetary governments of Hiroseke and Stewart, for instance, conferred placidly with each other; but in the iridium-mining colony they had founded together on Kalan, Japanese and Scotsmen were shooting at each other within five years.

The new colonizers had thought they would be able to control their colonies without military force. Their own experience had taught them to control space transport to the new colonies. Without the ability to sell its produce in markets of its own choice, a colony could not strike off on its own—as the homeworlds had themselves done.

But a colony could be forced into a pattern of logical subservience only if its populace were willing to be logical. If instead the settlers decided to eat their own guts out through internal warfare, the colony would become as commercially valueless as Germany in 1648. Inevitably, homeworlds attempted through military force to control and unify their colonies; also inevitably, they increased the disruption by their activities.

And even if some sort of a military solution *was* imposed, there remained the question of how to deal with the defeated troublemakers—however they were defined—to avoid a new outbreak of fighting. Ideally, they could be used as expendables in battles elsewhere. It was a course which had been followed with success often in the past—Germans in French Indo-China in 1948, and Scots borderers in Ulster in 1605, for two examples. The course required that there be other battles to fight—but there were other unruly colonies as well as backwater worlds whose produce would be useful if it could be controlled at acceptable cost. Perhaps the first case of this occurred in 2414 when Monument equipped four thoussand Sikh rebels from Ramadan and shipped them to Portales to take over that planet's tobacco trade, but there were many other examples later.

And in any case, there was always someone willing

to hire soldiers, somewhere. World after world armed
its misfits and sent them off to someone else's back
yard, to attack or defend, to kill or die—so long as
they were not doing it at home. Because of the
pattern of colonization, there were only a few planets
that were not so tense that they might snap into
bloody war if mercenaries from across the galaxy
were available.

Even for the stable elite of worlds, Friesland and
Kronstad, Ssu-ma and Wylie, the system was a losing
proposition. Wars and the warriors they spawned were
short-term solutions, binding the industrial worlds
into a fabric of short-term solutions. In the long run,
off-world markets were destroyed, internal investment was channelled into what were basically non-
productive uses, and the civil populace became restive
in the omnipresence of violence and a foreign policy
directed toward its continuance.

On rural worlds, the result was nothing so subtle
as decay. It was life and society shattered forever by
the sledge of war.

Caught in the Crossfire

MARGRITTE GRAPPLED with the nearest soldier in the instant her husband broke for the woods. The man in field-gray cursed and tried to jerk his weapon away from her, but Margritte's muscles were young and taut from shifting bales. Even when the mercenary kicked her ankles from under her, Margritte's clamped hands kept the gun barrel down and harmless.

Neither of the other two soldiers paid any attention to the scuffle. They clicked off the safety catches of their weapons as they swung them to their shoulders. Georg was running hard, fresh blood from his retorn calf muscles staining his bandages. The double slap of automatic fire caught him in midstride and whipsawed his slender body. His head and heels scissored to the ground together. They were covered by the mist of blood that settled more slowly.

Sobbing, Margritte loosed her grip and fell back on the ground. The man above her cradled his flechette gun again and looked around the village. "Well, aren't you going to shoot me too?" she cried.

"Not unless we have to," the mercenary replied quietly. He was sweating despite the stiff breeze, and he wiped his black face with his sleeve. "Helmuth," he ordered, "start setting up in the building. Landschein, you stay out with me, make sure none of these women try the same damned thing." He glanced out to where Georg lay, a bright smear on the stubbled, golden earth. "Best get that out of sight too," he added. "The convoy's due in an hour."

Old Leida had frozen to a statue in ankle-length muslin at the first scream. Now she nodded her head of close ringlets. "Myrie, Della," she called, gesturing to her daughters, "bring brush hooks and come along." She had not lost her dignity even during the shooting.

"Hold it," said Landschein, the shortest of the three soldiers. He was a sharp-featured man who had grinned in satisfaction as he fired. "You two got kids in there?" he asked the younger women. The muzzle of his flechette gun indicated the locked door to the dugout which normally stored the crop out of sun and heat; today it imprisoned the village's twenty-six children. Della and Myrie nodded, too dry with fear to speak.

"Then you go drag him into the woods," Landschein said, grinning again. "Just remember—you might manage to get away, but you won't much like what you'll find when you come back. I'm sure some true friend'll point your brats out to us quick enough to save her own."

Leida nodded a command, but Landschein's freckled hand clamped her elbow as she turned to follow her daughters. "Not you, old lady. No need for you to get that near to cover."

"Do you think *I* would run and risk—everyone?" Leida demanded.

"Curst if I know what you'd risk," the soldier said. "But we're risking plenty already to ambush one of Hammer's convoys. If anybody gets loose ahead of time to warn them, we can kiss our butts goodbye."

Margritte wiped the tears from her eyes, using her palms because of the gritty dust her thrashings had pounded into her knuckles. The third soldier, the broad-shouldered blond named Helmuth, had leaned his weapon beside the door of the hall and was lifting bulky loads from the nearby air cushion vehicle. The settlement had become used to whining gray columns of military vehicles, cruising the road at random. This truck, however, had eased over the second canopy of the forest itself. It was a flimsy cargo-hauler like the one in which Krauder picked up the cotton at season's end, harmless enough to look at. Only Georg, left behind for his sickle-ripped leg when a government van had carried off the other males the week before as "recruits," had realized what it meant that the newcomers wore field-gray instead of khaki.

"Why did you come here?" Margritte asked in a near-normal voice.

The black mercenary glanced at her as she rose, glanced back at the other women obeying orders by continuing to pick the iridescent boles of Terran cotton grown in Pohweil's soil. "We had the capital under siege," he said, "until Hammer's tanks punched a corridor through. We can't close the corridor, so we got to cut your boys off from supplies some other way. Otherwise the Cartel'll wish it had paid its taxes instead of trying to take over. You grubbers may have been pruning their wallets, but Lord! they'll be flayed alive if your counter-attack works."

He spat a thin, angry stream into the dust. "The traders hired us and four other regiments, and you grubbers sank the whole treasury into bringing in Hammer's armor. Maybe we can prove today those cocky bastards aren't all they're billed as. . . ."

"We didn't care," Margritte said. "We're no more the Farm Bloc than Krauder and his truck is the Trade Cartel. Whatever they do in the capital—*we* had no choice. I hadn't even seen the capital . . . oh dear Lord, Georg would have taken me there for our honeymoon except that there was fighting all over. . . ."

"How long we got, Sarge?" the blond man demanded from the stark shade of the hall.

"Little enough. Get those bloody sheets set up or we'll have to pop the cork bare-ass naked; and we got enough problems." The big noncom shifted his glance about the narrow clearing, wavering rows of cotton marching to the edge of the forest's dusky green. The road, an unsurfaced track whose ruts were not a serious hindrance to air cushion traffic, was the long axis. Beside it stood the hall, twenty meters by five and the only above-ground structure in the settlement. The battle with the native vegetation made dug-outs beneath the cotton preferable to cleared land wasted for dwellings. The hall became more than a social center and common refectory: it was the gaudiest of luxuries and a proud slap to the face of the forest.

Until that morning, the forest had been the village's only enemy.

"Georg only wanted—"

"God *damn* it!" the sergeant snarled. "Will you shut it off? Every man but your precious husband gone off to the siege—no, shut it off till I finish!

—and him running to warn the convoy. If you'd wanted to save his life, you should've grabbed him, not me. Sure, all you grubbers, you don't care about the war—not much! It's all one to you whether you kill us yourselves or your tankers do it, those bastards so high and mighty for the money they've got and the equipment. I tell you, girl, I don't take it personal that people shoot at me, it's just the way we both earn our livings. But it's fair, it's even . . . and Hammer thinks he's the Way made Flesh because nobody can bust his tanks."

The sergeant paused and his lips sucked in and out. His thick, gentle fingers rechecked the weapon he held. "We'll just see," he whispered.

"Georg said we'd all be killed in the crossfire if we were out in the fields when you shot at the tanks."

"If Georg had kept his face shut and his ass in bed, he'd have lived longer than he did. Just shut it off!" the noncom ordered. He turned to his blond underling, fighting a section of sponge plating through the door. "Via, Bornzyk!" he shouted angrily. "Move it!"

Helmuth flung his load down with a hollow clang. "Via, then lend a hand! The wind catches these and—"

"I'll help him," Margritte offered abruptly. Her eyes blinked away from the young soldier's weapon where he had forgotten it against the wall. Standing, she far lacked the bulk of the sergeant beside her, but her frame gave no suggestion of weakness. Golden dust soiled the back and sides of her dress with butterfly scales.

The sergeant gave her a sharp glance, his left hand spreading and closing where it rested on the black barrel-shroud of his weapon. "All right," he said, "you give him a hand and we'll see you under cover with us when the shooting starts. You're smarter than I gave you credit."

They had forgotten Leida was still standing beside them. Her hand struck like a spading fork. Margritte ducked away from the blow, but Leida caught her on the shoulder and gripped. When the mercenary's reversed gun-butt cracked the older woman loose, a long strip of Margritte's blue dress tore away with her. "Bitch," Leida mumbled through bruised lips. "You'd help these beasts after they killed your own man?"

Margritte stepped back, tossing her head. For a moment she fumbled at the tear in her dress; then, defiantly, she let it fall open. Landschein turned in time to catch the look in Leida's eyes. "Hey, you'll give your friends more trouble," he stated cheerfully, waggling his gun to indicate Della and Myrie as they returned gray-faced from the forest fringe. "Go on, get out and pick some cotton."

When Margritte moved, the white of her loose shift caught the sun and the small killer's stare. "Landschein!" the black ordered sharply, and Margritte stepped very quickly toward the truck and the third man struggling there.

Helmuth turned and blinked at the girl as he felt her capable muscles take the windstrain off the panel he was shifting. His eyes were blue and set wide in a face too large-boned to be handsome, too frank to be other than attractive. He accepted the help without question, leading the way into the hall.

The dining tables were hoisted against the rafters. The windows, unshuttered in the warm autumn and unglazed, lined all four walls at chest height. The long wall nearest the road was otherwise unbroken; the one opposite it was pierced in the middle by the single door. In the center of what should have been an empty room squatted the mercenaries' construct. The metal-ceramic panels had been locked into three sides of a square, a pocket of armor open only toward the door. It was hidden beneath the lower sills of the windows; nothing would catch the eye of an oncoming tanker.

"We've got to nest three layers together," the soldier explained as he swung the load, easily managed within the building, "or they'll cut us apart if they get off a burst this direction."

Margritte steadied a panel already in place as Helmuth mortised his into it. Each sheet was about five centimeters in thickness, a thin plate of gray metal on either side of a white porcelain sponge. The girl tapped it dubiously with a blunt finger. "This can stop bullets?"

The soldier—he was younger than his size suggested, no more than eighteen. Younger even than Georg, and he had a smile like Georg's as he raised his eyes with a blush and said, "P-powerguns, yeah; three layers of it ought to. . . . It's light, we could carry it in the truck where iridium would have bogged us down. But look, there's another panel and the rockets we still got to bring in."

"You must be very brave to fight tanks with just— this," Margritte prompted as she took one end of the remaining armor sheet.

"Oh, well, Sergeant Counsel says it'll work," the boy said enthusiastically. "They'll come by, two combat cars, then three big trucks, and another combat car. Sarge and Landschein buzzbomb the lead cars before they know what's happening. I reload them and they hit the third car when it swings wide to get a shot. Any shooting the blower jocks get off, they'll spread because they won't know—oh, cop I said it. . . ."

"They'll think the women in the fields may be

firing, so they'll kill us first," Margritte reasoned aloud. The boy's neck beneath his helmet turned brick red as he trudged into the building.

"Look," he said, but he would not meet her eyes, "we got to do it. It'll be fast—nobody much can get hurt. And your . . . the children, they're all safe. Sarge said that with all the men gone, we wouldn't have any trouble with the women if we kept the kids safe and under our thumbs."

"We didn't have time to have children," Margritte said. Her eyes were briefly unfocused. "You didn't give Georg enough time before you killed him."

"He was . . . ," Helmuth began. They were outside again and his hand flicked briefly toward the slight notch Della and Myrie had chopped in the forest wall. "I'm sorry."

"Oh, don't be sorry," she said. "He knew what he was doing."

"He was—I suppose you'd call him a patriot?" Helmuth suggested, jumping easily to the truck's deck to gather up an armload of cylindrical bundles. "He was really against the Cartel?"

"There was never a soul in this village who cared who won the war," Margritte said. "We have our own war with the forest."

"They joined the siege!" the boy retorted. "They cared that m-much, to fight us!"

"They got in the vans when men with guns told them to get in," the girl said. She took the gear Helmuth was forgetting to hand to her and shook a lock of hair out of her eyes. "Should they have run? Like Georg? No, they went off to be soldiers; praying like we did that the war might end before the forest had eaten up the village again. Maybe if we were really lucky, it'd end before this crop had spoiled in the fields because there weren't enough hands left here to pick it in time."

Helmuth cleared the back of the truck with his own load and stepped down. "Well, just the same your, your husband tried to hide and warn the convoy," he argued. "Otherwise why did he run?"

"Oh, he loved me—you know?" said Margritte. "Your sergeant said all of us should be out picking as usual. Georg knew, he *told* you, that the crossfire would kill everybody in the fields as sure as if you shot us deliberately. And when you wouldn't change your plan . . . well, if he'd gotten away you would have had to give up your ambush, wouldn't you? You'd have known it was suicide if the tanks learned that you were waiting for them. So Georg ran."

The dark-haired woman stared out at the forest for a moment. "He didn't have a prayer, did he? You could have killed him a hundred times before he got to cover."

"Here, give me those," the soldier said, taking the bundles from her instead of replying. He began to unwrap the cylinders one by one on the wooden floor. "We couldn't let him get away," he said at last. He added, his eyes still down on his work, "Flechettes when they hit . . . I mean, sh-shooting at his legs wouldn't, wouldn't have been a kindness, you see?"

Margritte laughed again. "Oh, I saw what they dragged into the forest, yes." She paused, sucking at her lower lip. "That's how we always deal with our dead, give them to the forest. Oh, we have a service; but we wouldn't have buried Georg in the dirt, if . . . if he'd died. But you didn't care, did you? A corpse looks bad, maybe your precious ambush, your own lives. . . . Get it out of the way, toss it in the woods."

"We'd have buried him afterwards," the soldier mumbled as he laid a fourth thigh-thick projectile beside those he had already unwrapped.

"Oh, of *course*," Margritte said. "And me, and all the rest of us murdered out there in the cotton. Oh, you're gentlemen, you are."

"Via!" Helmuth shouted, his flush mottling as at last he lifted his gaze to the girl's. "We'd have b-buried him. *I'd* have buried him. You'll be safe in here with us until it's all over, and by the Lord, then you can come back with us too! You don't have to stay here with these hard-faced bitches."

A bitter smile tweaked the left edge of the girl's mouth. "Sure, you're a good boy."

The young mercenary blinked between protest and pleasure, settled on the latter. He had readied all six of the finned, gray missles; now he lifted one of the pair of launchers. "It'll be really quick," he said shyly, changing the subject. The launcher was an arm-length tube with double handgrips and an optical sight. Helmuth's big hands easily inserted one of the buzzbombs to lock with a faint snick.

"Very simple," Margritte murmured.

"Cheap and easy," the boy agreed with a smile. "You can buy a thousand of these for what a combat car runs—Hell, maybe more than a thousand. And it's one for one today, one bomb to one car. Landschein says the crews are just a little extra, like weevils in your biscuit."

He saw her grimace, the angry tensing of a woman who had just seen her husband blasted into a spray of offal. Helmuth grunted with his own pain, his mouth dropping open as his hand stretched to touch her bare shoulder. "Oh, Lord—didn't mean to say . . ."

She gently detached his fingers. His breath caught and he turned away. Unseen, her look of hatred seared his back. His hand was still stretched toward her and hers toward him, when the door scraped to admit Landschein behind them.

"Cute, oh bloody cute," the little mercenary said. He carried his helmet by its strap. Uncovered, his cropped gray hair made him an older man. "Well, get on with it, boy—don't keep me 'n Sarge waiting. He'll be mad enough about getting sloppy thirds."

Helmuth jumped to his feet. Landschein ignored him, clicking across to a window in three quick strides. "Sarge," he called, "we're all set. Come on, we can watch the women from here."

"I'll run the truck into the woods," Counsel's voice burred in reply. "Anyhow, I can hear better from out here."

That was true. Despite the open windows, the wails of the children were inaudible in the hall. Outside, they formed a thin backdrop to every other sound.

Landschein set down his helmet. He snapped the safety on his gun's sideplate and leaned the weapon carefully against the nest of armor. Then he took up the loaded launcher and ran his hands over its tube and grips. Without changing expression, he reached out to caress Margritte through the tear in her dress.

Margritte screamed and clawed her left hand as she tried to rise. The launcher slipped into Landschein's lap and his arm, far swifter, locked hers and drew her down against him. Then the little mercenary himself was jerked upward. Helmuth's hand on his collar first broke Landschein's grip on Margritte, then flung him against the closed door.

Landschein rolled despite the shock and his glance flicked toward his weapon, but between gun and gunman crouched Helmuth, no longer a red-faced boy but the strongest man in the room. Grinning,

Helmuth spread fingers that had crushed ribs in past rough and tumbles. "Try it, little man," he said. "Try it and I'll rip your head off your shoulders."

"You'll do wonders!" Landschein spat, but his eyes lost their glaze and his muscles relaxed. He bent his mouth into a smile. "Hey, kid, there's plenty of slots around. We'll work out something afterwards, no need to fight."

Helmuth rocked his head back in a nod of acceptance with nothing of friendship in it. "You lay another hand on her," he said in a normal voice, "and you'd best have killed me first." He turned his back deliberately on the older man and the nearby weapons. Landschein clenched his left fist once, twice, but then he began to load the remaining launcher.

Margritte slipped the patching kit from her belt pouch. Her hands trembled, but the steel needle was already threaded. Her whip-stitches tacked the torn piece top and sides to the remaining material, close enough for decency. Pins were a luxury that a cotton settlement could well do without. Landschein glanced back at her once, but at the same time the floor creaked as Helmuth's weight shifted to his other leg. Neither man spoke.

Sergeant Counsel opened the door. His right arm cradled a pair of flechette guns and he handed one to Helmuth. "Best not to leave it in the dust," he said. "You'll be needing it soon."

"They coming, Sarge?" Landschein asked. He touched his tongue to thin, pale lips.

"Not yet." Counsel looked from one man to the other. "You boys get things sorted out?"

"All green here," Landschein muttered, smiling again but lowering his eyes.

"That's good," the big black said, "because we got

a job to do and we're not going to let anything stop us. Anything."

Margritte was putting away her needle. The sergeant looked at her hard. "You keep your head down, hear?"

"It won't matter," the girl said calmly, tucking the kit away. "The tanks, they won't be surprised to see a woman in here."

"Sure, but they'll shoot your bleeding head off," Landschein snorted.

"Do you think I care?" she blazed back. Helmuth winced at the tone; Sergeant Counsel's eyes took on an undesirable shade of interest.

"But you're helping us," the big noncom mused. He tapped his fingertips on the gun in the crook of his arm. "Because you like us so much?" There was no amusement in his words, only a careful mind picking over the idea, all ideas.

She stood and walked to the door, her face as composed as a priest's at the gravesite. "Have your ambush," she said. "Would it help us if the convoy came through before you were ready for it?"

"The smoother it goes, the faster . . ." Counsel agreed quietly, "then the better for all of you."

Margritte swung the door open and stood looking out. Eight women were picking among the rows east of the hall. They would be relatively safe there, not caught between the ambushers' rockets and the raking powerguns of their quarry. Eight of them safe and fourteen sure victims on the other side. Most of them could have been out of the crossfire if they had only let themselves think, only considered the truth that Georg had died to underscore.

"I keep thinking of Georg," Margritte said aloud. "I guess my friends are just thinking about their children, they keep looking at the storage room. But the children, they'll be all right; it's just that most of them are going to be orphans in a few minutes."

"It won't be that bad," Helmuth said. He did not sound as though he believed it either.

The older children had by now ceased the screaming begun when the door shut and darkness closed in on them. The youngest still wailed and the sound drifted through the open door.

"I told her we'd take her back with us, Sarge," Helmuth said.

Landschein chortled, a flash of instinctive humor he covered with a raised palm. Counsel shook his head in amazement. "You were wrong, boy. Now, keep watching those women or we may not be going back ourselves."

The younger man reddened again in frustration. "Look, we've got women in the outfit now, and I don't mean the rec troops. Captain Denzil told me there's six in Bravo Company alone—"

"Hoo, little Helmuth wants his own girlie friend to keep his bed warm," Landschein gibed.

"Landschein, I—" Helmuth began, clenching his right hand into a ridge of knuckles.

"Shut if off!"

"But, Sarge—"

"Shut it off, boy, or you'll have me to deal with!" roared the black. Helmuth fell back and rubbed his eyes. The noncom went on more quietly, "Landschein, you keep your tongue to yourself, too."

Both big men breathed deeply, their eyes shifting in concert toward Margritte who faced them in silence. "Helmuth," the sergeant continued, "some units take women, some don't. We've got a few, damned few, because not many women have the guts for our line of work."

Margritte's smile flickered. "The hardness, you mean. The callousness."

"Sure, words don't matter," Counsel agreed mildly. He smiled back at her as one equal to another. "This one, yeah; she might just pass. Via, you don't have to look like Landschein there to be tough. But you're missing the big point, boy."

Helmuth touched his right wrist to his chin. "Well, what?" he demanded.

Counsel laughed. "She wouldn't go with us. Would you, girl?"

Margritte's eyes were flat, and her voice was dead flat. "No," she said, "I wouldn't go with you."

The noncom grinned as he walked back to a window vantage. "You see, Helmuth, you want her to give up a whole lot to gain you a bunkmate."

"It's not like that," Helmuth insisted, thumping his leg in frustration. "I just mean—"

"Oh, *Lord!*" the girl said loudly, "can't you just get on with your ambush?"

"Well, not till Hammer's boys come through," chuckled the sergeant. "They're so good, they can't run a convoy to schedule."

"S-sergeant," the young soldier said, "she doesn't understand." He turned to Margritte and gestured with both hands, forgetting the weapon in his left. "They won't take you back, those witches out there. The . . . the rec girls at Base Denzil don't go home, they can't. And you know damned well that s-somebody's going to catch it out there when it drops in the pot. They'll crucify you for helping us set up, the ones that're left."

"It doesn't matter what they do," she said. "It doesn't matter at all."

"Your life matters!" the boy insisted.

Her laughter hooted through the room. "My life?"

Margritte repeated. "You splashed all that across the field an hour ago. You didn't give a damn when you did it, and I don't give one now—but I'd only follow you to Hell and hope your road was short."

Helmuth bit his knuckle and turned, pinched over as though he had been kicked. Sergeant Counsel grinned his tight, equals grin. "You're wasted here, you know," he said. "And we could use you. Maybe if—"

"Sarge!" Landschein called from his window. "Here they come."

Counsel scooped up a rocket launcher, probing its breech with his fingers to make finally sure of its load. "Now you keep down," he repeated to Margritte. "Backblast'll take your head off if their shooting don't." He crouched below the sill and the rim of the armor shielding him, peering through a periscope whose button of optical fibers was unnoticeable in the shadow. Faced inward toward the girl, Landschein hunched over the other launcher in the right corner of the protected area. His flechette gun rested beside him and one hand curved toward it momentarily, anticipating the instant he would raise it to spray the shattered convoy. Between them Helmuth knelt as stiffly as a statue of gray-green jade. He drew a buzzbomb closer to his right knee where it clinked against the barrel of his own weapon. Cursing nervously, he slid the flechette gun back out of the way. Both his hands gripped reloads, waiting.

The cars' shrill whine trembled in the air.

Margritte stood up by the door, staring out through the windows across the hall. Dust plumed where the long, straight roadway cut the horizon into two blocks of forest. The women in the fields had paused, straightening to watch the oncoming vehicles. But that was normal, nothing to alarm the khaki men in the bellies of their war cars; and if any woman thought of falling to hug the earth, the fans' wailing too nearly approximated that of the imprisoned children.

"Three hundred meters," Counsel reported softly as the blunt bow of the lead car gleamed through the dust. "Two-fifty." Landschein's teeth bared as he faced around, poised to spring.

Margritte swept up Helmuth's flechette gun and leveled it at waist height. The safety clicked off. Counsel had dropped his periscope and his mouth was open to cry an order. The deafening muzzle blast lifted him out of his crouch and pasted him briefly, voiceless, against the pocked inner face of the armor. Margritte swung her weapon like a flail into a triple splash of red. Helmuth died with only a reflexive jerk, but Landschein's speed came near to bringing his launcher to bear on Margritte. The stream of flechettes sawed across his throat. His torso dropped, headless but still clutching the weapon.

Margritte's gun silenced when the last needle slapped out of the muzzle. The aluminum barrel shroud had softened and warped during the long burst. Eddies in the fog of blood and propellant smoke danced away from it. Margritte turned as if in icy composure, but she bumped the door jamb and staggered as she stepped outside. The racket of the gun had drawn the sallow faces of every woman in the fields.

"It's over!" Margritte called. Her voice sounded thin in the fresh silence. Three of the nearer mothers ran toward the storage room.

Down the road, dust was spraying as the convoy skidded into a herringbone for defense. Gun muzzles searched: the running women; Margritte armed and motionless; the sudden eruption of children from the dugout. The men in the cars waited, their trigger fingers partly tensed.

Bergen, Della's six-year-old, pounded past Margritte to throw herself into her mother's arms. They clung together, each crooning to the other through their tears. "Oh, we were so afraid!" Bergen said, drawing away from her mother. "But now it's all right." She rotated her head and her eyes widened as they took in Margritte's tattered figure. "Oh, Margi," she gasped, "whatever happened to *you?*"

Della gasped and snatched her daughter back against her bosom. Over the child's loose curls, Della glared at Margritte with eyes like a hedge of pikes. Margritte's hand stopped half way to the child. She stood—gaunt, misted with blood as though sunburned. A woman who had blasted life away instead of suckling it. Della, a frightened mother, snarled at the killer who had been her friend.

Margritte began to laugh. She trailed the gun three steps before letting it drop unnoticed. The captain of the lead car watched her approach over his gunsights. His short, black beard fluffed out from under his helmet, twitching as he asked, "Would you like to tell us what's going on, honey, or do we got to comb it out ourselves?"

"I killed three soldiers," she answered simply. "Now there's nothing going on. Except that wherever you're headed, I'm going along. You can use my sort, soldier."

Her laughter was a crackling shadow in the sunlight.

Interlude: The
Bonding Authority

WARS RESULT when one side either misjudges its chances or wishes to commit suicide; and not even Masada *began* as a suicide attempt. In general, both warring parties expect to win. In the event, they are wrong more than half the time.

Employing mercenaries adds new levels of uncertainty to the already risky business of war. Too often in history a mercenary force has disappeared a moment before the battle; switched sides for a well-timed bribe; or even conquered its employer and brought about the very disasters it was hired to prevent.

Mercenaries, for their part, face the chances common to every soldier of being killed by the enemy. In addition, however, they must reckon with the possibility of being bilked of their pay or massacred to avoid its payment; of being used as cannon fodder by an employer whose distaste for "money-grubbing aliens" may exceed the enemy's; or of being abandoned far from home when defeat or political change erases their employer or his good will. As Xenophon and the Ten Thousand learned, in such circumstances the road home may be long—or as short as a shallow grave.

A solution to both sets of special problems was made possible by the complexity of galactic commerce. The recorded beginnings came early in the Twenty-seventh Century when several planets caught up in the Confederation Wars used the Terran firm of Felchow und Sohn as an escrow agent for their mercenaries' pay. Felchow was a commercial banking house which had retained its preeminence even after Terran industry had been in some measure supplanted by that of newer worlds. Neither Felchow nor Terra herself had any personal stake in the chaotic rise and fall of the Barnard Confederation; thus the house was the perfect neutral to hold the pay of the condottieri being hired by all parties. Payment was scrupulously made to mercenaries who performed according to their contracts. This included the survivors of the Dalhousie debacle who were able to buy passage off that ravaged world, despite the fact that less than ten percent of the populace which had hired them was still alive. Conversely, the pay of Wrangel's Legion, which had refused to assault the Confederation drop zone on Montauk, was forfeited to the Montauk government. The Third Armistice intervened and Wrangel's troops were hunted across the face of the planet by both sides, too faithless to use and too dangerous to ignore.

Felchow und Sohn had performed to the satisfaction of all honest parties when first used as an intermediary. Over the next three decades the house was similarly involved in other conflicts, a passive escrow agent and paymaster. It was only after the Ariete Incident of 2662 that the concept coalesced into the one stable feature of a galaxy at war.

The Ariete, a division recruited mostly from among the militias of the Aldoni System, was hired by the rebels on Paley. Their pay was banked with Felchow, since the rebels very reasonably doubted that anyone would take on the well-trained troops of the Republic of Paley if they had already been handed the carrot. But the Ariete fought very well indeed, losing an estimated thirty percent of its effectives before surrendering in the final collapse of the rebellion. The combat losses have to be estimated because the Republican forces, in defiance of the "Laws of War" and their own promises before the surrender, butchered all their fifteen or so thousand mercenary prisoners.

Felchow und Sohn, seeing an excuse for an action which would raise it to incredible power, reduced Paley to Stone Age savagery.

An industrialized world (as Paley was) is an interlocking whole. Off-planet trade may amount to no more than five percent of its GNP; but when that trade is suddenly cut off, the remainder of the economy resembles a car lacking two pistons. It may make whirring sounds for a time, but it isn't going anywhere.

Huge as Felchow was, a single banking house could not have cut Paley off from the rest of the galaxy. When Felchow, however, offered other commercial banks membership in a cartel and a share of the lucrative escrow business, the others joined gladly and without exception. No one would underwrite cargoes to or from Paley; and Paley, already wracked by a war and its aftermath, shuddered down into the slag heap of history.

Lucrative was indeed a mild word for the mercenary business. The escrowed money itself could be put to work, and the escrowing bank was an obvious agent for the other commercial transactions needed to run a war. Mercenaries replaced equipment, recruited men, and shipped themselves by the thousands across the galaxy. The new banking cartel served those needs smoothly—and maximized its own profits.

With the banks' new power came a new organization. The expanded escrow operations were made the responsibility of a Bonding Authority, still based in Bremen but managed independently of the cartel itself. The Authority's fees were high. In return, its Contracts Department was expert in preventing expensive misunderstandings from arising, and its investigative staff could neither be bribed nor deluded by a violator. Under the Authority's ruthless nurture, the business of war became as regular as any other commercial endeavor, and more profitable than most.

Hangman

THE LIGHT in the kitchen alcove glittered on Lieutenant Schilling's blond curls; glittered also on the frost-spangled window beside her and from the armor of the tank parked outside. All the highlights looked cold to Capt. Danny Pritchard as he stepped closer to the infantry lieutenant.

"Sal—" Pritchard began. From the orderly room behind them came the babble of the radios ranked against one wall and, less muted, the laughter of soldiers waiting for action. "You can't think like a Dutchman any more. We're Hammer's Slammers, all of us. We're mercs. Not Dutch, not Frisians—"

"You're not," Lieutenant Schilling snapped, looking up from the cup of bitter chocolate she had just drawn from the urn. She was a short woman and lightly built, but she had the unerring instinct of a bully who is willing to make a scene for a victim who is not willing to be part of one. "You're a farmer from

Dunstan, what d'you care about Dutch miners, whatever these bleeding French do to them. But a lot of us do care, Danny, and if you had a little compassion—"

"But Sal—" Pritchard repeated, only his right arm moving as he touched the blond girl's shoulder.

"Get your hands off me, Captain!" she shouted. "That's over!" She shifted the mug of steaming chocolate in her hand. The voices in the orderly room stilled. Then, simultaneously, someone turned up the volume of the radio and at least three people began to talk loudly on unconnected subjects.

Pritchard studied the back of his hand, turned it over to examine the callused palm as well. He smiled. "Sorry, I'll remember that," he said in a normal voice. He turned and stepped back into the orderly room, a brown-haired man of thirty-four with a good set of muscles to cover his moderate frame and nothing at all to cover his heart. Those who knew Danny Pritchard slightly thought him a relaxed man, and he looked relaxed even now. But waiting around the electric grate were three troopers who knew Danny very well indeed: the crew of the Plow, Pritchard's command tank.

Kowie drove the beast, a rabbit-eyed man whose fingers now flipped cards in another game of privy solitaire. His deck was so dirty that only familiarity allowed him to read the pips. Kowie's hands and eyes were just as quick at the controls of the tank, sliding its bulbous hundred and fifty metric tons through spaces that were only big enough to pass it. When he had to, he drove nervelessly through objects instead of going around. Kowie would never be more than a tank driver; but he was the best tank driver in the Regiment.

Rob Jenne was big and as blond as Lieutenant Schilling. He grinned up at Pritchard, his expression changing from embarrassment to relief as he saw that his captain was able to smile also. Jenne had transferred from combat cars to tanks three years back, after the Slammers had pulled out of Squire's World. He was sharp-eyed and calm in a crisis. Twice after his transfer Jenne had been offered a blower of his own to command if he would return to combat cars. He had refused both promotions, saying he would stay with tanks or buy back his contract, that there was no way he was going back to those open-topped coffins again. When a tank commander's slot came open, Jenne got it; and Pritchard had made the blond sergeant his own blower chief when a directional mine had retired the previous man. Now Jenne straddled a chair backwards, his hands flexing a collapsible torsion device that kept his muscles as dense and hard as they had been the day he was recruited from a quarry on Burlage.

Line tanks carry only a driver and the blower chief who directs the tank and its guns when they are not under the direct charge of the Regiment's computer. In addition to those two and a captain, command tanks have a Communications Technician to handle the multiplex burden of radio traffic focused on the vehicle. Pritchard's commo tech was Margritte Di-Manzo, a slender widow who cropped her lustrous hair short so that it would not interfere with the radio helmet she wore most of her waking hours. She was off-duty now, but she had not removed the bulky headgear which linked her to the six radios in the tank parked outside. Their simultaneous sound would have been unintelligible babbling to most listeners. The black-haired woman's training, both conscious and hypnotic, broke that babbling into a set of discrete conversations. When Pritchard reentered the room, Margritte was speaking to Jenne. She did not look up at her commander until Jenne's brightening expression showed her it was safe to do so.

Two commo people and a sergeant with Intelligence tabs were at consoles in the orderly room. They were from the Regiment's HQ Battalion, assigned to Sector Two here on Kobold but in no sense a part of the sector's combat companies: Captain Riis' S Company—infantry—and Pritchard's own tanks.

Riis was the senior captain and in charge of the sector, a matter which neither he nor Pritchard ever forgot. Sally Schilling led his first platoon. Her aide, a black-haired corporal, sat with his huge boots up, humming as he polished the pieces of his field-stripped powergun. Its barrel gleamed orange in the light of the electric grate. Electricity was more general on Kobold than on some wealthier worlds, since mining and copper smelting made fusion units a practical necessity. But though the copper in the transmission cable might well have been processed on Kobold, the wire had probably been drawn offworld and shipped back here. Aurore and Friesland had refused to allow even such simple manufactures here on their joint colony. They had kept Kobold a market and a supplier of raw materials, but never a rival.

"Going to snow tonight?" Jenne asked.

"Umm, too cold," Pritchard said, walking over to the grate. He pretended he did not hear Lieutenant Schilling stepping out of the alcove. "I figure—"

"Hold it," said Margritte, her index finger curling out for a volume control before the duty man had time to react. One of the wall radios boomed loudly to the whole room. Prodding another switch, Margritte patched the signal separately through the link implanted in Pritchard's right mastoid. "—guns and looks like satchel charges. There's only one man in each truck, but they've been on the horn too and we can figure on more Frenchies here any—"

"Red Alert," Pritchard ordered, facing his commo tech so that she could read his lips. "Where is this?"

The headquarters radiomen stood nervously, afraid to interfere but unwilling to let an outsider run their equipment, however ably. "Red Alert," Margritte was repeating over all bands. Then, through Pritchard's implant, she said, "It's Patrol Sigma three-nine, near Haacin. Dutch civilians've stopped three outbound provisions trucks from Barthe's Company."

"Scramble First Platoon," Pritchard said, "but tell 'em to hold for us to arrive." As Margritte coolly passed on the order, Pritchard picked up the commo helmet he had laid on his chair when he followed Lieutenant Schilling into the kitchen. The helmet gave him automatic switching and greater range than the bioelectric unit behind his ear.

The wall radio was saying, "—need some big friendlies fast or it'll drop in the pot for sure."

"Sigma three-niner," Pritchard said, "this is Michael One."

"Go ahead, Michael One," replied the distant squad leader. Pritchard's commo helmet added an airy boundlessness to his surroundings without really deadening the ambient noise.

"Hold what you've got, boys," the tank captain said. "There's help on the way."

The door of the orderly room stood ajar the way Pritchard's crewmen had left it. The captain slammed it shut as he too ran for his tank. Behind in the orderly room, Lieutenant Schilling was snapping out quick directions to her own platoon and to her awakened commander.

The Plow was already floating when Danny reached it. Ice crystals, spewed from beneath the skirts by the lift fans, made a blue-white dazzle in the vehicle's running lights. Frost whitened the ladder up the high side of the tank's plenum chamber and hull. Pritchard paused to pull on his gloves before mounting. Sergeant Jenne, anchoring himself with his left hand on the turret's storage rack, reached down and lifted his captain aboard without noticeable effort. Side by side, the two men slid through the hatches to their battle stations.

"Ready," Pritchard said over the intercom.

"Movin' on," replied Kowie, and with his words the tank slid forward over the frozen ground like grease on a hot griddle.

The command post had been a district road-maintenance center before all semblance of central government on Kobold had collapsed. The orderly room and officers' quarters were in the supervisor's house, a comfortable structure with shutters and mottoes embroidered in French on the walls. Some of the hangings had been defaced by short-range gunfire. The crew barracks across the road now served the troopers on headquarters duty. Many of the Slammers could read the Dutch periodicals abandoned there in the break-up. The equipment shed beside the barracks garaged the infantry skimmers because the battery-powered platforms could not shrug off the weather like the huge panzers of M Company. The shed doors were open, pluming the night with heated air as the duty platoon ran for its mounts. Some of the troopers had not yet donned their helmets and body armor. Jenne waved as the tank swept on by; then the road curved and the infantry was lost in the night.

Kobold was a joint colony of Aurore and Friesland.

When eighty years of French oppression had driven the Dutch settlers to rebellion, their first act was to hire Hammer's Slammers. The break between Hammer and Friesland had been sharp, but time has a way of blunting anger and letting old habits resume. The Regimental language was Dutch, and many of the Slammers' officers were Frisians seconded from their own service. Friesland gained from the men's experience when they returned home; Hammer gained company officers with excellent training from the Gröningen Academy.

To counter the Slammers, the settlers of Auroran descent had hired three Francophone regiments. If either group of colonists could have afforded to pay its mercenaries unaided, the fighting would have been immediate and brief. Kobold had been kept deliberately poor by its homeworlds, however; so in their necessities the settlers turned to those homeworlds for financial help.

And neither Aurore nor Friesland wanted a war on Kobold.

Friesland had let its settlers swing almost from the beginning, sloughing their interests for a half share of the copper produced and concessions elsewhere in its sphere of influence. The arrangement was still satisfactory to the Council of State, if Frisian public opinion could be mollified by apparent activity. Aurore was on the brink of war in the Zemla System. Her Parliament feared another proxy war which could in a moment explode full-fledged, even though Friesland had been weakened by a decade of severe internal troubles. So Aurore and Friesland reached a compromise. Then, under threat of abandonment, the warring parties were forced to transfer their mercenaries' contracts to the home worlds. Finally, Aurore and

Friesland mutually hired the four regiments: the Slammers; Compagnie de Barthe; the Alaudae; and Phenix Moirots. Mercs from either side were mixed and divided among eight sectors imposed on a map of inhabited Kobold. There the contract ordered them to keep peace between the factions; prevent the importation of modern weapons to either side; and—wait.

But Colonel Barthe and the Auroran leaders had come to a further, secret agreement; and although Hammer had learned of it, he had informed only two men—Major Steuben, his aide and bodyguard; and Captain Daniel Pritchard.

Pritchard scowled at the memory. Even without the details a traitor had sold Hammer, it would have been obvious that Barthe had his own plans. In the other sectors, Hammer's men and their French counterparts ran joint patrols. Both sides scattered their camps throughout the sectors, just as the villages of either nationality were scattered. Barthe had split his sectors in halves, brusquely ordering the Slammers to keep to the west of the River Aillet because his own troops were mining the east of the basin heavily. Barthe's Company was noted for its minefields. That skill was one of the reasons they had been hired by the French. Since most of Kobold was covered either by forests or by rugged hills, armor was limited to roads where well-placed mines could stack tanks like crushed boxes.

Hammer listened to Barthe's pronouncement and laughed, despite the anger of most of his staff officers. Beside him, Joachim Steuben had grinned and traced the line of his cut-away holster. When Danny Pritchard was informed, he had only shivered a little and called a vehicle inspection for the next morning. That had been three months ago. . . .

The night streamed by like smoke around the tank. Pritchard lowered his face shield, but he did not drop his seat into the belly of the tank. Vision blocks within gave a 360 degree view of the tank's surroundings, but the farmer in Danny could not avoid the feeling of blindness within the impenetrable walls. Jenne sat beside his captain in a cupola fitted with a three-barrelled automatic weapon. He too rode with his head out of the hatch, but that was only for comradeship. The sergeant much preferred to be inside. He would button up at the first sign of hostile action. Jenne was in no sense a coward; it was just that he had quirks. Most combat veterans do.

Pritchard liked the whistle of the black wind past his helmet. Warm air from the tank's resistance heaters jetted up through the hatch and kept his body quite comfortable. The vehicle's huge mass required the power of a fusion plant to drive its lift motors, and the additional burden of climate control was inconsequential.

The tankers' face shields automatically augmented the light of the moon, dim and red because the sun it reflected was dim and red as well. The boosted light level displayed the walls of forest, the boles snaking densely to either side of the road. At Kobold's perihelion, the thin stems grew in days to their full six-meter height and spread a ceiling of red-brown leaves the size of blankets. Now, at aphelion, the chilled, sapless trees burned with almost explosive intensity. The wood was too dangerous to use for heating, even if electricity had not been common; but it fueled the gasogene engines of most vehicles on the planet.

Jenne gestured ahead. "Blowers," he muttered on the intercom. His head rested on the gun switch though he knew the vehicles must be friendly. The Plow slowed.

Pritchard nodded agreement. "Michael First, this is Michael One," he said. "Flash your running lights so we can be sure it's you."

"Roger," replied the radio. Blue light flickered from the shapes hulking at the edge of the forest ahead. Kowie throttled the fans up to cruise, then chopped them and swung expertly into the midst of the four tanks of the outlying platoon.

"Michael One, this is Sigma One," Captain Riis' angry voice demanded in the helmet.

"Go ahead."

"Barthe's sent a battalion across the river. I'm moving Lieutenat Schilling into position to block 'em and called Central for artillery support. You hold your first platoon at Haacin for reserve and any partisans up from Portela. I'll take direct command of the rest of—"

"Negative, negative, Sigma One!" Pritchard snapped. The Plow was accelerating again, second in the line of five tanks. They were beasts of prey sliding across the landscape of snow and black trees at eighty kph and climbing. "Let the French through, Captain. There won't be fighting, repeat, negative fighting."

"There damned well *will* be fighting, Michael One, if Barthe tries to shove a battalion into my sector!" Riis thundered back. "Remember, this isn't your command or a joint command. *I'm* in charge here."

"Margritte, patch me through to Battalion," Pritchard hissed on intercom. The Plow's turret was cocked thirty degrees to the right. It covered the forest sweeping by to that side and anything which might be hiding there. Pritchard's mind was on Sally Schilling, riding a skimmer through forest like that flanking the tanks, hurrying with her fifty men to try to stop a battalion's hasty advance.

The commo helmet popped quietly to itself. Pritchard tensed, groping for the words he would need to convince Lieutenant Colonel Miezierk. Miezierk, under whom command of Sectors One and Two was grouped, had been a Frisian regular until five years ago. He was supposed to think like a merc, now, not like a Frisian; but . . .

The voice that suddenly rasped, "Override, override!" was not Miezierk's. "Sigma One, Michael One, this is Regiment."

"Go ahead," Pritchard blurted. Captain Riis, equally rattled, said, "Yes, *sir*!" on the three-way link.

"Sigma, your fire order is cancelled. Keep your troops on alert, but keep 'em the hell out of Barthe's way."

"But Colonel Hammer—"

"Riis, you're not going to start a war tonight. Michael One, can your panzers handle whatever's going on at Haacin without violating the contract?"

"Yes, sir." Pritchard flashed a map briefly on his face shield to check his position. "We're almost there now."

"If you can't handle it, Captain, you'd better hope you're killed in action," Colonel Hammer said bluntly. "I haven't nursed this regiment for twenty-three years to lose it because somebody forgets what his job is." Then, more softly—Pritchard could imagine the colonel flicking his eyes side to side to gauge bystanders' reactions—he added, "There's support if you need it, Captain—if they're the ones who breach the contract."

"Affirmative."

"Keep the lid on, boy. Regiment out."

The trees had drunk the whine of the fans. Now the road curved and the tanks banked greasily to join the main highway from Dimo to Portela. The tailings pile of the Haacin Mine loomed to the right and hurled the drive noise back redoubled at the vehicles. The steel skirts of the lead tank touched the road metal momentarily, showering the night with orange sparks. Beyond the mine were the now-empty wheat fields and then the village itself.

Haacin, the largest Dutch settlement in Sector Two, sprawled to either side of the highway. Its houses were two- and three-story lumps of cemented mine tailings. They were roofed with tile or plastic rather than shakes of native timber, because of the wood's lethal flammability. The highway was straight and broad. It gave Pritchard a good view of the three cargo vehicles pulled to one side. Men in local dress swarmed about them. Across the road were ten of Hammer's khaki-clad infantry, patrol S-39, whose ported weapons half-threatened, half-protected the trio of drivers in their midst. Occasionally a civilian turned to hurl a curse at Barthe's men, but mostly the Dutch busied themselves with off-loading cartons from the trucks.

Pritchard gave a brief series of commands. The four line tanks grounded in a hedgehog at the edge of the village. Their main guns and automatics faced outward in all directions. Kowie swung the command vehicle around the tank which had been leading it. He cut the fans' angle of attack, slowing the Plow without losing the ability to accelerate quickly. The command vehicle eased past the squad of infantry, then grounded behind the rearmost truck. Pritchard felt the fans' hum through the metal of the hull.

"Who's in charge here?" the captain demanded,

his voice booming through the command vehicle's public address system.

The Dutch unloading the trucks halted silently. A squat man in a parka of feathery native fur stepped forward. Unlike many of the other civilians, he was not armed. He did not flinch when Pritchard pinned him with the spotlight of the tank. "I am Paul van Oosten," the man announced in the heavy Dutch of Kobold. "I am Mayor of Haacin. But if you mean who leads us in what we are doing here, well . . . perhaps Justice herself does. Klaus, show them what these trucks were carrying to Portela."

Another civilian stepped forward, ripping the top off the box he carried. Flat plastic wafers spilled from it, glittering in the cold light: powergun ammunition, intended for shoulder weapons like those the infantry carried.

"They were taking powerguns to the beasts of Portela to use against us," van Oosten said. He used the slang term, "skepsels" to name the Francophone settlers. The Mayor's shaven jaw was jutting out in anger.

"Captain!" called one of Barthe's truck drivers, brushing forward through the ring of Hammer's men. "Let me explain."

One of the civilians growled and lifted his heavy musket. Rob Jenne rang his knuckles twice on the receiver of his tribarrel, calling attention to the muzzles as he swept them down across the crowd. The Dutchman froze. Jenne smiled without speaking.

"We were sent to pick up wheat the regiment had purchased," Barthe's man began. Pritchard was not familiar with Barthe's insigniae, but from the merc's age and bearing he was a senior sergeant. An unlikely choice to be driving a provisions truck. "One of the vehicles happened to be partly loaded. We didn't take the time to empty it because we were in a hurry to finish the run and go off duty—there was enough room and lift to handle that little bit of gear and the grain besides.

"In any case—" and here the sergeant began pressing, because the tank captain had not cut him off at the first sentence as expected—"you do not, and these fools *surely* do not, have the right to stop Colonel Barthe's transport. If you have questions about the way we pick up wheat, that's between your CO and ours. Sir."

Pritchard ran his gloved index finger back and forth below his right eyesocket. He was ice inside, bubbling ice that tore and chilled him and had nothing to do with the weather. He turned back to Mayor van Oosten. "Reload the trucks," he said, hoping that his voice did not break.

"You can't!" van Oosten cried. "These powerguns are the only chance my village, my *people* have to survive whan you leave. You know what'll happen, don't you? Friesland and Aurore, they'll come to an agreement, a *trade-off*, they'll call it, and all the troops will leave. It's our lives they're trading! The beasts in Dimo, in Portela if you let these go through, they'll have powerguns that *their* mercenaries gave them. And we—"

Pritchard whispered a prepared order into his helmet mike. The rearmost of the four tanks at the edge of the village fired a single round from its main gun. The night flared cyan as the 200 mm bolt struck the middle of the tailings pile a kilometer away. Stone, decomposed by the enormous energy of the shot, recombined in a huge gout of flame. Vapor, lava, and cinders spewed in every direction. After a moment, bits of high-flung rock began pattering down on the roofs of Haacin.

The bolt caused a double thunderclap, that of the heated air followed by the explosive release of energy at the point of impact. When the reverberations died away there was utter silence in Haacin. On the distant jumble of rock, a dying red glow marked where the charge had hit. The shot had also ignited some saplings rooted among the stones. They had blazed as white torches for a few moments but they were already collapsing as cinders.

"The Slammers are playing this by rules," Pritchard said. Loudspeakers flung his quiet words about the village like the echoes of the shot; but he was really speaking for the recorder in the belly of the tank, preserving his words for a later Bonding Authority hearing. "There'll be no powerguns in civilian hands. Load every bit of this gear back in the truck. Remember, there's satellites up there—" Pritchard waved generally at the sky—"that see everything that happens on Kobold. If one powergun is fired by a civilian in this sector, I'll come for him. I promise you."

The mayor sagged within his furs. Turning to the crowd behind him, he said, "Put the guns back on the truck. So that the Portelans can kill us more easily."

"Are you mad, van Oosten?" demanded the gunman who had earlier threatened Barthe's sergeant.

"Are *you* mad, Kruse?" the mayor shouted back without trying to hide his fury. "D'ye doubt what those tanks would do to Haacin? And do you doubt this butcher—" his back was to Pritchard but there was no doubt as to whom the mayor meant—"would use them on us? Perhaps tomorrow we could have . . ."

There was motion at the far edge of the crowd,

near the corner of a building. Margritte, watching
the vision blocks within, called a warning. Pritchard
reached for his panic bar—Rob Jenne was traversing
the tribarrel. All three of them were too late. The
muzzle flash was red and it expanded in Pritchard's
eyes as a hammer blow smashed him in the middle
of the forehead.

The bullet's impact heaved the tanker up and backwards. His shattered helmet flew off into the night.
The unyielding hatch coaming caught him in the
small of the back, arching his torso over it as if he
were being broken on the wheel. Pritchard's eyes
flared with sheets of light. As reaction flung him
forward again, he realized he was hearing the reports
of Jenne's powergun and that some of the hellish
flashes were real.

If the tribarrel's discharges were less brilliant than
that of the main gun, then they were more than a
hundred times as close to the civilians. The burst
snapped within a meter of one bystander, an old man
who stumbled backward into a wall. His mouth and
staring eyes were three circles of empty terror. Jenne
fired seven rounds. Every charge but one struck the
sniper or the building he sheltered against. Powdered concrete sprayed from the wall. The sniper's
body spun backwards, chest gobbled away by the
bolts. His right arm still gripped the musket he had
fired at Pritchard. The arm had been flung alone
onto the snowy pavement. The electric bite of ozone
hung in the air with the ghostly afterimages of the
shots. The dead man's clothes were burning, tiny
orange flames that rippled into smoke an inch from
their bases.

Jenne's big left hand was wrapped in the fabric of
Pritchard's jacket, holding the dazed officer upright.
"There's another rule you play by," the sergeant

roared to the crowd. "You shoot at Hammer's Slammers and you get your balls kicked between your ears. Sure as god, boys; sure as death." Jenne's right hand swung the muzzles of his weapon across the faces of the civilians. "Now, load the bleeding trucks like the captain said, heroes."

For a brief moment, nothing moved but the threatening powergun. Then a civilian turned and hefted a heavy crate back aboard the truck from which he had just taken it. Empty-handed, the colonist began to sidle away from the vehicle—and from the deadly tribarrel. One by one the other villagers reloaded the hijacked cargo, the guns and ammunition they had hoped would save them in the cataclysm they awaited. One by one they took the blower chief's unspoken leave to return to their houses. One who did not leave was sobbing out her grief over the mangled body of the sniper. None of her neighbors had gone to her side. They could all appreciate— now—what it would have meant if that first shot had led to a general firefight instead of Jenne's selective response.

"Rob, help me get him inside," Pritchard heard Margritte say.

Pritchard braced himself with both hands and leaned away from his sergeant's supporting arm. "No, I'm all right," he croaked. His vision was clear enough, but the landscape was flashing bright and dim with varicolored light.

The side hatch of the turret clanked. Margritte was beside her captain. She had stripped off her cold weather gear in the belly of the tank and wore only her khaki uniform. "Get back inside there," Pritchard muttered. "It's not safe." He was afraid of falling if he raised a hand to fend her away. He felt an injector prick the swelling flesh over his cheekbones.

The flashing colors died away though Pritchard's ears began to ring.

"They carried some into the nearest building," the noncom from Barthe's Company was saying. He spoke in Dutch, having sleep-trained in the language during the transit to Kobold just as Hammer's men had in French.

"Get it," Jenne ordered the civilians still near the trucks. Three of them were already scurrying toward the house the merc had indicated. They were back in moments, carrying the last of the arms chests.

Pritchard surveyed the scene. The cargo had been reloaded, except for the few spilled rounds winking from the pavement. Van Oosten and the furious Kruse were the only villagers still in sight. "All right," Pritchard said to the truck drivers, "get aboard and get moving. And come back by way of Bitzen, not here. I'll arrange an escort for you."

The French noncom winked, grinned, and shouted a quick order to his men. The infantrymen stepped aside silently to pass the truckers. The French mercenaries mounted their vehicles and kicked them to life. Their fans whined and the trucks lifted, sending snow crystals dancing. With gathering speed, they slid westward along the forest-rimmed highway.

Jenne shook his head at the departing trucks, then stiffened as his helmet spat a message. "Captain," he said, "we got company coming."

Pritchard grunted. His own radio helmet had been smashed by the bullet, and his implant would only relay messages on the band to which it had been verbally keyed most recently. "Margritte, start switching for me," he said. His slender commo tech was already slipping back inside through the side hatch. Pritchard's blood raced with the chemicals Margritte had shot into it. His eyes and mind worked perfectly, though all his thoughts seemed to have razor edges on them.

"Use mine," Jenne said, trying to hand the captain his helmet.

"I've got the implant," Pritchard said. He started to shake his head and regretted the motion instantly. "That and Margritte's worth a helmet any day."

"It's a whole battalion," Jenne explained quietly, his eyes scanning the Bever Road down which Command Central had warned that Barthe's troops were coming. "All but the artillery—that's back in Dimo, but it'll range here easy enough. Brought in the anti-tank battery and a couple calliopes, though."

"Slide us up ahead of Michael First," Pritchard ordered his driver. As the Plow shuddered, then spun on its axis, the captain dropped his seat into the turret to use the vision blocks. He heard Jenne's seat whirr down beside him and the cupola hatch snick closed. In front of Pritchard's knees, pale in the instrument lights, Margritte DiManzo sat still and open-eyed at her communications console.

"Little friendlies," Pritchard called through his loud-speakers to the ten infantrymen, "find yourselves a quiet alley and hope nothing happens. The Lord help you if you fire a shot without me ordering it." The Lord help us all, Pritchard thought to himself.

Ahead of the command vehicle, the beetle shapes of First Platoon began to shift position. "Michael First," Pritchard ordered sharply, "get back as you were. We're not going to engage Barthe, we're going to meet him." Maybe.

Kowie slid them alongside, then a little forward of the point vehicle of the defensive lozenge. They set down. All of the tanks were buttoned up, save for the hatch over Pritchard's head. The central vision block was a meter by 30 cm panel. It could be set for anything from a 360 degree view of the tank's surroundings to a one-to-one image of an object a kilometer away. Pritchard focused and ran the gain to ten magnifications, then thirty. At the higher power, motion curling along the snow-smoothed grainfields between Haacin and its mine resolved into men. Barthe's troops were clad in sooty-white coveralls and battle armor. The leading elements were hunched low on the meager platforms of their skimmers. Magnification and the augmented light made the skittering images grainy, but the tanker's practiced eye caught the tubes of rocket launchers clipped to every one of the skimmers. The skirmish line swelled at two points where self-propelled guns were strung like beads on the cord of men: anti-tank weapons, 50 mm powerguns firing high-intensity charges. They were supposed to be able to burn through the heaviest armor. Barthe's boys had come loaded for bear; oh yes. They thought they knew just what they were going up against. Well, the Slammers weren't going to show them they were wrong. Tonight:

"Running lights, everybody," Pritchard ordered. Then, taking a deep breath, he touched the lift on his seat and raised himself head and shoulders back into the chill night air. There was a hand light clipped to Pritchard's jacket. He snapped it on, aiming the beam down onto the turret top so that the burnished metal splashed diffused radiance up over him. It bathed his torso and face plainly for the oncoming infantry. Through the open hatch, Pritchard could hear Rob cursing. Just possibly Margritte was mumbling a prayer.

"Batteries at Dimo and Harfleur in Sector One have received fire orders and are waiting for a signal to execute," the implant grated. "If Barthe opens fire, Command Central will not, repeat, negative, use Michael First or Michael One to knock down the shells. Your guns will be clear for action, Michael One."

Pritchard grinned starkly. His face would not have been pleasant even if livid bruises were not covering almost all of it. The Slammers' central fire direction computer used radar and satellite reconnaissance to track shells in flight. Then the computer took control of any of the Regiment's vehicle-mounted powerguns and swung them onto the target. Central's message notified Pritchard that he would have full control of his weapons at all times, while guns tens or hundreds of kilometers away kept his force clear of artillery fire.

Margritte had blocked most of the commo traffic, Pritchard realized. She had let through only this message that was crucial to what they were about to do. A good commo tech; a very good person indeed.

The skirmish line grounded. The nearest infantrymen were within fifty meters of the tanks and their fellows spread off into the night like lethal wings. Barthe's men rolled off their skimmers and lay prone. Pritchard began to relax when he noticed that their rocket launchers were still aboard the skimmers. The anti-tank weapons were in instant reach, but at least they were not being leveled for an immediate salvo. Barthe didn't want to fight the Slammers. His targets were the Dutch civilians, just as Mayor van Oosten had suggested.

An air cushion jeep with a driver and two officers aboard drew close. It hissed slowly through the line of infantry, then stopped nearly touching the command vehicle's bow armor. One of the officers dismounted. He was a tall man who was probably very thin when he was not wearing insulated coveralls and battle armor. He raised his face to Pritchard atop the high curve of the blower, sweeping up his reflective face shield as he did so. He was Lieutenant Colonel Benoit, commander of the French mercenaries in Sector Two, a clean-shaven man with sharp features and a splash of gray hair displaced across his forehead by his helmet. Benoit grinned and waved at the muzzle of the 200 mm powergun pointed at him. Nobody had ever said Barthe's chief subordinate was a coward.

Pritchard climbed out of the turret to the deck, then slid down the bow slope to the ground. Benoit was several inches taller than the tanker, with a force of personality which was daunting in a way that height alone could never be. It didn't matter to Pritchard. He worked with tanks and with Colonel Hammer; nothing else was going to face down a man who was accustomed to those.

"Sergeant Major Oberlie reported how well and . . . firmly you handled their little affair, Captain," Benoit said, extending his hand to Pritchard. "I'll admit that I was a little concerned that I would have to rescue my men myself."

"Hammer's Slammers can be depended on to keep their contracts," the tanker replied, smiling with false warmth. "I told these squareheads that any civilian caught with a powergun was going to have to answer to me for it. Then we made sure nobody thinks we were kidding."

Benoit chuckled. Little puffs of vapor spurted from his mouth with the sounds. "You've been sent to the Gröningen Academy, have you not, Captain Pritchard?" the older man asked. "You understand that I take an interest in my opposite numbers in this sector."

Pritchard nodded. "The Old Man picked me for the two-year crash course on Friesland, yeah. Now and again he sends noncoms he wants to promote."

"But you're not a Frisian, though you have Frisian military training," the other mercenary continued, nodding to himself. "As you know, Captain, promotion in some infantry regiments comes much faster than it does in the . . . Slammers. If you feel a desire to speak to Colonel Barthe some time in the future, I assure you this evening's business will not be forgotten."

"Just doing my job, Colonel," Pritchard simpered. Did Benoit think a job offer would make a traitor of him? Perhaps. Hammer had bought Barthe's plans for very little, considering their military worth. "Enforcing the contract, just like you'd have done if things were the other way around."

Benoit chuckled again and stepped back aboard his jeep. "Until we meet again, Captain Pritchard," he said. "For the moment, I think we'll just proceed on into Portela. That's permissible under the contract, of course."

"Swing wide around Haacin, will you?" Pritchard called back. "The folks there're pretty worked up. Nobody wants more trouble, do we?"

Benoit nodded. As his jeep lifted, he spoke into his helmet communicator. The skirmish company rose awkwardly and set off in a counter-clockwise circuit of Haacin. Behind them, in a column reformed from their support positions at the base of the tailings heap, came the truck-mounted men of the other three companies. Pritchard stood and watched until the last of them whined past.

Air stirred by the tank's idling fans leaked out under the skirts. The jets formed tiny deltas of the snow which winked as Pritchard's feet caused eddy currents. In their cold precision, the tanker recalled Colonel Benoit's grin.

"Command Central," Pritchard said as he climbed his blower, "Michael One. Everything's smooth here. Over." Then, "Sigma One, this is Michael One. I'll be back as quick as fans'll move me, so if you have anything to say we can discuss it then." Pritchard knew that Captain Riis must have been burning the net up, trying to raise him for a report or to make demands. It wasn't fair to make Margritte hold the bag now that Pritchard himself was free to respond to the sector chief; but neither did the Dunstan tanker have the energy to argue with Riis just at the moment. Already this night he'd faced death and Colonel Benoit. Riis could wait another ten minutes.

The Plow's armor was a tight fit for its crew, the radios, and the central bulk of the main gun with its feed mechanism. The command vehicle rode glass-smooth over the frozen roadway, with none of the jouncing that a rougher surface might bring even through the air cushion. Margritte faced Pritchard over her console, her seat a meter lower than his so that she appeared a suppliant. Her short hair was the lustrous purple-black of a grackle's throat in sunlight. Hidden illumination from the instruments brought her face to life.

"Gee, Captain," Jenne was saying at Pritchard's side, "I wish you'd a let me pick up that squarehead's rifle. I know those groundpounders. They're just as apt as not to claim the kill credit themselves, and if I can't prove I stepped on the body they might get away with it. I remember on Paradise, me and Piet de Hagen—he was left wing gunner, I was right—both shot at a partisan. And then damned if Central didn't decide the slope had blown herself up with a hand grenade after we'd wounded her. So *neither* of us got the credit. You'd think—"

"Lord's *blood*, Sergeant," Pritchard snarled, "are you so damned proud of killing one of the poor bastards who hired us to protect them?"

Jenne said nothing. Pritchard shrank up inside, realizing what he had said and unable to take the words back. "Oh, Lord, Rob," he said without looking up, "I'm sorry. It . . . I'm shook, that's all."

After a brief silence, the blond sergeant laughed. "Never been shot in the head myself, Captain, but I can see it might shake a fellow, yeah." Jenne let the whine of the fans stand for a moment as the only further comment while he decided whether he would go on. Then he said, "Captain, for a week after I first saw action I meant to get out of the Slammers, even if I had to sweep floors on Curwin for the rest of my life. Finally I decided I'd stick it. I didn't like the . . . rules of the game, but I could learn to play by them.

"And I did, And one rule is, that you get to be as good as you can at killing the people Colonel Hammer wants killed. Yeah, I'm proud about that one just now. It was a tough snap shot and I made it. I don't care why we're on Kobold or who brought us here. But I know I'm supposed to kill anybody who shoots at us, and I will."

"Well, I'm glad you did," Pritchard said evenly as he looked the sergeant in the eyes. "You pretty well saved things from getting out of hand by the way you reacted."

As if he had not heard his captain, Jenne went on, "I was afraid if I stayed in the Slammers I'd turn into an animal, like the dogs we trained back home to kill rats in the quarries. And I was right. But it's the way I am now, so I don't seem to mind."

"You do care about those villagers, don't you?" Margritte asked Pritchard unexpectedly.

The captain looked down and found her eyes on him. They were the rich powder-blue of chicory flowers. "You're probably the only person in the Regiment who thinks that," he said bitterly. "Except for me. And maybe Colonel Hammer. . . ."

Margritte smiled, a quick flash and as quickly gone. "There're rule-book soldiers in the Slammers," she said, "captains who'd never believe Barthe was passing arms to the Auroran settlements since he'd signed a contract that said he wouldn't. You aren't that kind. And the Lord knows Colonel Hammer isn't, and he's backing you. I've been around you too long, Danny, to believe you like what you see the French doing."

Pritchard shrugged. His whole face was stiff with bruises and the drugs Margritte had injected to control them. If he'd locked the helmet's chin strap, the bullet's impact would have broken his neck even though the lead itself did not penetrate. "No, I don't like it," the brown-haired captain said. "It reminds me too much of the way the Combine kept us so poor on Dunstan that a thousand of us signed on for birdseed to fight off-planet. Just because it *was* off-planet. And if Kobold only gets cop from the worlds who settled her, then the French skim the best of that. Sure, I'll tell the Lord I feel sorry for the Dutch here."

Pritchard held the commo tech's eyes with his own as he continued, "But it's just like Rob said, Margritte: I'll do my job, no matter who gets hurt. We can't do a thing to Barthe or the French until they step over the line in a really obvious way. That'll mean a lot of people get hurt too. But that's what I'm waiting for."

Margritte reached up and touched Pritchard's hand where it rested on his knee. "You'll do something when you can," she said quietly.

He turned his palm up so that he could grasp the

woman's fingers. What if she knew he was planning an incident, not just waiting for one? "I'll do something, yeah," he said. "But it's going to be too late for an awful lot of people."

Kowie kept the Plow at cruising speed until they were actually in the yard of the command post. Then he cocked the fan shafts forward, lifting the bow and bringing the tank's mass around in a curve that killed its velocity and blasted an arc of snow against the building. Someone inside had started to unlatch the door as they heard the vehicle approach. The air spilling from the tank's skirts flung the panel against the inner wall and skidded the man within on his back.

The man was Captain Riis, Pritchard noted without surprise. Well, the incident wouldn't make the infantry captain any angrier than the rest of the evening had made him already.

Riis had regained his feet by the time Pritchard could jump from the deck of his blower to the fan-cleared ground in front of the building. The Frisian's normally pale face was livid now with rage. He was of the same somatotype as Lieutenant Colonel Benoit, his French counterpart in the sector: tall, thin, and proudly erect. Despite the fact that Riis was only twenty-seven, he was Pritchard's senior in grade by two years. He had kept the rank he held in Friesland's regular army when Colonel Hammer recruited him. Many of the Slammers were like Riis, Frisian soldiers who had transferred for the action and pay of a fighting regiment in which their training would be appreciated.

"You cowardly filth!" the infantryman hissed as Pritchard approached. A squad in battle gear stood within the orderly room beyond Riis. He pursed his fine lips to spit.

"Hey, Captain!" Rob Jenne called. Riis looked up. Pritchard turned, surprised that the big tank commander was not right on his heels. Jenne still smiled from the Plow's cupola. He waved at the officers with his left hand. His right was on the butterfly trigger of the tribarrel.

The threat, unspoken as it was, made a professional of Riis again. "Come on into my office," he muttered to the tank captain, turning his back on the armored vehicle as if it were only a part of the landscape.

The infantrymen inside parted to pass the captains. Sally Schilling was there. Her eyes were as hard as her porcelain armor as they raked over Pritchard. That didn't matter, he lied to himself tiredly.

Riis' office was at the top of the stairs, a narrow cubicle which had once been a child's bedroom. The sloping roof pressed in on the occupants, though a dormer window brightened the room during daylight. One wall was decorated with a regimental battle flag—not Hammer's rampant lion but a pattern of seven stars on a white field. It had probably come from the unit in which Riis had served on Friesland. Over the door hung another souvenir, a big-bore musket of local manufacture. Riis threw himself into the padded chair behind his desk. "Those bastards were carrying powerguns to Portela!" he snarled at Pritchard.

The tanker nodded. He was leaning with his right shoulder against the door jamb. "That's what the folks at Haacin thought," he agreed. "If they'll put in a complaint with the Bonding Authority, I'll testify to what I saw."

"Testify, testify!" Riis shouted. "We're not lawyers, we're soldiers! You should've seized the trucks right then and—"

"No, I should not have, Captain!" Pritchard shouted

back, holding up a mirror to Riis' anger. "Because if I had, Barthe would've complained to the Authority himself, and we'd at least've been fined. At least! The contract says the Slammers'll cooperate with the other three units in keeping peace on Kobold. Just because we suspect Barthe is violating the contract doesn't give us a right to violate it ourselves. Especially in a way any *simpleton* can see is a violation."

"If Barthe can get away with it, we can," Riis insisted, but he settled back in his chair. He was physically bigger than Pritchard, but the tanker had spent half his life with the Slammers. Years like those mark men; death is never very far behind their eyes.

"I don't think Barthe can get away with it," Pritchard lied quietly, remembering Hammer's advice on how to handle Riis and calm the Frisian without telling him the truth. Barthe's officers had been in on his plans; and one of them had talked. Any regiment might have one traitor.

The tanker lifted down the musket on the wall behind him and began turning it in his fingers. "If the Dutch settlers can prove to the Authority that Barthe's been passing out powerguns to the French," the tanker mused aloud, "well, they're responsible for half Barthe's pay, remember. It's about as bad a violation as you'll find. The Authority'll forfeit his whole bond and pay it over to whoever they decide the injured parties are. That's about three years' gross earnings for Barthe, I'd judge—he won't be able to replace it. And without a bond posted, well, he may get jobs, but they'll be the kind nobody else'd touch for the risk and the pay. His best troops'll sign on with other people. In a year or so, Barthe won't have a regiment any more."

"He's willing to take the chance," said Riis.

"Colonel Hammer isn't!" Pritchard blazed back.

"You don't know that. It isn't the sort of thing the colonel could say—"

"Say?" Pritchard shouted. He waved the musket at Riis. Its breech was triple-strapped to take the shock of the industrial explosive it used for propellant. Clumsy and large, it was the best that could be produced on a mining colony whose home worlds had forbidden local manufacturing. "Say? I bet my life against one of these tonight that the colonel wanted us to obey the contract. Do you have the guts to ask him flat out if he wants us to run guns to the Dutch?"

"I don't think that would be proper, Captain," said Riis coldly as he stood up again.

"Then try not to 'think it proper' to go do some bloody stupid stunt on your own—sir," Pritchard retorted. So much for good intentions. Hammer—and Pritchard—had expected Riis' support of the Dutch civilians. They had even planned on it. But the man seemed to have lost all his common sense. Pritchard laid the musket on the desk because his hands were trembling too badly to hang it back on the hooks.

"If it weren't for you, Captain," Riis said, "there's not a Slammer in this sector who'd object to our helping the only decent people on this planet the way we ought to. You've made your decision, and it sickens me. But I've made decisions too."

Pritchard went out without being dismissed. He blundered into the jamb, but he did not try to slam the door. That would have been petty, and there was nothing petty in the tanker's rage.

Blank-faced, he clumped down the stairs. His bunk was in a parlor which had its own door to the outside. Pritchard's crew was still in the Plow. There they had listened intently to his half of the argument with Riis, transmitted by the implant. If Pritchard had called for help, Kowie would have sent the command vehicle through the front wall buttoned up, with Jenne ready to shoot if he had to, to rescue his CO. A tank looks huge when seen close up. It is all howling steel and iridium, with black muzzles ready to spew death across a planet. On a battlefield, when the sky is a thousand shrieking colors no god ever made and the earth beneath trembles and gouts in sudden mountains, a tank is a small world indeed for its crew. Their loyalties are to nearer things than an abstraction like "The Regiment."

Besides, tankers and infantrymen have never gotten along well together.

No one was in the orderly room except two radiomen. They kept their backs to the stairs. Pritchard glanced at them, then unlatched his door. The room was dark, as he had left it, but there was a presence. Pritchard said, "Sal—" as he stepped within and the club knocked him forward into the arms of the man waiting to catch his body.

The first thing Pritchard thought as his mind slipped toward oblivion was that the cloth rubbing his face was homespun, not the hard synthetic from which uniforms were made. The last thing Pritchard thought was that there could have been no civilians within the headquarters perimeter unless the guards had allowed them; and that Lieutenant Schilling was officer of the guard tonight.

Pritchard could not be quite certain when he regained consciousness. A heavy felt rug covered and hid his trussed body on the floor of a clattering surface vehicle. He had no memory of being carried to the truck, though presumably it had been parked some distance from the command post. Riis and his confederates would not have been so open as to have civilians drive to the door to take a kidnapped officer, even if Pritchard's crew could have been expected to ignore the breach of security.

Kidnapped. Not for later murder, or he would already be dead instead of smothering under the musty rug. Thick as it was, the rug was still inadequate to keep the cold from his shivering body. The only lights Pritchard could see were the washings of icy color from the night's doubled shock to his skull.

That bone-deep ache reminded Pritchard of the transceiver implanted in his mastoid. He said in a husky whisper which he hoped would not penetrate the rug, "Michael One to any unit, any unit at all. Come in please, any Slammer."

Nothing. Well, no surprise. The implant had an effective range of less than twenty meters, enough for relaying to and from a base unit, but unlikely to be useful in Kobold's empty darkness. Of course, if the truck happened to be passing one of M Company's night defensive positions. . . . "Michael One to any unit," the tanker repeated more urgently.

A boot slammed him in the ribs. A voice in guttural Dutch snarled, "Shut up, you, or you get what you gave Henrik."

So he'd been shopped to the Dutch, not that there had been much question about it. And not that he might not have been safer in French hands, the way everybody on this cursed planet thought he was a traitor to his real employers. Well, it wasn't fair; but Danny Pritchard had grown up a farmer, and no farmer is ever tricked into believing that life is fair.

The truck finally jolted to a stop. Gloved hands jerked the cover from Pritchard's eyes. He was not surprised to recognize the concrete angles of Haacin as men passed him hand to hand into a cellar. The attempt to hijack Barthe's powerguns had been an accident, an opportunity seized; but the crew which had kidnapped Pritchard must have been in position before the call from S-39 had intervened.

"Is this wise?" Pritchard heard someone demand from the background. "If they begin searching, surely they'll begin in Haacin."

The two men at the bottom of the cellar stairs took Pritchard's shoulders and ankles to carry him to a spring cot. It had no mattress. The man at his feet called, "There won't be a search, they don't have enough men. Besides, the beasts'll be blamed—as they should be for so many things. If Pauli won't let us kill the turncoat, then we'll all have to stand the extra risk of him living."

"You talk too much," Mayor van Oosten muttered as he dropped Pritchard's shoulders on the bunk. Many civilians had followed the captive into the cellar. The last of them swung the door closed. It lay almost horizontal to the ground. When it slammed, dust sprang from the ceiling. Someone switched on a dim incandescent light. The scores of men and women in the storage room were as hard and fell as the bare walls. There were three windows at street level, high on the wall. Slotted shutters blocked most of their dusty glass.

"Get some heat in this hole or you may as well cut my throat," Pritchard grumbled.

A woman with a musket cursed and spat in his face. The man behind her took her arm before the gunbutt could smear the spittle. Almost in apology, the man said to Pritchard, "It was her husband you killed."

"You're being kept out of the way," said a husky

man—Kruse, the hothead from the hijack scene. His facial hair was pale and long, merging indistinguishably with the silky fringe of his parka. Like most of the others in the cellar, he carried a musket. "Without your meddling, there'll be a chance for us to . . . get ready to protect ourselves, after the tanks leave and the beasts come to finish us with their powerguns."

"Does Riis think I won't talk when this is over?" Pritchard asked.

"I told you—" one of the men shouted at van Oosten. The heavy-set mayor silenced him with a tap on the chest and a bellowed, "Quiet!" The rising babble hushed long enough for van Oosten to say, "Captain, you will be released in a very few days. If you—cause trouble, then, it will only be an embarrassment to yourself. Even if your colonel believes you were doing right, he won't be the one to bring to light a violation which was committed with—so you will claim—the connivance of his own officers."

The mayor paused to clear his throat and glower around the room. "Though in fact we had no help from any of your fellows, either in seizing you or in arming ourselves for our own protection."

"Are you all blind?" Pritchard demanded. He struggled with his elbows and back to raise himself against the wall. "Do you think a few lies will cover it all up? The only ships that've touched on Kobold in three months are the ones supplying us and the other mercs. Barthe maybe's smuggled in enough guns in cans of lube oil and the like to arm some civilians. He won't be able to keep that a secret, but maybe he can keep the Authority from proving who's responsible.

"That's with three months and pre-planning. If Riis tries to do anything on his own, that many of his own men are going to be short sidearms—they're all issued by serial number, Lord take it!—and a blind

Mongoloid could get enough proof to sink the Regiment."

"You think we don't understand," said Kruse in a quiet voice. He transferred his musket to his left hand, then slapped Pritchard across the side of the head. "We understand very well," the civilian said. "All the mercenaries will leave in a few days or weeks. If the French have powerguns and we do not, they will kill us, our wives, our children. . . . There's a hundred and fifty villages on Kobold like this one, Dutch, and as many French ones scattered between. It was bad before, with no one but the beasts allowed any real say in the government; but now if they win, there'll be French villages and French mines—and slave pens. Forever."

"You think a few guns'll save you?" Pritchard asked. Kruse's blow left no visible mark in the tanker's livid flesh, though a better judge than Kruse might have noted that Pritchard's eyes were as hard as his voice was mild.

"They'll help us save ourselves when the time comes," Kruse retorted.

"If you'd gotten powerguns from French civilians instead of the mercs directly, you might have been all right," the captain said. He was coldly aware that the lie he was telling was more likely to be believed in this situation than it would have been in any setting he might deliberately have contrived. There had to be an incident, the French civilians *had* to think they were safe in using their illegal weapons. . . . . "The Portelans, say, couldn't admit to having guns to lose. But anything you take from mercs—us or Barthe, it doesn't matter—we'll take back the hard way. You don't know what you're buying into."

Kruse's face did not change, but his fist drew back for another blow. The mayor caught the younger man's arm and snapped, "Franz, we're here to show him that it's not a few of us, it's every family in the village behind . . . our holding him." Van Oosten nodded around the room. "More of us than your colonel could dream of trying to punish," he added naively to Pritchard. Then he flashed back at Kruse, "If you act like a fool, he'll want revenge anyway."

"You may never believe this," Pritchard interjected wearily, "but I just want to do my job. If you let me go now, it—may be easier in the long run."

"Fool," Kruse spat and turned his back on the tanker.

A trap door opened in the ceiling, spilling more light into the cellar. "Pauli!" a woman shouted down the opening, "Hals is on the radio. There's tanks coming down the road, just like before!"

"The Lord's wounds!" van Oosten gasped. "We must—"

"They can't know!" Kruse insisted. "But we've got to get everybody out of here and back to their own houses. Everybody but me and him—" a nod at Pritchard—"and this." The musket lowered so that its round black eye pointed straight into the bound man's face.

"No, by the side door!" van Oosten called to the press of conspirators clumping up toward the street. "Don't run right out in front of them." Cursing and jostling, the villagers climbed the ladder to the ground floor, there presumably to exit on an alley.

Able only to twist his head and legs, Pritchard watched Kruse and the trembling muzzle of his weapon. The village must have watchmen with radios at either approach through the forests. If Hals was atop the heap of mine tailings—where Pritchard would have placed his outpost if he were in charge, certainly—then he'd gotten a nasty surprise when the main gun splashed the rocks with Hell. The captain grinned at the thought. Kruse misunderstood and snarled, "If they *are* coming for you, you're dead, you treacherous bastard!" To the backs of his departing fellows, the young Dutchman called, "Turn out the light here, but leave the trap door open. That won't show on the street, but it'll give me enough light to shoot by."

The tanks weren't coming for him, Pritchard knew, because they couldn't have any idea where he was. Perhaps his disappearance had stirred up some patrolling, for want of more directed action; perhaps a platoon was just changing ground because of its commander's whim. Pritchard had encouraged random motion. Tanks that freeze in one place are sitting targets, albeit hard ones. But whatever the reason tanks were approaching Haacin, if they whined by in the street outside they would be well within range of his implanted transmitter.

The big blowers were audible now, nearing with an arrogant lack of haste as if bears headed for a beehive. They were moving at about thirty kph, more slowly than Pritchard would have expected even for a contact patrol. From the sound there were four or more of them, smooth and gray and deadly.

"Kruse, I'm serious," the Slammer captain said. Light from the trap door back-lit the civilian into a hulking beast with a musket. "If you—"

"Shut up!" Kruse snarled, prodding his prisoner's bruised forehead with the gun muzzle. "One more word, any word, and—"

Kruse's right hand was so tense and white that the musket might fire even without his deliberate intent.

The first of the tanks slid by outside. Its cushion of air was so dense that the ground trembled even though none of the blower's 170 tonnes was in direct contact with it. Squeezed between the pavement and the steel curtain of the plenum chamber, the air spurted sideways and rattled the cellar windows. The rattling was inaudible against the howling of the fans themselves, but the trembling shutters chopped facets in the play of the tank's running lights. Kruse's face and the far wall flickered in blotched abstraction.

The tank moved on without pausing. Pritchard had not tried to summon it.

"That power," Kruse was mumbling to himself, "that should be for us to use to sweep the beasts—" The rest of his words were lost in the growing wail of the second tank in the column.

Pritchard tensed within. Even if a passing tank picked up his implant's transmission, its crew would probably ignore the message. Unless Pritchard identified himself, the tankers would assume it was babbling thrown by the ionosphere. And if he did identify himself, Kruse—

Kruse thrust his musket against Pritchard's skull again, banging the tanker's head back against the cellar wall. The Dutchman's voice was lost in the blower's howling, but his blue-lit lips clearly were repeating, "One word . . ."

The tank moved on down the highway toward Portela.

". . . and maybe I'll shoot you anyway," Kruse was saying. "That's the way to serve traitors, isn't it? *Mercenary!*"

The third blower was approaching. Its note seemed slightly different, though that might be the after-effect of the preceding vehicles' echoing din. Pritchard was cold all the way to his heart, because in a moment he was going to call for help. He knew that Kruse would shoot him, knew also that he would rather die now than live after hope had come so near but passed on, passed on. . . .

The third tank smashed through the wall of the house.

The Plow's skirts were not a bulldozer blade, but they were thick steel and backed with the mass of a 150 tonne command tank. The slag wall repowdered at the impact. Ceiling joists buckled into pretzel shape and ripped the cellar open to the floor above. Kruse flung his musket up and fired through the cascading rubble. The boom and red flash were lost in the chaos, but the blue-green fire stabbing back across the cellar laid the Dutchman on his back with his parka aflame. Pritchard rolled to the floor at the first shock. He thrust himself with corded legs and arms back under the feeble protection of the bunk. When the sound of falling objects had died away, the captain slitted his eyelids against the rock dust and risked a look upward.

The collision had torn a gap ten feet long in the house wall, crushing it from street level to the beams supporting the second story. The tank blocked the hole with its gray bulk. Fresh scars brightened the patina of corrosion etched onto its skirts by the atmospheres of a dozen planets. Through the buckled flooring and the dust whipped into arabesques by the idling fans, Pritchard glimpsed a slight figure clinging left-handed to the turret. Her right hand still threatened the wreckage with a submachinegun. Carpeting burned on the floor above, ignited by the burst that killed Kruse. Somewhere a woman was screaming in Dutch.

"Margritte!" Pritchard shouted. "Margritte! Down here!"

The helmeted woman swung up her face shield and tried to pierce the cellar gloom with her unaided eyes. The tank-battered opening had sufficed for the exchange of shots, but the tangle of structural members and splintered flooring was too tight to pass a man—or even a small woman. Sooty flames were beginning to shroud the gap. Margritte jumped to the ground and struggled for a moment before she was able to heave open the door. The Plow's turret swung to cover her, though neither the main gun nor the tribarrel in the cupola could depress enough to rake the cellar. Margritte ran down the steps to Pritchard. Coughing in the rock dust, he rolled out over the rubble to meet her. Much of the smashed sidewall had collapsed onto the street when the tank backed after the initial impact. Still, the crumpled beams of the ground floor sagged further with the additional weight of the slag on them. Head-sized pieces had splanged on the cot above Pritchard.

Margritte switched the submachinegun to her left hand and began using a clasp knife on her captain's bonds. The cord with which he was tied bit momentarily deeper at the blade's pressure.

Pritchard winced, then began flexing his freed hands. "You know, Margi," he said, "I don't think I've ever seen you with a gun before."

The commo tech's face hardened as if the polarized helmet shield had slipped down over it again. "You hadn't," she said. The ankle bindings parted and she stood, the dust graying her helmet and her foam-filled coveralls. "Captain, Kowie had to drive and we needed Rob in the cupola at the gun. That left me to—do anything else that had to be done. I did what had to be done."

Pritchard tried to stand, using the technician as a post on which to draw himself upright. Margritte looked frail, but with her legs braced she stood like a rock. Her arm around Pritchard's back was as firm as a man's.

"You didn't ask Captain Riis for help, I guess," Pritchard said, pain making his breath catch. The line tanks had two-man crews with no one to spare for outrider, of course.

"We didn't report you missing," Margritte said, "even to First Platoon. They just went along like before, thinking you were in the Plow giving orders." Together, captain and technician shuffled across the floor to the stairs. As they passed Kruse's body, Margritte muttered cryptically, "That's four."

Pritchard assumed the tremors beginning to shake the woman's body were from physical strain. He took as much weight off her as he could and found his numbed feet were beginning to function reasonably well. He would never have been able to board the Plow without Sergeant Jenne's grip on his arm, however.

The battered officer settled in the turret with a groan of comfort. The seat cradled his body with gentle firmness, and the warm air blown across him was just the near side of heaven.

"Captain," Jenne said, "what d'we do about the slopes who grabbed you? Shall we call in an interrogation team and—"

"We don't do anything," Pritchard interrupted. "We just pretend none of this happened and head back to . . ." He paused. His flesh wavered both hot and cold as Margritte sprayed his ankles with some of the apparatus from the medical kit. "Say, how did you find me, anyway?"

"We shut off coverage when you—went into your room," Jenne said, seeing that the commo tech herself did not intend to speak. He meant, Pritchard knew, they had shut off the sound when their captain had said, "Sal." None of the three of them were looking either of the other two in the eyes. "After a bit, though, Margi noticed the carrier line from your implant had dropped off her oscilloscope. I checked your room, didn't find you. Didn't see much point talking it over with the remfs on duty, either.

"So we got satellite recce and found two trucks'd left the area since we got back. One was Riis', and the other was a civvie junker before that. It'd been parked in the woods out of sight, half a kay up the road from the buildings. Both trucks unloaded in Haacin. We couldn't tell which load was you, but Margi said if we got close, she'd home on your carrier even though you weren't calling us on the implant. Some girl we got here, hey?"

Pritchard bent forward and squeezed the commo tech's shoulder. She did not look up, but she smiled. "Yeah, always knew she was something," he agreed, "but I don't think I realized quite what a person she was until just now."

Margritte lifted her smile. "Rob ordered First Platoon to fall in with us," she said. "He set up the whole rescue." Her fine-fingered hands caressed Pritchard's calves.

But there was other business in Haacin, now. Riis had been quicker to act than Pritchard had hoped. He asked, "You say one of the infantry's trucks took a load here a little bit ago?"

"Yeah, you want the off-print?" Jenne agreed, searching for the flimsy copy of the satellite picture. "What the Hell would they be doing, anyhow?"

"I got a suspicion," his captain said grimly, "and I suppose it's one we've got to check out."

"Michael First-Three to Michael One," the radio broke in. "Vehicles approaching from the east on the hardball."

"Michael One to Michael First," Pritchard said,

letting the search for contraband arms wait for this new development. "Reverse and form a line abreast beyond the village. Twenty meter intervals. The Plow'll take the road." More weapons from Riis? More of Barthe's troops when half his sector command was already in Portela? Pritchard touched switches beneath the vision blocks as Kowie slid the tank into position. He split the screen between satellite coverage and a ground-level view at top magnification. Six vehicles, combat cars, coming fast. Pritchard swore. Friendly, because only the Slammers had armored vehicles on Kobold, not that cars were a threat to tanks anyway. But no combat cars were assigned to this sector; and the unexpected is always bad news to a company commander juggling too many variables already.

"Platoon nearing Tango Sigma four-two, three-two, please identify to Michael One," Pritchard requested, giving Haacin's map coordinates.

Margritte turned up the volume of the main radio while she continued to bandage the captain's rope cuts. The set crackled, "Michael One, this is Alpha One and Alpha First. Stand by."

"God's bleeding cunt!" Rob Jenne swore under his breath. Pritchard was nodding in equal agitation. Alpha was the Regiment's special duty company. Its four combat car platoons were Colonel Hammer's bodyguards and police. The troopers of A Company were nicknamed the White Mice, and they were viewed askance even by the Slammers of other companies— men who prided themselves on being harder than any other combat force in the galaxy. The White Mice in turn feared their commander, Major Joachim Steuben; and if that slightly-built killer feared any-one, it was the man who was probably travelling with him this night. Pritchard sighed and asked the question. "Alpha One, this is Michael One. Are you flying a pennant, sir?"

"Affirmative, Michael One."

Well, he'd figured Colonel Hammer was along as soon as he heard what the unit was. What the Old Man was doing here was another question, and one whose answer Pritchard did not look forward to learning.

The combat cars glided to a halt under the guns of their bigger brethren. The tremble of their fans gave the appearance of heat ripples despite the snow. From his higher vantage point, Pritchard watched the second car slide out of line and fall alongside the Plow. The men at the nose and right wing guns were both short, garbed in nondescript battle gear. They differed from the other troopers only in that their helmet shields were raised and that the faces visible beneath were older than those of most Slammers: Col. Alois Hammer and his hatchetman.

"No need for radio, Captain," Hammer called in a husky voice. "What are you doing here?"

Pritchard's tongue quivered between the truth and a lie. His crew had been covering for him, and he wasn't about to leave them holding the bag. All the breaches of regulations they had committed were for their captain's sake. "Sir, I brought First Platoon back to Haacin to check whether any of the powerguns they'd hijacked from Barthe were still in civvie hands." Pritchard could feel eyes behind the cracked shutters of every east-facing window in the village.

"And have you completed your check?" the colonel pressed, his voice mild but his eyes as hard as those of Major Steuben beside him; as hard as the iridium plates of the gun shields.

Pritchard swallowed. He owed nothing to Captain Riis, but the young fool *was* his superior—and at least he hadn't wanted the Dutch to kill Pritchard.

He wouldn't put Riis' ass in the bucket if there were neutral ways to explain the contraband. Besides, they were going to need Riis and his Dutch contacts for the rest of the plan. "Sir, when you approached I was about to search a building where I suspect some illegal weapons are stored."

"And instead you'll provide back-up for the major here," said Hammer, the false humor gone from his face. His words rattled like shrapnel. "He'll retrieve the twenty-four powerguns which Captain Riis saw fit to turn over to civilians tonight. If Joachim hadn't chanced, *chanced* onto that requisition . . ." Hammer's left glove shuddered with the strength of his grip on the forward tribarrel. Then the colonel lowered his eyes and voice, adding, "The quartermaster who filled a requisition for twenty-four pistols from Central Supply is in the infantry again tonight. And Captain Riis is no longer with the Regiment."

Steuben tittered, loose despite the tension of everyone around him. The cold was bitter, but Joachim's right hand was bare. With it he traced the baroque intaglios of his holstered pistol. "Mr. Riis is lucky to be alive," the slight Newlander said pleasantly. "Luckier than some would have wished. But, Colonel, I think we'd best go pick up the merchandise before anybody nerves themself to use it on us."

Hammer nodded, calm again. "Interfile your blowers with ours, Captain," he ordered. "Your panzers watch street level while the cars take care of upper floors and roofs."

Pritchard saluted and slid down into the tank, relaying the order to the rest of his platoon. Kowie blipped the Plow's throttles, swinging the turreted mass in its own length and sending it back into the village behind the lead combat car. The tank felt light as a dancer, despite the constricting sidestreet

Kowie followed the car into. Pritchard scanned the full circuit of the vision blocks. Nothing save the wind and armored vehicles moved in Haacin. When Steuben had learned a line company was requisitioning two dozen extra sidearms, the major had made the same deductions as Pritchard had and had inspected the same satellite tape of a truck unloading. Either Riis was insane or he really thought Colonel Hammer was willing to throw away his life's work to arm a village—inadequately. Lord and Martyrs! Riis would have *had* to be insane to believe that!

Their objective was a nondescript two-story building separated from its neighbors by narrow alleys. Hammer directed the four rearmost blowers down a parallel street to block the rear. The searchlights of the vehicles chilled the flat concrete and glared back from the windows of the building. A battered surface truck was parked in the street outside. It was empty. Nothing stirred in the house.

Hammer and Steuben dismounted without haste. The major's helmet was slaved to a loudspeaker in the car. The speaker boomed, "Everyone out of the building. You have thirty seconds. Anyone found inside after that'll be shot. Thirty seconds!"

Though the residents had not shown themselves earlier, the way they boiled out of the doors proved they had expected the summons. All told there were eleven of them. From the front door came a well-dressed man and woman with their three children: a sexless infant carried by its mother in a zippered cocoon; a girl of eight with her hood down and her hair coiled in braids about her forehead; and a twelve-year-old boy who looked nearly as husky as his father. Outside staircases disgorged an aged couple on the one hand and four tough-looking men on the other.

Pritchard looked at his blower chief. The sergeant's right hand was near the gun switch and he mumbled an old ballad under his breath. Chest tightening, Pritchard climbed out of his hatch. He jumped to the ground and paced quietly over to Hammer and his aide.

"There's twenty-four pistols in this building," Joachim's amplified voice roared, "or at least you people know where they are. I want somebody to save trouble and tell me."

The civilians tensed. The mother half-turned to swing her body between her baby and the officers.

Joachim's pistol was in his hand, though Pritchard had not seen him draw it. "Nobody to speak?" Joachim queried. He shot the eight-year-old in the right knee. The spray of blood was momentary as the flesh exploded. The girl's mouth pursed as her buckling leg dropped her face-down in the street. The pain would come later. Her parents screamed, the father falling to his knees to snatch up the child as the mother pressed her forehead against the door jamb in blind panic.

Pritchard shouted, "You son of a bitch!" and clawed for his own sidearm. Steuben turned with the precision of a turret lathe. His pistol's muzzle was a white-hot ring from its previous discharge. Pritchard knew only that and the fact that his own weapon was not clear of its holster. Then he realized that Colonel Hammer was shouting, "*No!*" and that his open hand had rocked Joachim's head back.

Joachim's face went pale except for the handprint burning on his cheek. His eyes were empty. After a moment, he holstered his weapon and turned back to the civilians. "Now, who'll tell us where the guns are?" he asked in a voice like breaking glassware.

The tear-blind woman, still holding her infant,

gurgled, "Here! In the basement!" as she threw open the door. Two troopers followed her within at a nod from Hammer. The father was trying to close the girl's wounded leg with his hands, but his palms were not broad enough.

Pritchard vomited on the snowy street.

Margritte was out of the tank with a medikit in her hand. She flicked the civilian's hands aside and began freezing the wound with a spray. The front door banged open again. The two White Mice were back with their submachineguns slung under their arms and a heavy steel weapons-chest between them. Hammer nodded and walked to them.

"You could have brought in an interrogation team!" Pritchard shouted at the backs of his superiors. "You don't shoot children!"

"Machine interrogation takes time, Captain," Steuben said mildly. He did not turn to acknowledge the tanker. "This was just as effective."

"That's a little girl!" Pritchard insisted with his hands clenched. The child was beginning to cry, though the local anesthetic in the skin-sealer had probably blocked the physical pain. The psychic shock of a body that would soon end at the right knee would be worse, though. The child was old enough to know that no local doctor could save the limb. "This isn't something that human beings *do*!"

"Captain," Steuben said, "they're lucky I haven't shot all of them."

Hammer closed the arms chest. "We've got what we came for," he said. "Let's go."

"Stealing guns from my colonel," the Newlander continued as if Hammer had not spoken. The handprint had faded to a dull blotch. "I really ought to—"

"Joachim, shut it off!" Hammer shouted. "We're going to talk about what happened tonight, you and

I. I'd rather do it when we were alone—but I'll tell you now if I have to. Or in front of a court-martial."

Steuben squeezed his forehead with the fingers of his left hand. He said nothing.

"Let's go," the colonel repeated.

Pritchard caught Hammer's arm. "Take the kid back to Central's medics," he demanded.

Hammer blinked. "I should have thought of that," he said simply. "Some times I lose track of . . . things that aren't going to shoot at me. But we don't need this sort of reputation."

"I don't care cop for public relations," Pritchard snapped. "Just save that little girl's leg."

Steuben reached for the child, now lying limp. Margritte had used a shot of general anesthetic. The girl's father went wild-eyed and swung at Joachim from his crouch. Margritte jabbed with the injector from behind the civilian. He gasped as the drug took hold, then sagged as if his bones had dissolved. Steuben picked up the girl.

Hammer vaulted aboard the combat car and took the child from his subordinate's arms. Cutting himself into the loudspeaker system, the stocky colonel thundered to the street, "Listen you people. If you take guns from mercs—either Barthe's men or my own—we'll grind you to dust. Take 'em from civilians if you think you can. You may have a chance, then. If you rob mercs, you just get a chance to die."

Hammer nodded to the civilians, nodded again to the brooding buildings to either side. He gave an unheard command to his driver. The combat cars began to rev their fans.

Pritchard gave Margritte a hand up and followed her. "Michael One to Michael First," he said. "Head back with Alpha First."

*   *   *

Pritchard rode inside the turret after they left Haacin, glad for once of the armor and the cabin lights. In the writhing tree-limbs he had seen the Dutch mother's face as the shot maimed her daughter.

Margritte passed only one call to her commander. It came shortly after the combat cars had separated to return to their base camp near Midi, the planetary capital. The colonel's voice was as smooth as it ever got. It held no hint of the rage which had blazed out in Haacin. "Captain Pritchard," Hammer said, "I've transferred command of Sigma Company to the leader of its First Platoon. The sector, of course, is in your hands now. I expect you to carry out your duties with the ability you've already shown."

"Michael One to Regiment," Pritchard replied curtly. "Acknowledged."

Kowie drew up in front of the command post without the furious caracole which had marked their most recent approach. Pritchard slid his hatch open. His crewmen did not move. "I've got to worry about being sector chief for a while," he said, "but you three can sack out in the barracks now. You've put in a full tour in my book."

"Think I'll sleep here," Rob said. He touched a stud, rotating his seat into a couch alongside the receiver and loading tube of the main gun.

Pritchard frowned. "Margritte?" he asked.

She shrugged. "No, I'll stay by my set for a while." Her eyes were blue and calm.

On the intercom, Kowie chimed in with, "Yeah, you worry about the sector, we'll worry about ourselves. Say, don't you think a tank platoon'd be better for base security than these pongoes?"

"Shut up, Kowie," Jenne snapped. The blond Burlager glanced at his captain. "Everything'll be fine, so long as we're here," he said from one elbow. He patted the breech of the 200 mm gun.

Pritchard shrugged and climbed out into the cold night. He heard the hatch grind shut behind him.

Until Pritchard walked in the door of the building, it had not occurred to him that Riis' replacement was Sally Schilling. The words "First Platoon leader" had not been a name to the tanker, not in the midst of the furor of his mind. The little blonde glanced up at Pritchard from the map display she was studying. She spat cracklingly on the electric stove and faced around again. Her aide, the big corporal, blinked in some embarrassment. None of the headquarters staff spoke.

"I need the display console from my room," Pritchard said to the corporal.

The infantryman nodded and got up. Before he had taken three steps, Lieutenant Schilling's voice cracked like pressure-heaved ice, "Corporal Webbert!"

"Sir?" The big man's face went tight as he found himself a pawn in a game whose stakes went beyond his interest.

"Go get the display console for our new commander. It's in his room."

Licking his lips with relief, the corporal obeyed. He carried the heavy four-legged console back without effort.

Sally was making it easier for him, Pritchard thought. But how he wished that Riis hadn't made so complete a fool of himself that he had to be removed. Using Riis to set up a double massacre would have been a lot easier to justify when Danny awoke in the middle of the night and found himself remembering. . . .

Pritchard positioned the console so that he sat with his back to the heater. It separated him from

Schilling. The top of the instrument was a slanted, 40 cm screen which glowed when Pritchard switched it on. "Sector Two display," he directed. In response to his words the screen sharpened into a relief map. "Population centers,' he said. They flashed on as well, several dozen of them ranging from a few hundred souls to the several thousand of Haacin and Dimo. Portela, the largest Francophone settlement west of the Aillet, was about twenty kilometers west of Haacin.

And there were now French mercenaries on both sides of that division line. Sally had turned from her own console and stood up to see what Pritchard was doing. The tanker said, "All mercenary positions, confirmed and calculated."

The board spangled itself with red and green symbols, each of them marked in small letters with a unit designation. The reconnaissance satellites gave unit strengths very accurately, and computer analysis of radio traffic could generally name the forces. In the eastern half of the sector, Lieutenant Colonel Benoit had spread out one battalion in platoon-strength billets. The guardposts were close enough to most points to put down trouble immediately. A full company near Dimo guarded the headquarters and two batteries of rocket howitzers.

The remaining battalion in the sector, Benoit's own, was concentrated in positions blasted into the rocky highlands ten kays west of Portela. It was not a deployment that would allow the mercs to effectively police the west half of the sector, but it was a very good defensive arrangement. The forest that covered the center of the sector was ideal for hit-and-run sniping by small units of infantry. The tree boles were too densely woven for tanks to plow through them. Because the forest was so flammable at this season, however, it would be equally dangerous to ambushers. Benoit was wise to concentrate in the barren high-ground.

Besides the highlands, the fields cleared around every settlement were the only safe locations for a modern firefight. The fields, and the broad swathes cleared for roads through the forest. . . .

"Incoming traffic for Sector Chief," announced a radioman. "It's from the skepsel colonel, sir." He threw his words into the air, afraid to direct them at either of the officers in the orderly room.

"Voice only, or is there visual?" Pritchard asked. Schilling held her silence.

"Visual component, sir."

"Patch him through to my console," the tanker decided. "And son—watch your language. Otherwise, you say 'beast' when you shouldn't."

The map blurred from the display screen and was replaced by the hawk features of Lieutenant Colonel Benoit. A pick-up on the screen's surface threw Pritchard's own image onto Benoit's similar console.

The Frenchman blinked. "Captain Pritchard? I'm very pleased to see you, but my words must be with Captain Riis directly. Could you wake him?"

"There've been some changes," the tanker said. In the back of his mind, he wondered what had happened to Riis. Pulled back under arrest, probably. "I'm in charge of Sector Two, now. Co-charge with you, that is."

Benoit's face steadied as he absorbed the information without betraying an opinion about it. Then he beamed like a feasting wolf and said, "Congratulations, Captain. Some day you and I will have to discuss the . . . events of the past few days. But what I was calling about is far less pleasant, I'm afraid."

Benoit's image wavered on the screen as he paused.

Pritchard touched his tongue to the corner of his mouth. "Go ahead, Colonel," he said. "I've gotten enough bad news today that a little more won't signify."

Benoit quirked his brow in what might or might not have been humor. "When we were proceeding to Portela," he said, "some of my troops mistook the situation and set up passive tank interdiction points. Mines, all over the sector. They're booby-trapped, of course. The only safe way to remove them is for the troops responsible to do it. They will of course be punished later."

Pritchard chuckled. "How long do you estimate it'll take to clear the roads, Colonel?" he asked.

The Frenchman spread his hands, palms up. "Weeks, perhaps. It's much harder to clear mines safely than to lay them, of course."

"But there wouldn't be anything between *here* and Haacin, would there?" the tanker prodded. It was all happening just as Hammer's informant had said Barthe planned it. First, hem the tanks in with nets of forest and minefields; then, break the most important Dutch stronghold while your mercs were still around to back you up. . . . "The spur road to our HQ here wasn't on your route; and besides, we just drove tanks over it a few minutes ago."

Behind Pritchard, Sally Schilling was cursing in a sharp, carrying voice. Benoit could probably hear her, but the colonel kept his voice as smooth as milk as he said, "Actually, I'm afraid there *is* a field—gas, shaped charges, and glass-shard antipersonnel mines— somewhere on that road, yes. Fortunately, the field was signal activated. It wasn't primed until after you had passed through. I assure you, Captain Pritchard, that all the roads west of the Aillet may be too dangerous to traverse until I have cleared them. I

warn you both as a friend and so that we will not be
charged with damage to any of your vehicles—and
men. You have been fully warned of the danger;
anything that happens now is your responsibility."

Pritchard leaned back in the console's integral seat,
chuckling again. "You know, Colonel," the tank captain said, "I'm not sure that the Bonding Authority
wouldn't find those mines were a hostile act justify-
ing our retaliation." Benoit stiffened, more an internal hardness than anything that showed in his muscles.
Pritchard continued to speak through a smile. "We
won't, of course. Mistakes happen. But one thing,
Colonel Benoit—"

The Frenchman nodded, waiting for the edge to
bite. He knew as well as Pritchard did that, at best,
if there were an Authority investigation, Barthe would
have to throw a scapegoat out. A high-ranking
scapegoat.

"Mistakes happen," Pritchard repeated, "but they
can't be allowed to happen twice. You've got my
permission to send out a ten-man team by daylight—
only by daylight—to clear the road from Portela to
Bever. That'll give you a route back to your side of
the sector. If any other troops leave their present
position, for any reason, I'll treat it as an attack."

"Captain, this demarcation within the sector was
not a part of the contract—"

"It was at the demand of Colonel Barthe," Pritchard
snapped, "and agreed to by the demonstrable practice of both regiments over the past three months."
Hammer had briefed Pritchard very carefully on the
words to use here, to be recorded for the benefit of
the Bonding Authority. "You've heard the terms,
Colonel. You can either take them or we'll put the
whole thing—the minefields and some other matters

that've come up recently—before the Authority right now. Your choice."

Benoit stared at Pritchard, apparently calm but tugging at his upper lip with thumb and forefinger. "I think you are unwise, Captain, in taking full responsibility for an area in which your tanks cannot move; but that is your affair, of course. I will obey your mandate. We should have the Portela-Haacin segment cleared by evening; tomorrow we'll proceed to Bever. Good day."

The screen segued back to the map display. Pritchard stood up. A spare helmet rested beside one of the radiomen. The tank captain donned it—he had forgotten to requisition a replacement from stores— and said, "Michael One to all Michael units." He paused for the acknowledgment lights from his four platoons and the command vehicle. Then, "Hold your present positions. Don't attempt to move by road, any road, until further notice. The roads have been mined. There are probably safe areas, and we'll get you a map of them as soon as Command Central works it up. For the time being, just stay where you are. Michael One, out."

"Are you really going to take that?" Lieutenant Schilling demanded in a low, harsh voice.

"Pass the same orders to your troops, Sally," Pritchard said. "I know they can move through the woods where my tanks can't, but I don't want any friendlies in the forest right now either." To the intelligence sergeant on watch, Pritchard added, "Samuels, get Central to run a plot of all activity by any of Benoit's men. That won't tell us where they've laid mines, but it'll let us know where they can't have."

"What happens if the bleeding skepsels ignore you?" Sally blazed. "You've bloody taught them to ignore you, haven't you? Knuckling under every time somebody whispers 'contract'? You can't move a tank to stop them if they do leave their base, and I've got 198 effectives. A battalion'd laugh at me, *laugh!*"

Schilling's arms were akimbo, her face as pale with rage as the snow outside. Speaking with deliberate calm, Pritchard said, 'I'll call in artillery if I need to. Benoit only brought two calliopes with him, and they can't stop all the shells from three firebases at the same time. The road between his position and Portela's just a snake-track cut between rocks. A couple firecracker rounds going off above infantry strung out there—Via, it'll be a butcher shop."

Schilling's eyes brightened. "Then for tonight, the sector's just like it was before we came," she thought out loud. "Well, I suppose you know best," she added in false agreement, with false nonchalance. "I'm going back to the barracks. I'll brief First Platoon in person and radio the others from there. Come along, Webbert."

The corporal slammed the door behind himself and his lieutenant. The gust of air that licked about the walls was cold, but Pritchard was already shivering at what he had just done to a woman he loved.

It was daylight by now, and the frosted windows turned to flame in the ruddy sun. Speaking to no one but his console's memory, Pritchard began to plot tracks from each tank platoon. He used a topographic display, ignoring the existence of the impenetrable forest which covered the ground.

Margritte's resonant voice twanged in the implant, "Captain, would you come to the blower for half a sec?"

"On the way," Pritchard said, shrugging into his coat. The orderly room staff glanced up at him.

Margritte poked her head out of the side hatch. Pritchard climbed onto the deck to avoid some of the generator whine. The skirts sang even when the fans were cut off completely. Rob Jenne, curious but at ease, was visible at his battle station beyond the commo tech. "Sir," Margritte said, "we've been picking up signals from—there." The blue-eyed woman thumbed briefly at the infantry barracks without letting her pupils follow the gesture.

Pritchard nodded. "Lieutenant Schilling's passing on my orders to her company."

"Danny, the transmission's in code, and it's not a code of ours." Margritte hesitated, then touched the back of the officer's gloved left hand. "There's answering signals, too. I can't triangulate without moving the blower, of course, but the source is in line with the tailings pile at Haacin."

It was what he had planned, after all. Someone the villagers could trust had to get word of the situation to them. Otherwise they wouldn't draw the Portelans and their mercenary backers into a fatal mistake. Hard luck for the villagers who were acting as bait, but very good luck for every other Dutchman on Kobold. . . . Pritchard had no reason to feel anything but relief that it had happened. He tried to relax the muscles which were crushing all the breath out of his lungs. Margritte's fingers closed over his hand and squeezed it.

"Ignore the signals," the captain said at last. "We've known all along they were talking to the civilians, haven't we?" Neither of his crewmen spoke. Pritchard's eyes closed tightly. He said, "We've known for months, Hammer and I, every damned thing that Barthe's been plotting with the skepsels. They want a chance to break Haacin now, while they're around to cover for the Portelans. We'll give them their chance and ram it up their ass crosswise. The Old Man hasn't spread the word for fear the story'd get out, the same way Barthe's plans did. We're all mercenaries, after all. But I want you three to know. And I'll be glad when the only thing I have to worry about is the direction the shots are coming from."

Abruptly, the captain dropped back to the ground. "Get some sleep," he called. "I'll be needing you sharp tonight."

Back at his console, Pritchard resumed plotting courses and distances. After he figured each line, he called in a series of map coordinates to Command Central. He knew his radio traffic was being monitored and probably unscrambled by Barthe's intelligence staff; knew also that even if he had read the coordinates out in clear, the French would have assumed it was a code. The locations made no sense unless one knew they were ground zero for incendiary shells.

As Pritchard worked, he kept close watch on the French battalions. Benoit's own troops held their position, as Pritchard had ordered. They used the time to dig in. At first they had blasted slit trenches in the rock. Now they dug covered bunkers with the help of mining machinery trucked from Portela by civilians. Five of the six anti-tank guns were sited atop the eastern ridge of the position. They could rake the highway as it snaked and switched back among the foothills west of Portela.

Pritchard chuckled grimly again when Sergeant Samuels handed him high-magnification off-prints from the satellites. Benoit's two squat, bulky calliopes were sited in defilade behind the humps of the eastern ridge line. There the eight-barrelled powerguns were safe from the smashing fire of M Company's tanks, but their ability to sweep artillery shells from the sky was degraded by the closer horizon. The Slammers did not bother with calliopes themselves. Their central fire director did a far better job by working through the hundreds of vehicle-mounted weapons. How much better, Benoit might learn very shortly.

The mine-sweeping team cleared the Portela-Haacin road, as directed. The men returned to Benoit's encampment an hour before dusk. The French did not come within five kilometers of the Dutch village.

Pritchard watched the retiring mine sweepers, then snapped off the console. He stood. "I'm going out to my blower," he said.

His crew had been watching for him. A hatch shot open, spouting condensate, as soon as Pritchard came out the door. The smooth bulk of the tank blew like a restive whale. On the horizon, the sun was so low that the treetops stood out in silhouette like a line of bayonets.

Wearily, the captain dropped through the hatch into his seat. Jenne and Margritte murmured greeting and waited, noticeably tense. "I'm going to get a couple hours' sleep," Pritchard said. He swung his seat out and up, so that he lay horizontal in the turret. His legs hid Margritte's oval face from him. "Punch up coverage of the road west of Haacin, would you?" he asked. "I'm going to take a tab of Glirine. Slap me with the antidote when something moves there."

"If something moves," Jenne amended.

"When." Pritchard sucked down the pill. "The squareheads think they've got one last chance to smack Portela and hijack the powerguns again. Thing is, the Portelans'll have already distributed the guns and be waiting for the Dutch to come through. It'll be a damn short fight, that one. . . ." The drug took hold and Pritchard's consciousness began to flow away like a sugar cube in water. "Damn short. . . ."

* * *

At first Pritchard felt only the sting on the inside of his wrist. Then the narcotic haze ripped away and he was fully conscious again.

"There's a line of trucks, looks like twenty, moving west out of Haacin, sir. They're blacked out, but the satellite has 'em on infra-red."

"Red Alert," Pritchard ordered. He locked his seat upright into its combat position. Margritte's soft voice sounded the general alarm. Pritchard slipped on his radio helmet. "Michael One to all Michael units. Check off." Five green lights flashed their silent acknowledgements across the top of the captain's face-shield display. "Michael One to Sigma One," Pritchard continued.

"Go ahead, Michael One." Sally's voice held a note of triumph.

"Sigma One, pull all your troops into large, clear areas—the fields around the towns are fine, but stay the hell away from Portela and Haacin. Get ready to slow down anybody coming this way from across the Aillet. Over."

"Affirmative, Danny, affirmative!" Sally replied. Couldn't she use the satellite reconnaissance herself and see the five blurred dots halfway between the villages? They were clearly the trucks which had brought the Portelans into their ambush positions. What would she say when she realized how she had set up the villagers she was trying to protect? Lambs to the slaughter. . . .

The vision block showed the Dutch trucks more clearly than the camouflaged Portelans. The crushed stone of the roadway was dark on the screen, cooler than the surrounding trees and the vehicles upon it. Pritchard patted the breech of the main gun and looked across it to his blower chief. "We got a basic load for this aboard?" he asked.

"Do bears cop in the woods?" Jenne grinned. "We gonna get a chance to bust caps tonight, Captain?"

Pritchard nodded. "For three months we've been here, doing nothing but selling rope to the French. Tonight they've bought enough that we can hang 'em with it." He looked at the vision block again. "You alive, Kowie?" he asked on intercom.

"Ready to slide any time you give me a course," said the driver from his closed cockpit.

The vision block sizzled with bright streaks that seemed to hang on the screen though they had passed in microseconds. The leading blobs expanded and brightened as trucks blew up.

"Michael One to Fire Central," Pritchard said.

"Go ahead, Michael One," replied the machine voice.

"Prepare Fire Order Alpha."

"Roger, Michael One."

"Margritte, get me Benoit."

"Go ahead, Captain."

"Slammers to Benoit. Pritchard to Benoit. Come in please, Colonel."

"Captain Pritchard, Michel Benoit here." The colonel's voice was smooth but too hurried to disguise the concern underlying it. "I assure you that none of my men are involved in the present fighting. I have a company ready to go out and control the disturbance immediately, however."

The tanker ignored him. The shooting had already stopped for lack of targets. "Colonel, I've got some artillery aimed to drop various places in the forest. It's coming nowhere near your troops or any other human beings. If you interfere with this necessary shelling, the Slammer'll treat it as an act of war. I speak with my colonel's authority."

"Captain, I don't—"

Pritchard switched manually. "Michael One to Fire Central. Execute Fire Order Alpha."

"On the way, Michael One."

"Michael One to Michael First, Second, Fourth. Command Central has fed movement orders into your map displays. Incendiary clusters are going to burst over marked locations to ignite the forest. Use your own main guns to set the trees burning in front of your immediate positions. One round ought to do it. Button up and you can move through the fire— the trees just fall to pieces when they've burned."

The turret whined as it slid under Rob's control. "Michael Third, I'm attaching you to the infantry. More Frenchmen're apt to be coming this way from the east. It's up to you to see they don't slam a door on us."

The main gun fired, its discharge so sudden that the air rang like a solid thing. Seepage from the ejection system filled the hull with the reek of super-heated polyurethane. The side vision blocks flashed cyan, then began to flood with the mounting white hell-light of the blazing trees. In the central block, still set on remote, all the Dutch trucks were burning as were patches of forest which the ambush had ignited. The Portelans had left the concealment of the trees and swept across the road, mopping up the Dutch.

"Kowie, let's move," Jenne was saying on intercom, syncopated by the mild echo of his voice in the turret. Margritte's face was calm, her lips moving subtly as she handled some traffic that she did not pass on to her captain. The tank slid forward like oil on a lake. From the far distance came the thumps of incendiary rounds scattering their hundreds of separate fireballs high over the trees.

Pritchard slapped the central vision block back on direct; the tank's interior shone white with transmitted fire. The Plow's bow slope sheared into a thicket of blazing trees. The wood tangled and sagged, then gave in a splash of fiery splinters whipped aloft by the blower's fans. The tank was in Hell on all sides, Kowie steering by instinct and his inertial compass. Even with his screens filtered all the way down, the driver would not be able to use his eyes effectively until more of the labyrinth had burned away.

Benoit's calliopes had not tried to stop the shelling. Well, there were other ways to get the French mercs to take the first step over the line. For instance—

"Punch up Benoit again," Pritchard ordered. Even through the dense iridium plating, the roar of the fire was a subaural presence in the tank.

"Go ahead," Margritte said, flipping a switch on her console. She had somehow been holding the French officer in conversation all the time Pritchard was on other frequencies.

"Colonel," Pritchard said, "we've got clear running through this fire. We're going to chase down everybody who used a powergun tonight; then we'll shoot them. We'll shoot everybody in their families, everybody with them in this ambush, and we'll blow up every house that anybody involved lived in. That's likely to be every house in Portela, isn't it?"

More than the heat and ions of the blazing forest distorted Benoit's face. He shouted, "Are you mad? You can't think of such a thing, Pritchard!"

The tanker's lips parted like a wolf's. He could think of mass murder, and there were plenty of men in the Slammers who would really be willing to carry out the threat. But Pritchard wouldn't have to, because Benoit was like Riis and Schilling: too much of a nationalist to remember his first duty as a merc. . . . "Colonel Benoit, the contract demands we keep the peace and stay impartial. The record shows how we treated people in Haacin for *having* powerguns. For what the Portelans did tonight—don't worry, we'll be impartial. And they'll never break the peace again."

"Captain, I will not allow you to massacre French civilians," Benoit stated flatly.

"Move a man out of your present positions and I'll shoot him dead," Pritchard said. "It's your choice, Colonel. Over and out."

The Plow bucked and rolled as it pulverized fire-shattered trunks, but the vehicle was meeting nothing solid enough to slam it to a halt. Pritchard used a side block on remote to examine Benoit's encampment. The satellite's enhanced infra-red showed a stream of sparks flowing from the defensive positions toward the Portela road: infantry on skimmers. The pair of larger, more diffuse blobs were probably anti-tank guns. Benoit wasn't moving his whole battalion, only a reinforced company in a show of force to make Pritchard back off.

The fool. Nobody was going to back off now.

"Michael One to all Michael and Sigma units," Pritchard said in a voice as clear as the white flames around his tank. "We're now in a state of war with Barthe's Company and its civilian auxiliaries. Michael First, Second and Fourth, we'll rendezvous at the ambush site as plotted on your displays. Anybody between there and Portela is fair game. If we take any fire from Portela, we go down the main drag in line and blow the cop out of it. If any of Barthe's people are in the way, we keep on sliding west.

Sigma One, mount a fluid defense, don't push, and wait for help. It's coming. If this works, it's Barthe against Hammer—and that's wheat against the scythe. Acknowledged?"

As Pritchard's call board lit green, a raspy new voice broke into the sector frequency. "Wish I was with you, panzers. We'll cover your butts and the other sectors—if anybody's dumb enough to move. Good hunting!"

"I wish you *were* here and not me, Colonel," Pritchard whispered, but that was to himself . . . and perhaps it was not true even in his heart. Danny's guts were very cold, and his face was as cold as death.

To Pritchard's left, a lighted display segregated the area of operations. It was a computer analog, not direct satellite coverage. Doubtful images were brightened and labeled—green for the Slammers, red for Barthe; blue for civilians unless they were fighting on one side or the other. The green dot of the Plow converged on the ambush site at the same time as the columns of First and Fourth Platoons. Second was a minute or two farther off. Pritchard's breath caught. A sheaf of narrow red lines was streaking across the display toward his tanks. Barthe had ordered his Company's artillery to support Benoit's threatened battalion.

The salvo frayed and vanished more suddenly than it had appeared. Other Slammers' vehicles had ripped the threat from the sky. Green lines darted from Hammer's own three firebases, off-screen at the analog's present scale. The fighting was no longer limited to Sector Two. If Pritchard and Hammer had played their hand right, though, it would stay limited to only the Slammers and Compagnie de Barthe. The other Francophone regiments would fear to join an unexpected battle which certainly resulted from someone's contract violation. If the breach were Hammer's, the Dutch would not be allowed to profit by the fighting. If the breach were Barthe's, anybody who joined him would be punished as sternly by the Bonding Authority.

So violent was the forest's combustion that the flames were already dying down into sparks and black ashes. The command tank growled out into the broad avenue of the road west of Haacin. Dutch trucks were still burning—fabric, lubricants, and the very paint of their frames had been ignited by the powerguns. Many of the bodies sprawled beside the vehicles were smoldering also. Some corpses still clutched their useless muskets. The dead were victims of six centuries of progress which had come to Kobold pre-packaged, just in time to kill them. Barthe had given the Portelans only shoulder weapons, but even that meant the world here. The powerguns were repeaters with awesome destruction in every bolt. Without answering fire to rattle them, even untrained gunmen could be effective with weapons which shot line-straight and had no recoil. Certainly the Portelans had been effective.

Throwing ash and fire like sharks in the surf, the four behemoths of First Platoon slewed onto the road from the south. Almost simultaneously, Fourth joined through the dying hellstorm to the other side. The right of way was fifty meters wide and there was no reason to keep to the center of it. The forest, ablaze or glowing embers, held no ambushes any more.

The Plow lurched as Kowie guided it through the bodies. Some of them were still moving. Pritchard wondered if any of the Dutch had lived through the night, but that was with the back of his mind. The Slammers were at war, and nothing else really mattered. "Triple line ahead," he ordered. "First to the left, Fourth to the right; the Plow'll take the center alone till Second joins. Second, wick up when you hit the hardball and fall in behind us. If it moves, shoot it."

At one hundred kph, the leading tanks caught the Portelans three kilometers east of their village. The settlers were in the trucks that had been hidden in the forest fringe until the fires had been started. The ambushers may not have known they were being pursued until the rearmost truck exploded. Rob Jenne had shredded it with his tribarrel at five kilometers' distance. The cyan flicker and its answering orange blast signaled the flanking tanks to fire. They had just enough parallax to be able to rake the four remaining trucks without being blocked by the one which had blown up. A few snapping discharges proved that some Portelans survived to use their new powerguns on tougher meat than before. Hits streaked ashes on the tanks' armor. No one inside noticed.

From Portela's eastern windows, children watched their parents burn.

A hose of cyan light played from a distant roof top. It touched the command tank as Kowie slewed to avoid a Portelan truck. The burst was perfectly aimed, an automatic weapon served by professionals. Professionals should have known how useless it would be against heavy armor. A vision block dulled as a few receptors fused. Jenne cursed and trod the footswitch of the main gun. A building leaped into dazzling prominence in the microsecond flash. Then it and most of the block behind collapsed into internal fires, burying the machinegun and everything else in the neighborhood. A moment later, a salvo of Hammer's high explosive got through the calliopes' inade-

quate screen. The village began to spew skyward in
white flashes.

The Portelans had wanted to play soldier, Pritchard thought. He had dammed up all pity for the
villagers of Haacin; he would not spend it now on
these folk.

"Line ahead—First, Fourth, and Second," Pritchard ordered. The triple column slowed and reformed
with the Plow the second vehicle in the new line.
The shelling lifted from Portela as the tanks plunged
into the village. Green trails on the analog termi-
nated over the road crowded with Benoit's men and
over the main French position, despite anything the
calliopes could do. The sky over Benoit's bunkers
rippled and flared as firecracker rounds sleeted down
their thousands of individual bomblets. The defensive fire cut off entirely. Pritchard could imagine the
carnage among the unprotected calliope crews when
the shrapnel whirred through them.

The tanks were firing into the houses on either
side, using tribarrels and occasional wallops from
their main guns. The blue-green flashes were so intense they colored even the flames they lit among
the wreckage. At fifty kph the thirteen tanks swept
through the center of town, hindered only by the
rubble of houses spilled across the street. Barthe's
men were skittering white shadows who burst when
powerguns hit them point blank.

The copper mine was just west of the village and
three hundred meters north of the highway. As the
lead tank bellowed out around the last houses, a
dozen infantrymen rose from where they had sheltered in the pit head and loosed a salvo of buzzbombs.
The tank's automatic defense system was live. White
fire rippled from just above the skirts as the charges
there flailed pellets outward to intersect the rockets.

Most of the buzzbombs exploded ten meters distant against the steel hail. One missile soared harmlessly over its target, its motor a tiny flare against the flickering sky. Only one of the shaped charges burst alongside the turret, forming a bell of light momentarily bigger than the tank. Even that was only a near miss. It gouged the iridium armor like a misthrust rapier which tears skin but does not pierce the skull.

Main guns and tribarrels answered the rockets instantly. Men dropped, some dead, some reloading. "Second Platoon, go put some HE down the shaft and rejoin," Pritchard ordered. The lead tank now had expended half its defensive charges. "Michael First-Three, fall in behind First-One. Michael One leads," he went on.

Kowie grunted acknowledgement. The Plow revved up to full honk. Benoit's men were on the road, those who had not reached Portela when the shooting started or who had fled when the artillery churned the houses to froth. The infantry skimmers were trapped between sheer rocks and sheer drop-offs, between their own slow speed and the onrushing frontal slope of the Plow. There were trees where the rocks had given them purchase. Scattered incendiaries had made them blazing cressets lighting a charnel procession.

Jenne's tribarrel scythed through body armor and dismembered men in short bursts. One of the anti-tank guns—was the other buried in Portela?—lay skewed against a rock wall, its driver killed by a shell fragment. Rob put a round from the main gun into it. So did each of the next two tanks. At the third shot, the ammunition ignited in a blinding secondary explosion.

The anti-tank guns still emplaced on the ridge line had not fired, though they swept several stretches of the road. Perhaps the crews had been rattled by the shelling, perhaps Benoit had held his fire for fear of hitting his own men. A narrow defile notched the final ridge. The Plow heaved itself up the rise, and at the top three bolts slapped it from different angles.

Because the bow was lifted, two of the shots vaporized portions of the skirt and the front fans. The tank nosed down and sprayed sparks with half its length. The third bolt grazed the left top of the turret, making the iridium ring as it expanded. The interior of the armor streaked white though it was not pierced. The temperature inside the tank rose thirty degrees. Even as the Plow skidded, Sergeant Jenne was laying his main gun on the hot spot that was the barrel of the leftmost anti-tank weapon. The Plow's shot did what heavy top cover had prevented Hammer's rocket howitzers from accomplishing with shrapnel. The anti-tank gun blew up in a distance-muffled flash. One of its crewmen was silhouetted high in the air by the vaporizing metal of his gun.

Then the two remaining weapons ripped the night and the command blower with their charges.

The bolt that touched the right side of the turret spewed droplets of iridium across the interior of the hull. Air pistoned Pritchard's eardrums. Rob Jenne lurched in his harness, right arm burned away by the shot. His left hand blackened where it touched bare metal that sparked and sang as circuits shorted. Margritte's radios were exploding one by one under the overloads. The vision blocks worked and the turret hummed placidly as Pritchard rotated it to the right with his duplicate controls.

"Cut the power! Rob's burning!" Margritte was shrieking. She had torn off her helmet. Her thick hair stood out like tendrils of bread mold in the gathering charge. Then Pritchard had the main gun bearing and it lit the ridge line with another second-ary explosion.

"Danny, our ammunition! It'll—"

Benoit's remaining gun blew the tribarrel and the cupola away deafeningly. The automatic's loading tube began to gang-fire down into the bowels of the tank. It reached a bright column up into the sky, but the turret still rolled.

Electricity crackled around Pritchard's boot and the foot trip as he fired again. The bolt stabbed the night. There was no answering blast. Pritchard held down the switch, his nostrils thick with ozone and superheated plastic and the sizzling flesh of his friend. There was still no explosion from the target bunker. The rock turned white between the cyan flashes. It cracked and flowed away like sun-melted snow, and the anti-tank gun never fired again.

The loading tube emptied. Pritchard slapped the main switch and cut off the current. The interior light and the dancing arcs died, leaving only the dying glow of the bolt-heated iridium. Tank after tank edged by the silent command vehicle and roared on toward the ridge. Benoit's demoralized men were already beginning to throw down their weapons and surrender.

Pritchard manually unlatched Jenne's harness and swung it horizontal. The blower chief was breathing but unconscious. Pritchard switched on a battery-powered handlight. He held it steady as Margritte began to spray sealant on the burns. Occasionally she paused to separate clothing from flesh with a stylus.

"It had to be done," Pritchard whispered. By sac-rificing Haacin, he had mousetrapped Benoit into starting a war the infantry could not win. Hammer was now crushing Barthe's Company, one on one, in an iridium vise. Friesland's Council of State would not have let Hammer act had they known his intentions, but in the face of a stunning victory they simply could not avoid dictating terms to the French.

"It had to be done. But I look at *what* I did—" Pritchard swung his right hand in a gesture that would have included both the fuming wreck of Portela and the raiders from Haacin, dead on the road beyond. He struck the breech of the main gun instead. Clenching his fist, he slammed it again into the metal in self-punishment. Margritte cried out and blocked his arm with her own.

"Margi," Pritchard repeated in anguish, "it isn't something that human beings *do* to each other."

But soldiers do.

And hangmen.

Interlude: Table of Organization and Equipment, Hammer's Regiment

Sec I: Headquarters Battalion

Except for Artillery and Replacement, all the support elements were grouped for administrative convenience in HQ Battalion. In practice, a large percentage of the strength of these units was parcelled out to line companies according to need.

a) Headquarters Company—Colonel Hammer and his personal staff, including battalion officers; satellite launch and maintenance personnel; finance; and a security element. Total: 153 effectives.

b) Maintenance—Capable of handling anything short of full hull rebuilds and internal work on fusion units. Company included three tank and six combat car transporters, stretched-chassis vehicles with fans at either end; ACVs cannot, of course, be towed. Total: 212 effectives.

c) Communications—Included not only the staff of

Command Central, but the staffs of local headquarters with area responsibilities. Total: 143 effectives.

d) Medical—Twenty-four first line medics with medicomps linked to Central, and a field hospital with full life-support capability. Total: 60 effectives.

e) Supply—Included Mess and Quartermaster functions. Total: 143 effectives.

f) Intelligence—Order of Battle was performed mostly by computer. Imagery Interpretation, study of satellite recce, was in large measure still a human function. There were three mechanical interrogation (i.e., mind probe) teams. Total: 84 effectives.

g) Transport—312 men (heavily supplemented from Replacement Battalion) and 288 air cushion trucks for local unit supply from spaceport or planetary logistics centers. True aircraft, flying above the nape of the earth, would have been suicidally vulnerable to powerguns.

h) Combat Engineers—Carried out bridging, clearing, mine-sweeping, and very frequently fighting tasks. Formed in three 16-man platoons, each mounted on a pair of tank-chassis Engineer Vehicles. Total: 50 effectives.

i) Recreation—Field brothels. The strength and composition of this unit varied from world to world. Generally, teams of 3–6 were put under the direct control of company supply personnel.

Sec II: Combat Cars

Eight combat car companies, each of a command section (one car) and four line platoons. Each platoon contained a command car and five combat cars, or six combat cars. Company total: 100 effectives.

Sec III: Tanks

Four tank companies, each of a command tank and four line platoons. Each line platoon contained four tanks. Company total: 36 effectives.

Sec IV: Infantry

Four companies, each of four platoons. Each platoon contained four 10-man line squads; two 2-man tribarrel teams (jeep-mounted); one 2-man 100 mm mortar team (jeep-mounted); and a command element. All but Heavy Weapons were on 1-man skimmers. Buzzbombs could be issued for special purposes; but in general, support from the armored vehicles allowed the Slammers' infantry to travel lighter than most pongoes. Company total: 202 effectives.

Sec V: Artillery

Three batteries of self-propelled 200 mm rocket howitzers. Each battery contained six tubes; one command car; and two munitions haulers. Battery total: 37 effectives.

Sec VI: Replacement

The training and reserve component of the Slammers, normally totalling 1500 men (including cadre) with about ten tanks, twenty-five combat cars, and a hundred trucks. Because Hammer had no permanent base world, training had to be performed wherever the Regiment was located. Because men were more vulnerable than the armored vehicles they rode, and the vehicles were too valuable to run undercrewed or held out of service while replacements were trained, a pool of trained men had to be on hand to fill gaps immediately. Until they were needed in combat slots, they acted as extra drivers, loading crews, camp police, and firebase security.

Note: As personal weapons line infantry were issued 2 cm shoulder powerguns and grenades. Vehicle and Heavy Weapons crewmen carried 1 cm pistols (unless they had picked up shoulder arms on their own). Officers carried pistols or 1 cm submachineguns as they desired.

Standing Down

"LOOK, I'M NOT about to wear a goon suit like that, even to my wedding," Colonel Hammer said, loudly enough to be heard through the chatter. There were a dozen officers making last-minute uniform adjustments in the crowded office and several civilians besides. "Joachim, where's Major Pritchard? I want him in the car with us, and it's curst near jump-off now."

Joachim Steuben was settled nonchalantly on the corner of a desk, unconcerned about the state of his dress because he knew it was perfect—as always. He shrugged. "Pritchard hasn't called in," the Newlander said. His fine features brightened in a smile. "But go ahead, Alois, put the armor on."

"Yes indeed, sir," said the young civilian. He was holding the set of back-and-breast armor carefully by the edges so as not to smear its bright chrome. Rococo whorls and figures decorated the plastron,

but despite its ornateness, the metal/ceramic sandwich beneath the brightwork was quite functional.
"Really, the image you'll project to the spectators
will be ideal, quite ideal. And there couldn't be a
better time for it, either."

Lieutenant Colonel Miezierk frowned, wrinkling his
forehead to the middle of his bald skull. He said, "Yes,
Colonel. After all, Mr. van Meter's firm studied the
matter very carefully and I think—" Joachim snickered;
Miezierk's scalp reddened but he went on—"that
you ought to follow his advice here."

"Lord!" Hammer said, but he thrust his hands
through the armholes and let Miezierk lock the clam-
shell back.

Someone tapped on the door. A lieutenant was
leaning over the front desk, combing his hair in the
screen of the display console. He cursed and straightened so that the door could open to admit Captain
Fallman. The Intelligence captain was duty officer
for the afternoon, harried by the inevitable series of
last-minute emergencies. "Colonel," he said, "there's
a Mr. Wang here to see you."

"Lord curse it, Fallman, he can wait till tomorrow!" Hammer blazed. "He can wait till Hell freezes
over. Miezierk, get this bloody can off me, it's driving the stylus in my pocket clear through my rib
cage."

"Sir, we can take the stylus—" Miezierk began.

"Sir, he's from the Bonding Authority," Fallman
was saying. "It's about President Theismann's—death."

Hammer swore, brushing the startled Miezierk's
hands away. The room grew very silent. "Joachim,
what's in the office next door?" Hammer asked.

"Dust, three walls, and some stains from the Iron
Guards who decided to make a stand there," the
Newlander replied.

"Bring him next door, Captain, I'll talk to him there," Hammer said. He met his bodyguard's eyes. "Come along too, Joachim."

At the door the colonel paused, looking back at his still-faced officers. "Don't worry," he said. "Everything's going to work out fine."

The closing door cut off the babble of nervous speculation from within.

A moment after Hammer and his aide had entered the side office, Captain Fallman ushered in a heavy Oriental. Joachim bowed to the civilian and closed the door, leaving the duty officer alone in the hallway.

An automatic weapon had punched through the outer wall of the office, starting fires which the grenade thrown in a moment later had snuffed. There was still a scorched-plastic afterstench mingling with that of month-dead meat. Joachim had been serious about the Iron Guards.

"I'm Hammer," the colonel said, smiling but not offering the Authority representative his hand for fear it might be refused.

"Wang An-wei," said the Oriental, nodding curtly. He held a flat briefcase. It seemed to be more an article of dress than a tool he intended to use this morning. "I was sent here as Site Officer when Councillor Theismann—"

"President Theismann, he preferred," interjected Hammer. He seated himself in feigned relaxation on a blast-warped chair.

Wang's answering smile was brief and as sharp as the lightning. "He was never awarded the title by a quorum of the Council," the Terran said. "As you no doubt are aware, Site Officers are expected to be precise. If I may continue?"

Hammer nodded. Steuben snickered. His left thumb was hooked in the belt which tucked his tailored blouse in at the waist, but his right hand dangled loose at his side.

"When Councillor Theismann hired you to make him dictator," Wang continued coolly. "Naturally I have been investigating the death of your late employer. There have been—and I'm sure you're aware of this—accusations that you murdered Councillor Theismann yourself in order to replace him as head of the successful coup."

The Site Officer looked at the men in turn. The two Slammers looked back.

"I started with the autopsy data. In addition, I have interrogated the Councillor's guards, both his personal contingent and the platoon of—White Mice—on security detail here at Government House." Wang stared at Hammer. "I assume you were informed of this?"

Hammer nodded curtly. "I signed off before they'd let you mind-probe my men."

"I used mechanical interrogation on all troops below officer rank involved," Wang agreed, "as your bond agreement specifies the Site Officer may require." When Hammer made no reply, he continued, "The evidence is uncontroverted that Councillor Theismann, accompanied by you, Colonel—" Hammer nodded again—"stepped out onto his balcony and was struck in the forehead by a pistol bolt."

Wang paused again. The room was very tense. "The pistol must have been fired from at least a kilometer away. Because of the distance and the fact that fighting was going on at several points within the city, I have reported to my superiors that it was a stray shot, and that the Councillor's death was accidental."

Joachim's fingers ceased toying with the butt of the powergun holstered high on his right hip. "We were clearing some of van Vorn's people out of the Hotel Zant," he said. "Pistol and submachinegun work. There might have been a stray shot from that. It'd be very difficult to brain a man that far away with a pistol, wouldn't it?"

"Impossible, of course," Wang said. His gaze flicked to Steuben's ornate pistol, flicked up to the bodyguard's eyes. For the first time the Oriental looked startled. He looked away from Steuben very quickly and said, "Since the investigation has cleared you, and your employment has ended for the time, I'll be returning to Earth now. I wish you good fortune, and I hope we may do business again in the near future."

Hammer laughed, clapping the civilian on the shoulder with his left hand while their right hands shook. "That's all over, Mr. Wang. The Slammers're out of the merc business for good, now. But I appreciate your wishes."

Wang turned to the door, smiling by reflex. He looked at Joachim's face again: the Cupid grin and unlined cheeks; the hair which, though naturally graying, still fell across the Newlander's forehead in an attractive page-boy; and the eyes. Wang was shivering as he stepped into the hall.

Danny Pritchard stood outside the door, watching the Site Officer leave. He was dressed in civilian clothing.

Spaceport buses did not serve the cargo ships for the man or two they might bring, so Rob Jenne hiked toward the barrier on foot. At first he noticed only that the short man marching toward the terminal from the other recently-landed freighter was also

missing an arm. Then the other's crisp stride rang a
bell in Jenne's mind. He shouted, "Top! Sergeant
Horthy! What the hell're *you* doing here?"

Horthy turned with the wary quickness of a man
uncertain as to any caller's interest. At Jenne's grin
he broke into a smile himself. The two men dropped
their bags and shook hands awkwardly, Jenne's left
in Horthy's right. "Same thing you're doing, trooper,"
Horthy said. The Magyar's goatee was white against
his swarthy skin, but his grip was as firm as it had
been when Rob Jenne was Horthy's right wing gunner. "Comin' here to help the colonel put some
backbone in this place. You don't know how glad I
was when the call came, snake."

"Don't I though?" Jenne murmured. Side by side,
talking simultaneously, the two veterans walked
toward the spaceport barrier. There was already a line
waiting at the customs kiosk. Jenne knew very well
what his old sergeant meant. Seven years of retire-
ment had been hard on the younger man, too. He
hadn't lacked money—his pension put him well above
the norm for the Burlage quarrymen to whom he had
returned —but he was useless. To himself, to Burlage,
to the entire human galaxy. Jenne had shouted for
joy when Colonel Hammer summoned all pensioned
Slammers who wanted to come. The Old Man needed
supervisors and administrators, now. It didn't matter
any more that gaseous iridium had burned off Jenne's
right arm, right eye, and his gonads; it was enough
that Hammer knew where his loyalties lay.

A gray bus with wire-mesh windows and SECURITY
stencilled on its side pulled up to the barrier. The
faces and clothing of the prisoners within were as
drab as the air cushion vehicle's exterior. A guard
wearing the blue of the civil police stepped out and

walked to the barrier. His submachinegun was slung carelessly under his right arm.

Horthy nudged his companion. "It's a load a' politicals for the Borgo Mines," he muttered. "Bet they're bein' hauled out on the ship that brought me in. *And* I'll bet that bus'll be heading back to wherever the colonel is, just as quick as it unloads. Let's see if that cop'll offer us a ride, snake."

As he spoke, the Magyar veteran stepped to the waist-high barrier. The customs official bustled over from his kiosk and shouted in Horthy's face. Horthy ignored him. The official unsnapped the flap of his pistol holster. Other travellers waiting for entry scattered, more afraid of losing their lives than their places in line. Jenne, his good eye flashing across the tension, knowing as well as any man alive that his muscles were nothing to the blast of a powergun, cursed and closed the Magyar's rear.

A second bus, civilian in stripes of white and bright orange, pulled up behind the prison vehicle. The policeman turned and waved angrily. The bus hissed and settled to the pavement despite him. The policeman fumbled with his submachinegun.

A shot from the bus cut him down.

A man with a pistol swung to the loading step of the striped vehicle. He roared, "Just hold it, everybody. We got a load of hostages here. Either we get out of here with our friends or nobody gets out!"

The customs official had paused, staring with his mouth open and his fingers brushing the butt of the gun whose existence he had forgotten. Horthy, behind him, drew the pistol and fired. The rebel doubled over, his jacket afire over his sternum. Someone aboard the civilian bus screamed. Another gun fired. Horthy was prone, his pistol punching out windows in answer to the burst that had sawed the customs official in half.

Rob rolled over the barrier, coming up with the guard's automatic weapon.

The striped bus was moving, dragging the fallen gunman's torso on the concrete. The ex-tanker's mind raced in the old channels. The fans of the bus were not armored like those of a military vehicle. Rob aimed low. A powergun bolt sprayed lime dust over his head and shoulders. His own burst ripped across the plenum chamber. The driving fans disintegrated, flaying the air with steel like a bursting shell. The bus rolled over on its left side. Metal and humans screamed together. A gray-suited prisoner jumped from the door of the government bus. Horthy shot her in the face.

The ruptured fuel cell of the overturned vehicle ignited. The explosion slapped the area with a pillow of warm air. The screaming took a minute to die. Then there was just the rush of wind feeding the fire, and the nearing wail of sirens.

Jenne's cheek and shoulder-stub were oozing where the concrete had ground against them. He rose to his knees, keeping his eye and the submachinegun trailed on the gray bus. No one else was trying to get out of it. The police could sort through whatever had happened inside in their own good time.

Horthy stood, heat rippling from the barrel of the weapon he had appropriated. He glanced at the mangled customs official as if he would rather have spit on the body. "Oh, yes," the veteran said. "They need us here, trooper. They need people to teach 'em the facts of life."

*   *   *

"Pritchard, where the Hell have you been?" Hammer demanded, pretending that he did not understand the implications of his subordinate's business suit.

"I need to talk to you, Colonel," the brown-haired major said.

Hammer stood aside. "Then come on in. Joachim, we'll join the group next door in a moment. Wait for us there, if you will."

Pritchard took a step forward. He hesitated when he realized that Joachim was not moving. The Newlander had been as relaxed as a sunning adder during the interview with Wang An-wei. Now he was white and tense. "Colonel, he's a traitor to you," Joachim said. "He's going to walk out." His voice was quiet but not soft.

"Joachim, I told you—"

"You don't talk to traitors, Colonel. What you do to traitors—" The Newlander's hand was dipping to his gunbutt. Hammer grappled with him. He was not as fast as his aide, but he knew Joachim's mind even better than the gunman did himself. The extra fraction of a second saved Pritchard's life.

The two men stood, locked like wrestlers or lovers. Pritchard did not move, knowing that emphasizing his presence would be the worst possible course under the circumstances. Hammer said, "Joachim, are you willing to shoot me?"

The bodyguard winced, a tic that momentarily disfigured his face. "Alois! You know I wouldn't. . . ."

"Then do as I say. Or you'll have to shoot me. To keep me from shooting you."

Hammer stepped away from his aide. Joachim lurched through the doorway, bumping Pritchard as he passed because his eyes had filled with tears.

Pritchard swung the door shut behind him. "I told

you last week I was going to resign from the Slammers, sir."

Hammer nodded. "And I told you you weren't."

Pritchard looked around at the dust and rubble of the room, the bloodstains. "I've decided there's been enough killing, Colonel. For me. We're going somewhere else."

"Danny, the killing's over!"

The taller man gave a short snap of his head. He said, "No, it'll never be over—not any place you are." He spread his hands, then clenched them. He was staring at his knuckles because he would not look at his commander. "Right now we're chasing van Vorn's guards like rabbits, shooting 'em down or sticking 'em behind wire where they're not a curse a' good to you or themselves or this planet."

He faced Hammer, the outrage bubbling out at a human being, not the colonel he had served for all his adult life. "And the ones we kill—doesn't every one a' them have a wife or a brother or a nephew? And they'll put a knife in a Slammer some night and be shot the same way because of it!"

"All right," said Hammer calmly. "What else?"

"How about the Social Unity Party, then?" Pritchard blazed. "Maybe the one chance to get this place a work force that *works* instead of the robots the Great Houses've been trying to make them. And does anybody listen? Hell, no! The Council tinkers with the franchise to make sure they don't get a majority of the Estates-General; van Vorn outlaws the party and makes their leaders terrorists instead of politicians. And you, *you* ship them off-planet to rot in state-owned mines on Kobold!"

"All right," Hammer repeated. He sat down again, his stillness as compelling as that of the shattered room around him. "What would you do?"

Pritchard's eyes narrowed. He stretched his left hand out to the wall, not leaning on it but touching its firmness, its chill. "What do you care?" he asked quietly. "I didn't say the Slammers couldn't keep you in power here the rest of your life. I just don't want to be a part of it, is all."

Without warning, Hammer stood and slammed his fist into the wall. He turned back to his aide. His bleeding knuckles had flecked the panel more brightly than the remains of the Iron Guards. "Is that what you think?" he demanded. "That I'm a bandit who's found himself a bolthole? That for the past thirty years I've fought wars because that's the best way to make bodies?"

"Sir, I . . ." But Pritchard had nothing more to say or need to say it.

Hammer rubbed his knuckles. He grinned wryly at his subordinate, but the grin slipped away. "It's my own fault," he said. "I don't tell people much. That's how it's got to be when you're running a tank regiment, but . . . that's not where we are now.

"Danny, this is my *home*." Hammer began to reach out to the taller man but stopped. He said, "You've been out there. You've seen how every world claws at every other one, claws its own guts too. The whole system's about to slag down, and there's nothing to stop it if *we* don't."

"You don't create order by ramming it down peoples' throats on a bayonet! It doesn't work that way."

"Then show me a way that *does* work!" Hammer cried, gripping his subordinate's right hand with his own. "Are things going to get better because you're sitting on your butt in some farmhouse, living off the money *you* made killing? Danny, I *need* you. My *son* will need you."

Pritchard touched his tongue to his lips. "What is it you're asking me to do?" he said.

"Do you have a way to handle the Unionists?" Hammer shot back at him. "And the Iron Guards?"

"Maybe," Pritchard said with a frown. "Amnesty won't be enough—they won't believe it's real, for one thing. But a promise of authority . . . administrative posts in education, labor, maybe even security —that'd bring out a few of the Unionists because they couldn't afford *not* to take the chance. Most of the rest of them might follow when they saw you really were paying off."

The brown-haired man's enthusiasm was building without the hostility that had marked it before. "The Guards, that'll be harder because they're rigid, most of them. But if you *can* find some way to convince them there's nothing to gain by staying out, and— Hell, there'll be counter-protests, but work the ones who turn over their guns into the civil police. Not in big dollops, but scattered all over the planet. They'll feel more secure that way, and you can keep an eye on them easier anyhow."

Hammer nodded. "All right, bring me a preliminary assessment of both proposals by, say, 0800 Tuesday. No, make that noon, you're going to waste the rest of today watching a wedding from the front row. You'll have the backing you'll need, but these are *your* projects—I've got too much blood on my hands to run them." His eyes held Pritchard's. "Or don't you have the guts to try?"

The taller man hesitated, then squeezed Hammer's hand in return. "I rode your lead tank," he said. "I ran your lead company. If you need me now, you've got me." His face clouded. "Only, Colonel—"

Hammer tightened. "Spit it out."

"I'm not ashamed of anything. But I swore to

Margritte I'd never wear another uniform or carry
another gun. And I won't."

Hammer cleared his throat. "Right now I don't
need a major as much as I do a conscience," he said.
He cleared his throat again. "Now let's go. We've got
a wedding to get to."

Cosimo Barracks was a fortress in the midst of
estates which had belonged for three hundred years
to the family of the late President van Vorn. The
Slammers had bypassed Cosimo in the blitzkrieg which
replaced van Vorn with Theismann, their employer.
But now, a month after van Vorn had poisoned himself in Government House and three weeks after
someone else had burst Theismann's skull with a
powergun, the fortress still refused to surrender.
Sally Schilling, leading a "battalion" made up of S
Company and six hundred local recruits, was on
hand to do something about the situation.

A burst of automatic fire combed the rim of the
dugout, splashing Captain Schilling with molten granite. "Via!" she snapped to the frightened recruit,
"keep your coppy head down and don't draw fire."

The sergeant who shared the dugout with Schilling
and the recruit shook his own head in disgust. In her
mind, Schilling seconded the opinion. To police a
planet, Hammer needed more men than the five
thousand he had brought with him. He wanted to
give the new troops at least a taste of combat in the
mopping-up operations. Schilling could understand
that desire, but it was a pain in the ass trying to do
her own job and act as baby-sitter besides.

She looked again through the eyepiece of her periscope. The machinegun had ceased firing, though
cyan flickers across the perimeter showed someone
else was catching it. The Iron Guards were political

bullies rather than combat soldiers, but their fortress here was as tough as anything the Slammers had faced in their history. The fiber-optics periscope showed Cosimo Barracks only as a rolling knob. The grass covering the rock was streaked yellow in fans pointing back to hidden gunports. The ports themselves were easy enough targets, but the weapons within were on disappearing carriages and popped up only long enough to fire. The rest of the fortress, with an estimated five hundred Iron Guards plus enough food, water and ammunition to last a century, was deep underground.

Schilling glanced down at her console. On it Cosimo Barracks showed as a red knot of tunnels drawn from plans found in Government House. "Sigma Battalion," she said, "check off." Points of green light winked on the screen, an emerald necklace ringing the fortress. Each point was a squad guarding nearly one hundred meters of front. That was adequate; the infantry was on hand primarily to prevent a breakout.

"Fire Central," Schilling said, "prepare Fire Order Tango-Niner."

"Ready," squawked the helmet.

"Ma'am," said the recruit, "w-why don't the tanks attack instead of us?"

"Shut it off, boy!" the sergeant snapped.

"No, Webbert, we're supposed to be teaching them," Schilling said. She gestured toward the knob. The recruit automatically raised his head. Webbert shoved him back down before another burst could decapitate him. The captain sighed. "Mines're as thick up there as flies on a fresh turd," she said, "and they've got more guns in that hill than the light stuff they've been using on us. Besides, *we* aren't going to attack."

The recruit nodded with his mouth and eyes both

wide open. He began to rub the stock of his unfamiliar powergun.

"Fire Central, execute Tango-Niner," Schilling ordered.

"On the way."

Nothing happened. After a long half minute, the recruit burst out, "What went wrong? Dear Lord, will they make us charge—"

"Boy!" the sergeant shouted, his own knuckles tight on his weapon.

"Webbert!"

The sergeant cursed and turned away.

Schilling said, "The hogs're a long way away. It takes time, that's all. Everything takes time."

"Shot," said the helmet. Five seconds to impact. The sky overhead began to howl. The recruit was trembling, his own throat working as if to scream along with the shells.

The explosions were almost anticlimactic. They were only a rumbling through the bedrock, more noticed by one's feet than one's ears. Schilling, at the periscope, caught the spurts of earth as the first penetrator rounds struck. The detonations seconds later were lost in the shriek of further shells landing on the same points. Each tube's first shell ripped sod to the granite. The second salvo struck gravel; the third, sand. By the tenth salvo, the charges were bursting in the guts of Cosimo Barracks, thirty meters down. A magazine went off there, piercing earth and sky in a cyan blast that made the sun pale.

"Not an oyster born yet but a starfish can drill a hole through it," muttered Webbert. He had been a fisherman long years before when he saw one of Hammer's recruiting brochures.

"Sigma One, this is Sigma Eight-Six," said the

helmet. "Our sensors indicate all three fortress elevators are rising."

With the words, circuits of meadow gaped. "Sigma Battalion," Schilling said as she rose and aimed over the lip of the dugout, "time to earn our pay. And remember—no prisoners!"

Because of the way the ground pitched, it was hard for the captain to keep her submachinegun trained on the rising elevator car. But there were eight hundred guns firing simultaneously at the three elevator heads. The bolts converged like suns burning into the heart of the hillside.

"They were sending up their families!" the recruit suddenly screamed. "The children!"

Sally Schilling slid a fresh gas cylinder in place in the butt of her weapon, then reached for another magazine as well. "They had three months to turn in their guns," she said. "Half the ones down there were troops we beat at Maritschoon and paroled. So this was the second time, and *I'm* not going to have my ass blown away because I gave somebody three chances to do it. As for the families, well . . . there's a couple thousand more of van Vorn's folks mooching around in the Kronburg, and they won't know it was an accident: when word of this gets around, the ones that're still out are going to think again."

The fortress guns had fallen silent as the elevator cars rose. Now a few weapons opened up again, but in long, suicidal bursts which flailed the world until the Slammers' fire silenced them forever.

President van Vorn's Iron Guards had planned to use the garage beneath Government House for a last stand; which in a manner of speaking was what they did. The political soldiers had naively failed to consider gas. The Slammers introduced KD7 into the forced ventilation system, then spent three days neutralizing the toxin before they could safely enter the garage and remove the bloated corpses. Now the concrete walls, unmarred by shots or grenade fragments, echoed to the fans of two dozen combat cars readying for the parade.

"There's three layers a' gold foil," the bald maintenance chief was saying as he rapped the limousine's myrmillon bubble. "That'll diffuse most of a two see-emma bolt, but the folks, they'll still be able to *see* you, you see?"

"What I don't see is my wife," Hammer snapped to the stiff-faced noble acting as the Council's liaison with their new overlord. "She's agreed, I've agreed. If *you* think that the Great Houses can back out of this now—"

"Colonel," interrupted Pritchard, pointing at the closed car which was just entering the garage. The armored doors to the mews slammed shut behind the vehicle, cutting off the wash of sunlight which had paled the glow strips by comparison. The car hissed slowly between armored vehicles and support pillars, coming to a halt beside Hammer and his aides. Two men got out, dressed in the height of conservative fashion. The colors of Great Houses slashed their collar flares. A moment later, a pair of women stepped out between them.

One of them was sixty, as tall and heavy as either of the men. Her black garments were as harsh as the glare she turned on Hammer when he nodded to her.

The other woman was short enough to be petite. It was hard to tell, however, because she wore a dress of misty, layered fabric which gave the impression of spiderweb but hid even the outline of her body. The celagauze veil hanging from her cap-brim blurred her face similarly. Before any of those around her could interfere, she had reached up and removed the cap.

"Anneke!" cried the woman in black. One of the escorting nobles shifted. Danny Pritchard motioned him back, using his left hand by reflex.

Anneke sailed the cap into the intake of a revving combat car. Shreds of white fabric softened the floor of the garage. "What, Aunt Ruth?" she asked. Her voice was clearly audible over the fans and the engines. "That's the idea, isn't it? Prove to the citizens that the Great Houses are still in charge because the colonel is marrying one of us? But then they've got to see who I am, don't they?"

Hammer stepped forward. "Lady Brederode," he said, repeating his nod. The older woman looked away as if Hammer were a spot of offal on the pavement. "Lady Tromp."

Anneke Tromp extended her right hand. She had fine bones and skin as soft as the lining of a jewelry box. The fingernails looked metallic.

The colonel knelt to kiss her hand, the gesture stiffened by his armor. "Well, Lady Tromp," he said, "are you ready?"

The woman smiled. Hammer became the commander again. He waved dismissingly toward his bride's aunt and escort. "I've made provisions for your seating at the church," he said, "but you'll not be needed for the procession. Lady Tromp will ride in my vehicle. We'll be accompanied by majors—that is, by Major Steuben and Mr. Pritchard."

Anneke nodded graciously to the aides flanking Hammer. Unexpectedly, Joachim giggled. His eyes were red. "Your family and I go back a long way, Lady," he said. "Did you know that I shot your

father on Melpomene? Between the eyes, so that he
could see it coming."

The colonel's face changed, but he grinned as he
turned. He threw an arm around his bodyguard's
shoulders. "Joachim," he said, "let's talk in the car
for a moment." Steuben looked away, blazing hatred
at everyone else in the room, but he followed his
commander into the soundproofed compartment.

As the car door thudded shut, Anneke Tromp
stepped idly to Pritchard's side. She was still smiling. Without looking at the limousine's bubble, she
said, "That's a very jealous man, Mr. Pritchard. And
jealous not only of me, I should think."

Danny shrugged. "Joachim's been with the colonel a long time," he said. "He's not an . . . evil . . .
man. Just loyal."

"A razor blade in a melon isn't evil, Mr. Pritchard," the woman said, gesturing as though they were
discussing the markings of the nearest combat car.
"It's just too dangerous to be permitted to exist."

Pritchard swallowed. Part of his duties involved
checking the roster of veterans returning to the colors. He was remembering a big man with an engag-
ing grin—as good a tank commander as had ever
served under Pritchard, and the lightest touch he
knew on the trigger of an automatic weapon. "We'll
see," Danny said without looking at the woman.

"When I was a little girl," she murmured, "my
father ruled Friesland. I want to live to see my son
rule."

The car door opened and both men got out.
"Joachim has decided to ride up front with the driver
instead of with us in back," Hammer said with a false
smile. He held the door. "Shall we?"

Pritchard sat on a jump seat across from Hammer
and Lady Tromp. The armored bubble was cloudy,

like the sky on the morning of a snowstorm. Hammer touched a plate on the console. "Six-two," he said. "Move 'em out."

Fans revved. The garage door lifted and began passing combat cars out into the mews. Hammer's driver slid the limousine into the line of cars waiting to exit. More armored vehicles edged in behind them. They accelerated up the ramp and into the Frisian sunlight. The whole west quarter of Government House had burned in the fighting, darkening the vitril panels there.

Pritchard leaned forward. "You don't really think that you can turn Friesland around, much less the galaxy?" he asked.

Hammer shrugged. "If I don't, they'll at least say that I died trying."

The limousine glided through the archway into Independence Boulevard. Tank companies were already closing either end of the block, eight tanks abreast. The panzers had been painted dazzlingly silver for the celebration. The combat cars aligned themselves in four ranks between the double caps of bigger vehicles, leaving the limousine to tremble alone in the midst of the waves of heavy armor. Hammer's breastplate was a sunblazed eye in the center of all.

On the front bench beside the driver, Joachim was trying nervously to scan the thousands of civilians. He knew that despite the armored bubble, the right man could kill Hammer as easily as he himself had murdered Councillor Theismann. He wished he could kill every soul in the crowd.

Pritchard checked the time, then radioed a command. The procession began to slip forward toward the throngs lining the remaining three kilometers of the boulevard, all the way to the Church of the First Landfall.

"I've been a long time coming back to Friesland," said Hammer softly. He was not really speaking to his companions. "But now I'm back. And I'm going to put this place in order."

Anneke Tromp touched him. Her glittering finger-nails lay like knife-blades across the back of his hand. "*We're* going to put it in order," she said.

"We'll see," said Danny Pritchard.

"Hammer!" shouted the crowd.

"Hammer!"

"Hammer!"

"Hammer!"

The Tank

Lords

Lords

THEY WERE the tank lords.

The Baron had drawn up his soldiers in the court-yard, the twenty men who were not detached to his estates on the border between the Kingdom of Ganz and the Kingdom of Marshall—keeping the uneasy truce and ready to break it if the Baron so willed.

I think the King sent mercenaries in four tanks to our palace so that the Baron's will would be what the King wished it to be . . . though of course we were told they were protection against Ganz and the mercenaries of the Lightning Division whom Ganz employed.

The tanks and the eight men in them were from Hammer's Slammers, and they were magnificent.

Lady Miriam and her entourage rushed back from the barred windows of the women's apartments on the second floor, squealing for effect. The tanks were so huge that the mirror-helmeted men watching from

261

the turret hatches were nearly on a level with the upper story of the palace.

I jumped clear, but Lady Miriam bumped the chair I had dragged closer to stand upon and watch the arrival over the heads of the women I served.

"Leesh!" cried the Lady, false fear of the tanks replaced by real anger at me. She slapped with her fan of painted ox-horn, cutting me across the knuckles because I had thrown a hand in front of my eyes.

I ducked low over the chair, wrestling it out of the way and protecting myself with its cushioned bulk. Sarah, the Chief Maid, rapped my shoulder with the silver-mounted brush she carried for last-minute touches to the Lady's hair. "A monkey would make a better page than you, Elisha," she said. "A gelded monkey."

But the blow was a light one, a reflexive copy of her mistress' act. Sarah was more interested in reclaiming her place among the others at the windows now that modesty and feminine sensibilities had been satisfied by the brief charade. I didn't dare slide the chair back to where I had first placed it; but by balancing on tiptoes on the carven arms, I could look down into the courtyard again.

The Baron's soldiers were mostly off-worlders themselves. They had boasted that they were better men than the mercenaries if it ever came down to cases. The fear that the women had mimed from behind stone walls seemed real enough now to the soldiers whose bluster and assault rifles were insignificant against the iridium titans which entered the courtyard at a slow walk, barely clearing the posts of gates which would have passed six men marching abreast.

Even at idle speed, the tanks roared as their fans maintained the cushions of air that slid them over the ground. Three of the Baron's men dodged back through the palace doorway, their curses inaudible over the intake whine of the approaching vehicles.

The Baron squared his powerful shoulders within his dress cloak of scarlet, purple, and gold. I could not see his face, but the back of his neck flushed red and his left hand tugged his drooping moustache in a gesture as meaningful as the angry curses that would have accompanied it another time.

Beside him stood Wolfitz, his Chamberlain; the tallest man in the courtyard; the oldest; and, despite the weapons the others carried, the most dangerous.

When I was first gelded and sold to the Baron as his Lady's page, Wolfitz had helped me continue the studies I began when I was training for the Church. Out of his kindness, I thought, or even for his amusement . . . but the Chamberlain wanted a spy, or another spy, in the women's apartments. Even when I was ten years old, I knew that death lay on that path—and life itself was all that remained to me.

I kept the secrets of all. If they thought me a fool and beat me for amusement, then that was better than the impalement which awaited a boy who was found meddling in the affairs of his betters.

The tanks sighed and lowered themselves the last finger's breadth to the ground. The courtyard, clay and gravel compacted over generations to the density of stone, crunched as the plenum-chamber skirts settled visibly into it.

The man in the turret of the nearest tank ignored the Baron and his soldiers. Instead, the reflective face shield of the tanker's helmet turned and made a slow, arrogant survey of the barred windows and the women behind them. Maids tittered; but the Lady Miriam did not, and when the tanker's face shield suddenly lifted, the mercenary's eyes and broad smile were toward the Baron's wife.

The tanks whispered and pinged as they came into balance with the surroundings which they dominated. Over those muted sounds, the man in the turret of the second tank to enter the courtyard called, "Baron Hetziman, I'm Lieutenant Kiley and this is my number two—Sergeant Commander Grant. Our tanks have been assigned to you as a Protective Reaction Force until the peace treaty's signed."

"You do us honor," said the Baron curtly. "We trust your stay with us will be pleasant as well as short. A banquet—"

The Baron paused, and his head turned to find the object of the other tanker's attention.

The lieutenant snapped something in a language that was not ours, but the name "Grant" was distinctive in the sharp phrase.

The man in the nearest turret lifted himself out gracefully by resting his palms on the hatch coaming and swinging up his long, powerful legs without pausing for footholds until he stood atop the iridium turret. The hatch slid shut between his booted feet. His crisp moustache was sandy blond, and the eyes which he finally turned on the Baron and the formal welcoming committee were blue. "Rudy Grant at your service, Baron," he said, with even less respect in his tone than in his words.

They did not need to respect us. They were the tank lords.

"We will go down and greet our guests," said the Lady Miriam, suiting her actions to her words. Even as she turned, I was off the chair, dragging it toward the inner wall of imported polychrome plastic.

"But, Lady . . . ," said Sarah nervously. She let her voice trail off, either through lack of a firm objection or unwillingness to oppose a course on which her mistress was determined.

With coos and fluttering skirts, the women swept out the door from which the usual guard had been removed for the sake of the show in the courtyard. Lady Miriam's voice carried back: "We were to meet them at the banquet tonight. We'll just do so a little earlier."

If I had followed the women, one of them would have ordered me to stay and watch the suite—though everyone, even the tenants who farmed the plots of the home estate here, was outside watching the arrival of the tanks. Instead, I waited for the sounds to die away down the stair tower—and I slipped out the window.

Because I was in a hurry, I lost one of the brass buttons from my jacket—my everyday livery of buff; I'd be wearing the black plush jacket when I waited in attendance at the banquet tonight, so the loss didn't matter. The vertical bars were set close enough to prohibit most adults, and few of the children who could slip between them would have had enough strength to then climb the bracing strut of the roof antenna, the only safe path since the base of the West Wing was a thicket of spikes and razor ribbon.

I was on the roof coping in a matter of seconds, three quick hand-over-hand surges. The women were only beginning to file out through the doorway. Lady Miriam led them, and her hauteur and lifted chin showed she would brook no interference with her plans.

Most of the tankers had, like Grant, stepped out of their hatches, but they did not wander far. Lieutenant Kiley stood on the sloping bow of his vehicle, offering a hand which the Baron angrily refused as he mounted the steps recessed into the tank's armor.

"Do you think I'm a child?" rumbled the Baron, but only his pride forced him to touch the tank when the mercenary made a hospitable offer. None of the Baron's soldiers showed signs of wanting to look into the other vehicles. Even the Chamberlain, aloof if not afraid, stood at arm's length from the huge tank which even now trembled enough to make the setting sun quiver across the iridium hull.

Because of the Chamberlain's studied unconcern about the vehicle beside him, he was the first of the welcoming party to notice Lady Miriam striding toward Grant's tank, holding her skirts clear of the ground with dainty, bejeweled hands. Wolfitz turned to the Baron, now leaning gingerly against the curve of the turret so that he could look through the hatch while the lieutenant gestured from the other side. The Chamberlain's mouth opened to speak, then closed again deliberately.

There were matters in which he too knew better than to become involved.

One of the soldiers yelped when Lady Miriam began to mount the nearer tank. She loosed her dress in order to take the hand which Grant extended to her. The Baron glanced around and snarled an inarticulate syllable. His wife gave him a look as composed as his was suffused with rage. "After all, my dear," said the Lady Miriam coolly, "our lives are in the hands of these brave men and their amazing vehicles. Of *course* I must see how they are arranged."

She was the King's third daughter, and she spoke now as if she were herself the monarch.

"That's right, milady," said Sergeant Grant. Instead of pointing through the hatch, he slid back into the interior of his vehicle with a murmur to the Lady.

She began to follow.

I think Lady Miriam and I, alone of those on the estate, were not nervous about the tanks for their size and power. I loved them as shimmering beasts, whom no one could strike in safety. The Lady's love was saved for other subjects.

"Grant, that won't be necessary," the lieutenant called sharply—but he spoke in our language, not his own, so he must have known the words would have little effect on his subordinate.

The Baron bellowed, "*Mir*—" before his voice caught. He was not an ungovernable man, only one whose usual companions were men and women who lived or died as the Baron willed. The Lady squeezed flat the flounces of her skirt and swung her legs within the hatch ring.

"Murphy," called the Baron to his chief of soldiers. "Get up there with her." The Baron roared more often than he spoke quietly. This time his voice was not loud, but he would have shot Murphy where he stood if the soldier had hesitated before clambering up the bow of the tank.

"Vision blocks in both the turret and the driver's compartment," said Lieutenant Kiley, pointing within his tank, "give a three-sixty-degree view at any wavelength you want to punch in."

Murphy, a grizzled man who had been with the Baron a dozen years, leaned against the turret and looked down into the hatch. Past him, I could see the combs and lace of Lady Miriam's elaborate coiffure. I would have given everything I owned to be there within the tank myself—and I owned nothing but my life.

The hatch slid shut. Murphy yelped and snatched his fingers clear.

Atop the second tank, the Baron froze and his flushed cheeks turned slatey. The mercenary lieutenant touched a switch on his helmet and spoke too softly for anything but the integral microphone to hear the words.

The order must have been effective, because the hatch opened as abruptly as it had closed—startling Murphy again.

Lady Miriam rose from the turret on what must have been a power lift. Her posture was in awkward contrast to the smooth ascent, but her face was composed. The tank and its apparatus were new to the Lady, but anything that could have gone on within the shelter of the turret was a familiar experience to her.

"We have seen enough of your equipment," said the Baron to Lieutenant Kiley in the same controlled voice with which he had directed Murphy. "Rooms have been prepared for you—the guest apartments alongside mine in the East Wing, not the barracks below. Dinner will be announced—" he glanced at the sky. The sun was low enough that only the height of the tank's deck permitted the Baron to see the orb above the courtyard wall "—in two hours. Make yourselves welcome."

Lady Miriam turned and backed her way to the ground again. Only then did Sergeant Grant follow her out of the turret. The two of them were as powerful as they were arrogant—but neither a king's daughter nor a tank lord is immortal.

"Baron Hetziman," said the mercenary lieutenant. "Sir—" the modest honorific for the tension, for the rage which the Baron might be unable to control even at risk of his estates and his life. "That building, the gatehouse, appears disused. We'll doss down there, if you don't mind."

The Baron's face clouded, but that was his normal reaction to disagreement. The squat tower to the left of the gate had been used only for storage for a generation. A rusted harrow, upended to fit farther within the doorway, almost blocked access now.

The Baron squinted for a moment at the structure, craning his short neck to look past the tank from which he had just climbed down. Then he snorted and said, "Sleep in a hog byre if you choose, Lieutenant. It might be cleaner at that."

"I realize," explained Lieutenant Kiley as he slid to the ground instead of using the steps, "that the request sounds odd, but Colonel Hammer is concerned that commandos from Ganz or the Lightning Division might launch an attack. The gatehouse is separated from everything but the outer wall—so if we have to defend it, we can do so without endangering any of your people."

The lie was a transparent one; but the mercenaries did not have to lie at all if they wished to keep us away from their sleeping quarters. So considered, the statement was almost generous, and the Baron chose to take it that way. "Wolfitz," he said offhandedly as he stamped toward the entrance. "Organize a party of tenants—" he gestured sharply toward the pattern of drab garments and drab faces lining the walls of the courtyard "—and clear the place, will you?"

The Chamberlain nodded obsequiously, but he continued to stride along at his master's heel.

The Baron turned, paused, and snarled, "*Now*," in a voice as grim as the fist he clenched at his side.

"My Lord," said Wolfitz with a bow that danced the line between brusque and dilatory. He stepped hastily toward the soldiers who had broken their rank in lieu of orders—a few of them toward the tanks and their haughty crews but most back to the stone shelter of the palace.

"You men," the Chamberlain said, making circling

motions with his hands. "Fifty of the peasants, *quickly*. Everything is to be turned out of the gatehouse, thrown beyond the wall for the time being. *Now*. *Move* them."

The women followed the Baron into the palace. Several of the maids glanced over their shoulders, at the tanks—at the tankers. Some of the women would have drifted closer to meet the men in khaki uniforms, but Lady Miriam strode head high and without hesitation.

She had accomplished her purposes; the purposes of her entourage could wait.

I leaned from the roof ledge for almost a minute further, staring at the vehicles which were so smooth-skinned that I could see my amorphous reflection in the nearest. When the sound of women's voices echoed through the window, I squirmed back only instants before the Lady reentered her apartment.

They would have beaten me because of my own excitement had they not themselves been agog with the banquet to come—and the night which would follow it.

The high-arched banquet hall was so rarely used that it was almost as unfamiliar to the Baron and his household as it was to his guests. Strings of small lights had been led up the cast-concrete beams, but nothing could really illuminate the vaulting waste of groins and coffers that formed the ceiling.

The shadows and lights trembling on flexible fastenings had the look of the night sky on the edge of an electrical storm. I gazed up at the ceiling occasionally while I waited at the wall behind Lady Miriam. I had no duties at the banquet—that was for house servants, not body servants like myself—but my presence was required for show and against the chance that the Lady would send me off with a message.

That chance was very slight. Any messages Lady Miriam had were for the second-ranking tank lord, seated to her left by custom: Sergeant-Commander Grant.

Only seven of the mercenaries were present at the moment. I saw mostly their backs as they sat at the high table, interspersed with the Lady's maids. Lieutenant Kiley was in animated conversation with the Baron to his left, but I thought the officer wished primarily to distract his host from the way Lady Miriam flirted on the other side.

A second keg of beer—estate stock; not the stuff brewed for export in huge vats—had been broached by the time the beef course followed the pork. The serving girls had been kept busy with the mugs—in large part, the molded-glass tankards of the Baron's soldiers, glowering at the lower tables, but the metal-chased crystal of the tank lords was refilled often as well.

Two of the mercenaries—drivers, separated by the oldest of Lady Miriam's maids—began arguing with increasing heat while a tall, black-haired server watched in amusement. I could hear the words, but the language was not ours. One of the men got up, struggling a little because the arms of his chair were too tight against those to either side. He walked toward his commander, rolling slightly.

Lieutenant Kiley, gesturing with his mug toward the roof peak, was saying to the Baron, "Has a certain splendor, you know. Proper lighting and it'd look like a cross between a prison and a barracks, but the way you've tricked it out is—"

The standing mercenary grumbled a short, forceful

paragraph, a question or a demand, to the lieutenant who broke off his own sentence to listen.

"Ah, Baron," Kiley said, turning again to his host. "Question is, what, ah, sort of regulations would there be on my boys dating local women. That one there—" his tankard nodded toward the black-haired servant. The driver who had remained seated was caressing her thigh "—for instance?"

"Regulations?" responded the Baron in genuine surprise. "On *servants*? None, of course. Would you like me to assign a group of them for your use?"

The lieutenant grinned, giving an ironic tinge to the courteous shake of his head. "I don't think that'll be necessary, Baron," he said.

Kiley stood up to attract his men's attention. "Open season on the servants, boys," he said, speaking clearly and in our language, so that everyone at or near the upper table would understand him. "Make your own arrangements. Nothing rough. And no less than two men together."

He sat down again and explained what the Baron already understood: "Things can happen when a fellow wanders off alone in a strange place. He can fall and knock his head in, for instance."

The two drivers were already shuffling out of the dining hall with the black-haired servant between them. One of the men gestured toward another buxom server with a pitcher of beer. She was not particularly well-favored, as men describe such things; but she was close, and she was willing—as any of the women in the hall would have been to go with the tank lords. I wondered whether the four of them would get any farther than the corridor outside.

I could not see the eyes of the maid who watched the departure of the mercenaries who had been seated beside her.

Lady Miriam watched the drivers leave also. Then she turned back to Sergeant Grant and resumed the conversation they held in voices as quiet as honey flowing from a ruptured comb.

In the bustle and shadows of the hall, I disappeared from the notice of those around me. Small and silent, wearing my best jacket of black velvet, I could have been but another patch of darkness. The two mercenaries left the hall by a side exit. I slipped through the end door behind me, unnoticed save as a momentary obstacle to the servants bringing in compotes of fruits grown locally and imported from across the stars.

My place was not here. My place was with the tanks, now that there was no one to watch me dreaming as I caressed their iridium flanks.

The sole guard at the door to the women's apartments glowered at me, but he did not question my reason for returning to what were, after all, my living quarters. The guard at the main entrance would probably have stopped me for spite: he was on duty while others of the household feasted and drank the best quality beer.

I did not need a door to reach the courtyard and the tanks parked there.

Unshuttering the same window I had used in the morning, I squeezed between the bars and clambered to the roof along the antenna mount. I was fairly certain that I could clear the barrier of points and edges at the base of the wall beneath the women's suite, but there was no need to take that risk.

Starlight guided me along the stone gutter, jumping the pipes feeding the cistern under the palace cellars. Buildings formed three sides of the courtyard, but the north was closed by a wall and the gatehouse. There was no spiked barrier beneath the wall, so I stepped to the battlements and jumped to the ground safely.

Then I walked to the nearest tank, silently from reverence rather than in fear of being heard by someone in the palace. I circled the huge vehicle slowly, letting the tip of my left index finger slide over the metal. The iridium skin was smooth, but there were many bumps and irregularities set into the armor: sensors, lights, and strips of close-range defense projectors to meet an enemy or his missile with a blast of pellets.

The tank was sleeping but not dead. Though I could hear no sound from it, the armor quivered with inner life like that of a great tree when the wind touches its highest branches.

I touched a recessed step. The spring-loaded fairing that should have covered it was missing, torn away or shot off—perhaps on a distant planet. I climbed the bow slope, my feet finding each higher step as if they knew the way.

It was as if I were a god.

I might have attempted no more than that, than to stand on the hull with my hand touching the stubby barrel of the main gun—raised at a sixty-degree angle so that it did not threaten the palace. But the turret hatch was open and, half-convinced that I was living in a hope-induced dream, I lifted myself to look in.

"Freeze," said the man looking up at me past his pistol barrel. His voice was calm. "And then we'll talk about what you think you're doing here."

The interior of the tank was coated with sulphurous light. It was too dim to shine from the hatch, but it provided enough illumination for me to see the little man in the khaki coveralls of the tank lords. The bore of the powergun in his hand shrank from the devouring cavity it had first seemed. Even the 1 cm bore of reality would release enough energy to splash the brains from my skull, I knew.

"I wanted to see the tanks," I said, amazed that I was not afraid. All men die, even kings; what better time than this would there be for me? "They would never let me, so I sneaked away from the banquet. I—it was worth it. Whatever happens now."

"Via," said the tank lord, lowering his pistol. "You're just a kid, ain'tcha?"

I could see my image foreshortened in the vision screen behind the mercenary, my empty hands shown in daylit vividness at an angle which meant the camera must be in another of the parked tanks.

"My Lord," I said—straightening momentarily but overriding the reflex so that I could meet the mercenary's eyes. "I am sixteen."

"Right," he said, "and I'm Colonel Hammer. Now—"

"Oh Lord!" I cried, forgetting in my joy and embarrassment that someone else might hear me. My vision blurred and I rapped my knees on the iridium as I tried to genuflect. "Oh, Lord Hammer, forgive me for disturbing you!"

"Blood and *martyrs*, boy!" snapped the tank lord. A pump whirred and the seat from which, cross-legged, he questioned me rose. "Don't be an idiot! Me name's Curran and I drive this beast, is all."

The mercenary was head and shoulders out of the hatch now, watching me with a concerned expression. I blinked and straightened. When I knelt, I had almost slipped from the tank; and in a few moments, my bruises might be more painful than my present embarrassment.

"I'm sorry, Lord Curran," I said, thankful for once that I had practice in keeping my expression calm after a beating. "I have studied, I have dreamed about your tanks ever since I was placed in my present status six years ago. When you came I—I'm afraid I lost control."

"You're a little shrimp, even alongside me, ain'tcha?" said Curran reflectively.

A burst of laughter drifted across the courtyard from a window in the corridor flanking the dining hall.

"Aw, Via," the tank lord said. "Come take a look, seein's yer here anyhow."

It was not a dream. My grip on the hatch coaming made the iridium bite my fingers as I stepped into the tank at Curran's direction; and besides, I would never have dared to dream this paradise.

The tank's fighting compartment was not meant for two, but Curran was as small as he had implied and I—I had grown very little since a surgeon had fitted me to become the page of a high-born lady. There were screens, gauges, and armored conduits across all the surfaces I could see.

"Drivers'll tell ye," said Curran, "the guy back here, he's just along for the ride 'cause the tank does it all for 'em. Been known t' say that myself, but it ain't really true. Still—"

He touched the lower left corner of a screen. It had been black. Now, it became gray unmarked save by eight short orange lines radiating from the edge of a two-centimeter circle in the middle of the screen.

"Fire control," Curran said. A hemispherical switch was set into the bulkhead beneath the screen. He touched the control with an index finger, rotating it slightly. "That what the Slammer's all about, ain't we? Firepower and movement, and the tricky part—movement—the driver handles from up front. Got it?"

"Yes, My Lord," I said, trying to absorb everything around me without taking my eyes from what Curran was doing. The West Wing of the palace, guest and baronial quarters above the ground-floor barracks, slid up the screen as brightly illuminated as if it were daylight.

"Now *don't* touch nothin'!" the tank lord said, the first time he had spoken harshly to me. "Got it?"

"Yes, My Lord."

"Right," said Curran, softly again. "Sorry, kid. Lieutenant'll have my ass if he sees me twiddlin' with the gun, and if we blow a hole in Central Prison here—" he gestured at the screen, though I did not understand the reference "—the Colonel'll likely shoot me hisself."

"I won't touch anything, My Lord," I reiterated.

"Yeah, well," said the mercenary. He touched a four-position toggle switch beside the hemisphere. "We just lowered the main gun, right? I won't spin the turret, 'cause they'd hear that likely inside. Matter of fact—"

Instead of demonstrating the toggle, Curran fingered the sphere again. The palace dropped off the screen and, now that I knew to expect it, I recognized the faint whine that must have been the gun itself gimbaling back up to a safe angle. Nothing within the fighting compartment moved except the image on the screen.

"So," the tanker continued, flipping the toggle to one side. An orange numeral 2 appeared in the upper left corner of the screen. "There's a selector there too—" he pointed to the pistol grip by my head, attached to the power seat which had folded up as soon as it lowered me into the tank at Curran's direction.

His finger clicked the switch to the other side—1

appeared in place of 2 on the screen—and then straight up—3. "Main gun," he said, "co-ax—that's the tribarrel mounted just in front of the hatch. You musta seen it?"

I nodded, but my agreement was a lie. I had been too excited and too overloaded with wonder to notice the automatic weapon on which I might have set my hand.

"And 3," Curran went on, nodding also, "straight up—that's both guns together. Not so hard, was it? You're ready to be a tank commander now—and—" he grinned, "—with six months and a little luck, I could teach ye t' drive the little darlin' besides."

"Oh, My Lord," I whispered, uncertain whether I was speaking to God or to the man beside me. I spread my feet slightly in order to keep from falling in a fit of weakness.

"*Watch* it!" the tank lord said sharply, sliding his booted foot to block me. More gently, he added, "Don't be touching *nothing*, remember? That—" he pointed to a pedal on the floor which I had not noticed "—that's the foot trip. Touch it and we give a little fireworks demonstration that nobody's gonna be very happy about."

He snapped the toggle down to its original position; the numeral disappeared from the screen. "Shouldn't have it live nohow," he added.

"But—all this," I said, gesturing with my arm close to my chest so that I would not bump any of the close-packed apparatus. "If shooting is so easy, then why is—*everything*—here?"

Curran smiled. "Up," he said, pointing to the hatch. As I hesitated, he added, "I'll give you a leg-up, don't worry about the power lift."

Flushing, sure that I was being exiled from Paradise because I had overstepped myself—somehow—

with the last question, I jumped for the hatch coaming and scrambled through with no need of the tanker's help. I supposed I was crying, but I could not tell because my eyes burned so.

"Hey, slow down, kid," called Curran as he lifted himself with great strength but less agility. "It's just Whichard's about due t' take over guard, and we don't need him t' find you inside. Right?"

"Oh," I said, hunched already on the edge of the tank's deck. I did not dare turn around for a moment. "Of course, My Lord."

"The thing about shootin'," explained the tank lord to my back, "ain't *how* so much's when and what. You got all this commo and sensors that'll handle any wavelength or take remote feeds. But *still* somebody's gotta decide which data t' call up—and decide what it means. And decide t' pop it er not—" I turned just as Curran leaned over to slap the iridium barrel of the main gun for emphasis. "Which is a mother-huge decision for whatever's down-range, ye know."

He grinned broadly. He had a short beard, rather sparse, which partly covered the pockmarks left by some childhood disease. "Maybe even puts tank commander up on a level with driver for tricky, right?"

His words opened a window in my mind, the frames branching and spreading into a spidery, infinite structure: responsibility, the choices that came with the power of a tank.

"Yes, My Lord," I whispered.

"Now, you better get back t' whatever civvies do," Curran said, a suggestion that would be snarled out as an order if I hesitated. "And *don't* be shootin' off yer mouth about t'night, right?"

"No, My Lord," I said as I jumped to the ground. Tie-beams between the wall and the masonry gatehouse would let me climb back to the path I had followed to get here.

"And thank you," I added, but varied emotions choked the words into a mumble.

I thought the women might already have returned, but I listened for a moment, clinging to the bars, and heard nothing. Even so I climbed in the end window. It was more difficult to scramble down without the aid of the antenna brace, but a free-standing wardrobe put that window in a sort of alcove.

I didn't know what would happen if the women saw me slipping in and out through the bars. There would be a beating—there was a beating whenever an occasion offered. That didn't matter, but it was possible that Lady Miriam would also have the openings cross-barred too straitly for even my slight form to pass.

I would have returned to the banquet hall, but female voices were already greeting the guard outside the door. I had only enough time to smooth the plush of my jacket with Sarah's hairbrush before they swept in, all of them together and their mistress in the lead as usual.

By standing against a color-washed wall panel, I was able to pass unnoticed for some minutes of the excited babble without being guilty of "hiding" with the severe flogging that would surely entail. By the time Lady Miriam called, "Leesh? *Elisha!*" in a querulous voice, no one else could have sworn that I hadn't entered the apartment with the rest of the entourage.

"Yes, My Lady?" I said, stepping forward.

Several of the women were drifting off in pairs to help one another out of their formal costumes and coiffures. There would be a banquet every night that the tank lords remained—providing occupation to fill the otherwise featureless lives of the maids and their mistress.

That was time consuming, even if they did not become more involved than public occasion required.

"Leesh," said Lady Miriam, moderating her voice unexpectedly. I was prepared for a blow, ready to accept it unflinchingly unless it were aimed at my eyes and even then to dodge as little as possible so as not to stir up a worse beating.

"Elisha," the Lady continued in a honeyed tone— then, switching back to acid sharpness and looking at her Chief Maid, she said, "Sarah, what *are* all these women doing here? Don't they have rooms of their own?"

Women who still dallied in the suite's common room—several of the lower-ranking stored their garments here in chests and clothes presses—scurried for their sleeping quarters while Sarah hectored them, arms akimbo.

"I need you to carry a message for me, Leesh," explained Lady Miriam softly. "To one of our guests. You—you do know, don't you, boy, which suite was cleared for use by our guests?"

"Yes, My Lady," I said, keeping my face blank. "The end suite of the East Wing, where the King slept last year. But I thought—"

"Don't think," said Sarah, rapping me with the brush which she carried on all but formal occasions. "And don't interrupt milady."

"Yes, My Lady," I said, bowing and rising.

"I don't want you to *go* there, boy," said the Lady with an edge of irritation. "If Sergeant Grant has any questions, I want you to point the rooms out to him—from the courtyard."

She paused and touched her full lips with her

tongue while her fingers played with the fan. "Yes," she said at last, then continued, "I want you to tell Sergeant Grant oh-four hundred and to answer any questions he may have."

Lady Miriam looked up again, and though her voice remained mild, her eyes were hard as knife points. "Oh. And Leesh? This is business which the Baron does not wish to be known. Speak to Sergeant Grant in private. And never speak to anyone else about it—even to the Baron if he tries to trick you into an admission."

"Yes, My Lady," I said bowing.

I understood what the Baron would do to a page who brought him that news—and how he would send a message back to his wife, to the king's daughter whom he dared not impale in person.

Sarah's shrieked order carried me past the guard at the women's apartment, while Lady Miriam's signet was my pass into the courtyard after normal hours. The soldier there on guard was muzzy with drink. I might have been able to slip unnoticed by the hall alcove in which he sheltered.

I skipped across the gravel-in-clay surface of the courtyard, afraid to pause to touch the tanks again when I knew Lady Miriam would be peering from her window. Perhaps on the way back . . . but no, she would be as intent on hearing how the message was received as she was anxious to know that it had been delivered. I would ignore the tanks—

"*Freeze*, buddy!" snarled someone from the turret of the tank I had just run past.

I stumbled with shock and my will to obey. Catching my balance, I turned slowly—to the triple muzzles of the weapon mounted on the cupola, not a pistol as Lord Curran had pointed. The man who spoke wore a shielded helmet, but there would not have been enough light to recognize him anyway.

"Please, My Lord," I said. "I have a message for Sergeant-Commander Grant?"

"From who?" the mercenary demanded. I knew now that Lieutenant Kiley had been serious about protecting from intrusion the quarters allotted to his men.

"My Lord, I . . ." I said and found no way to proceed.

"Yeah, Via," the tank lord agreed in a relaxed tone. "None a' my affair." He touched the side of his helmet and spoke softly.

The gatehouse door opened with a spill of light and the tall, broad-shouldered silhouette of Sergeant Grant. Like the mercenary on guard in the tank, he wore a communications helmet.

Grant slipped his face shield down, and for a moment my own exposed skin tingled—or my mind *thought* it perceived a tingle—as the tank lord's equipment scanned me.

"C'mon, then," he grunted, gesturing me toward the recessed angle of the building and the gate leaves. "We'll step around the corner and talk."

There was a trill of feminine laughter from the upper story of the gatehouse: a servant named Maria, whose hoots of joy were unmistakable. Lieutenant Kiley leaned his head and torso from the window above us and shouted to Grant, his voice and his anger recognizable even though the words themselves were not.

The sergeant paused, clenching his left fist and reaching for me with his right because I happened to be closest to him. I poised to run—survive this first, then worry about what Lady Miriam would say—but the tank lord caught himself, raised his shield, and called to his superior in a tone on the safe side of insolent, "All right, all right. I'll stay right here where Cermak can see me from the tank."

Apparently Grant had remembered Lady Miriam also, for he spoke in our language so that I—and the principal for whom I acted—would understand the situation.

Lieutenant Kiley banged his shutters closed.

Grant stared for a moment at Cermak until the guard understood and dropped back into the interior of his vehicle. We could still be observed through the marvelous vision blocks, but we had the miminal privacy needed for me to deliver my message.

"Lady Miriam," I said softly, "says oh-four hundred."

I waited for the tank lord to ask me for directions. His breath and sweat exuded sour echoes of the strong estate ale.

"Won't go," the tank lord replied unexpectedly. "I'll be clear at oh-three *to* oh-four." He paused before adding, "You tell her, kid, she better not be playin' games. Nobody plays prick-tease with *this* boy and likes what they get for it."

"Yes, My Lord," I said, skipping backward because I had the feeling that this man would grab me and shake me to emphasize his point.

I would not deliver his threat. My best small hope for safety at the end of this affair required that Lady Miriam believe I was ignorant of what was going on, and a small hope it was.

That *was* a slim hope anyway.

"Well, go on, then," the tank lord said.

He strode back within the gatehouse, catlike in his grace and lethality, while I ran to tell my mistress of the revised time.

An hour's pleasure seemed a little thing against the risk of two lives—and my own.

*   *   *

My "room" was what had been the back staircase before it was blocked to convert the second floor of the West Wing into the women's apartment. The dank cylinder was furnished only with the original stone stair treads and whatever my mistress and her maids had chosen to store there over the years. I normally slept on a chair in the common room, creeping back to my designated space before dawn.

Tonight I slept *beneath* one of the large chairs in a corner; not hidden, exactly, but not visible without a search.

The two women were quiet enough to have slipped past someone who was not poised to hear them as I was, and the tiny flashlight the leader carried threw a beam so tight that it could scarcely have helped them see their way. But the perfume they wore— imported, expensive, and overpowering—was more startling than a shout.

They paused at the door. The latch rattled like a tocsin though the hinges did not squeal.

The soldier on guard, warned and perhaps awakened by the latch, stopped them before they could leave the apartment. The glowlamp in the sconce beside the door emphasized the ruddy anger on his face.

Sarah's voice, low but cutting, said, "Keep silent, my man, or it will be the worse for you." She thrust a gleam of gold toward the guard, not payment but a richly-chased signet ring, and went on, "Lady Miriam knows and approves. Keep still and you'll have no cause to regret this night. Otherwise . . ."

The guard's face was not blank, but emotions chased themselves across it too quickly for his mood to be read. Suddenly he reached out and harshly squeezed the Chief Maid's breast. Sarah gasped, and the man snarled, "What've they got that *I* don't, tell me, huh? You're *all* whores, that's all you are!"

The second woman was almost hidden from the soldier by the Chief Maid and the panel of the half-opened door. I could see a shimmer of light as her hand rose, though I could not tell whether it was a blade or a gun barrel.

The guard flung his hand down from Sarah and turned away. "Go on, then," he grumbled. "What do I care? Go *on*, sluts."

The weapon disappeared, unused and unseen, into the folds of an ample skirt, and the two women left the suite with only the whisper of felt slippers. They were heavily veiled and wore garments coarser than any I had seen on the Chief Maid before—but Lady Miriam was as recognizable in the grace of her walk as Sarah was for her voice.

The women left the door ajar to keep the latch from rattling again, and the guard did not at first pull it to. I listened for further moments against the chance that another maid would come from her room or that the Lady would rush back, driven by fear or conscience—though I hadn't seen either state control her in the past.

I was poised to squeeze between the window-bars again, barefoot for secrecy and a better grip, when I heard the hum of static as the guard switched his belt radio live. There was silence as he keyed it, then his low voice saying, "They've left, sir. They're on their way toward the banquet hall."

There was another pause and a radio voice too thin for me to hear more than the fact of it. The guard said, "Yes, Chamberlain," and clicked off the radio.

He latched the door.

I was out through the bars in one movement and well up the antenna brace before any of the maids could have entered the common room to investigate the noise.

I knew where the women were going, but not whether the Chamberlain would stop them on the way past the banquet hall or the Baron's personal suite at the head of East Wing. The fastest, safest way for me to cross the roof of the banquet hall was twenty feet up the side, where the builders' forms had left a flat, thirty-centimeter path in the otherwise sloping concrete.

Instead, I decided to pick my way along the trash-filled stone gutter just above the windows of the corridor on the courtyard side. I could say that my life—my chance of life—depended on knowing what was going on . . . and it did depend on that. But crawling through the starlit darkness, spying on my betters, was also the only way I had of asserting myself. The need to assert myself had become unexpectedly pressing since Lord Curran had showed me the tank, and since I had experienced what a man *could* be.

There was movement across the courtyard as I reached the vertical extension of the load-bearing wall that separated the West Wing from the banquet hall. I ducked beneath the stone coping, but the activity had nothing to do with me. The gatehouse door had opened and, as I peered through dark-adapted eyes, the mercenary on guard in a tank exchanged with the man who had just stepped out of the building.

The tank lords talked briefly. Then the gatehouse door shut behind the guard who had been relieved while his replacement climbed into the turret of the vehicle parked near the West Wing—Sergeant Grant's tank. I clambered over the wall extension and stepped carefully along the gutter, regretting now that I had not worn shoes for protection. I heard nothing from the corridor below, although the casements were pivoted outward to catch any breeze that would relieve the summer stillness.

Gravel crunched in the courtyard as the tank lord on guard slid from his vehicle and began to stride toward the end of the East Wing.

He was across the courtyard from me—faceless behind the shield of his commo helmet and at best only a shadow against the stone of the wall behind him. But the man was Sergeant Grant beyond question, abandoning his post for the most personal of reasons.

I continued, reaching the East Wing as the tank lord disappeared among the stone finials of the outside staircase at the wing's far end. The guest suites had their own entrance, more formally ornamented than the doorways serving the estate's own needs. The portal was guarded only when the suites were in use—and then most often by a mixed force of the Baron's soldiers and those of the guests.

That was not a formality. The guest who would entrust his life solely to the Baron's good will was a fool.

A corridor much like that flanking the banquet hall ran along the courtyard side of the guest suites. It was closed by a cross-wall and door, separating the guests from the Baron's private apartment, but the door was locked and not guarded.

Lady Miriam kept a copy of the door's microchip key under the plush lining of her jewel box. I had found it but left it there, needless to me so long as I could slip through window grates.

The individual guest suites were locked also, but as I lowered myself from the gutter to a window ledge I heard a door snick closed. The sound was minuscule, but it had a crispness that echoed in the lightless hall.

Skirts rustled softly against the stone, and Sarah gave a gentle, troubled sigh as she settled herself to await her mistress.

I waited on the ledge, wondering if I should climb back to the roof—or even return to my own room. The Chamberlain 'had not blocked the assignation, and there was no sign of an alarm. The soldiers, barracked on the ground floor of this wing, would have been clearly audible had they been aroused.

Then I did hear something—or feel it. There had been motion, the ghost of motion, on the other side of the door closing the corridor. Someone had entered or left the Baron's apartment, and I had heard them through the open windows.

It could have been one of the Baron's current favorites—girls from the estate, the younger and more vulnerable, the better. They generally used the little door and staircase on the outer perimeter of the palace—where a guard *was* stationed against the possibility that an axe-wielding relative would follow the lucky child.

I lifted myself back to the roof with particular care, so that I would not disturb the Chief Maid waiting in the hallway. Then I followed the gutter back to the portion of roof over the Baron's apartments.

I knew the wait would be less than an hour, the length of Sergeant Grant's guard duty, but it did not occur to me that the interval would be as brief as it actually was. I had scarcely settled myself again to wait when I thought I heard a door unlatch in the guest suites. That could have been imagination or Sarah, deciding to wait in a room instead of the corridor; but moments later the helmeted tank lord paused on the outside staircase.

By taking the risk of leaning over the roof coping, I could see Lord Grant and a woman embracing on the landing before the big mercenary strode back across the courtyard toward the tank where he was supposed to be on guard. Desire had not waited on its accomplishment, and mutual fear had prevented the sort of dalliance after the event that the women dwelt on so lovingly in the privacy of their apartment . . . while Leesh, the Lady's page and no man, listened of necessity.

The women's slippers made no sound in the corridor, but their dresses brushed one another to the door which clicked and sighed as it let them out of the guest apartments and into the portion of the East Wing reserved to the Baron.

I expected shouts, then; screams, even gunfire as the Baron and Wolfitz confronted Lady Miriam. There was no sound except for skirts continuing to whisper their way up the hall, returning to the women's apartment. I stood up to follow, disappointed despite the fact that bloody chaos in the palace would endanger everyone—and me, the usual scapegoat for frustrations, most of all.

The Baron said in a tight voice at the window directly beneath me, "Give me the goggles, Wolfitz," and surprise almost made me fall.

The strap of a pair of night-vision goggles rustled over the Baron's grizzled head. Their frames clucked against the stone sash as my master bent forward with the unfamiliar headgear.

For a moment, I was too frightened to breathe. If he leaned out and turned his head, he would see me poised like a terrified gargoyle above him. Any move

I made—even flattening myself behind the wall coping—risked a sound and disaster.

"You're right," said the Baron in a voice that would have been normal if it had any emotion behind it. There was another sound of something hard against the sash, a metallic clink this time.

"*No*, My Lord!" said the Chamberlain in a voice more forceful than I dreamed any underling would use to the Baron. Wolfitz must have been seizing the nettle firmly, certain that hesitation or uncertainty meant the end of more than his plans. "If you shoot him now, the others will blast everything around them to glowing slag."

"Wolfitz," said the Baron, breathing hard. They had been struggling. The flare-mouthed mob gun from the Baron's nightstand—scarcely a threat to Sergeant Grant across the courtyard—extended from the window opening, but the Chamberlain's bony hand was on the Baron's wrist. "If you tell me I must let those arrogant outworlders pleasure *my* wife in *my* palace, I will kill you."

He sounded like an architect discussing a possible staircase curve.

"There's a better way, My Lord," said the Chamberlain. His voice was breathy also, but I thought exertion was less to account for that than was the risk he took. "We'll be ready the next time the—outworlder gives us the opportunity. We'll take him in, in the crime; but quietly so that the others aren't aroused."

"Idiot!" snarled the Baron, himself again in all his arrogant certainty. Their hands and the gun disappeared from the window ledge. The tableau was the vestige of an event the men needed each other too much to remember. "No matter what we do with the body, the others will blame us. Blame *me*."

His voice took a dangerous coloration as he added, "Is that what you had in mind, Chamberlain?"

Wolfitz said calmly, "The remainder of the platoon here will be captured—or killed, it doesn't matter—by the mercenaries of the Lightning Division, who will also protect us from reaction by King Adrian and Colonel Hammer."

"But . . ." said the Baron, the word a placeholder for the connected thought which did not form in his mind after all.

"The King of Ganz won't hesitate an instant if you offer him your fealty," the Chamberlain continued, letting the words display their own strength instead of speaking loudly in a fashion his master might take as badgering.

The Baron still held the mob gun, and his temper was doubtful at the best of times.

"The mercenaries of the Lightning Division," continued Wolfitz with his quiet voice and persuasive ideas, "will accept any risk in order to capture four tanks undamaged. The value of that equipment is beyond any profit the Lightning Division dreamed of earning when they were hired by Ganz."

"But . . ." the Baron repeated in an awestruck voice. "The truce?"

"A matter for the kings to dispute," said the Chamberlain offhandedly. "But Adrian will find little support among his remaining barons if you were forced into your change of allegiance. When the troops he billeted on you raped and murdered Lady Miriam, that is."

"How quickly can you make the arrangements?" asked the Baron. I had difficulty in following the words: not because they were soft, but because he growled them like a beast.

"The delay," Wolfitz replied judiciously, and I

could imagine him lacing his long fingers together
and staring at them, "will be for the next opportunity
your—Lady Miriam and her lover give us, I shouldn't
imagine that will be longer than tomorrow night."

The Baron's teeth grated like nutshells being ground
against stone.

"We'll have to use couriers, of course," Wolfitz
added. "The likelihood of the Slammers intercepting
any other form of communication is too high. . . .
But all Ganz and its mercenaries have to do is ready
a force to dash here and defend the palace before
Hammer can react. Since these tanks *are* the forward
picket, and they'll be unmanned while Sergeant Grant
is—otherwise occupied—the Lightning Division will
have almost an hour before an alarm can be given.
Ample time, I'm sure."

"Chamberlain," the Baron said in a voice from
which amazement had washed all the anger. "You
think of everything. See to it."

"Yes, My Lord," said Wolfitz humbly.

The tall Chamberlain *did* think of everything, or
very nearly; but he'd had much longer to plan than
the Baron thought. I wondered how long Wolfitz had
waited for an opportunity like this one; and what
payment he had arranged to receive from the King of
Ganz if he changed the Baron's allegiance?

A door slammed closed, the Baron returning to his
suite and his current child-mistress. Chamberlain
Wolfitz's rooms adjoined his master's, but my ears
followed his footsteps to the staircase at the head of
the wing.

By the time I had returned to the West Wing and
was starting down the antenna brace, a pair of the
Baron's soldiers had climbed into a truck and gone
rattling off into the night. It was an unusual event

but not especially remarkable: the road they took led off to one of the Baron's outlying estates.

But the road led to the border with Ganz, also; and I had no doubt as to where the couriers' message would be received.

The tank lords spent most of the next day busy with their vehicles. A squad of the Baron's soldiers kept at a distance the tenants and house servants who gawked while the khaki-clad tankers crawled through access plates and handed fan motors to their fellows. The bustle racks welded to the back of each turret held replacement parts as well as the crew's personal belongings.

It was hard to imagine that objects as huge and powerful as the tanks would need repair. I had to remember that they were not ingots of iridium but vastly complicated assemblages of parts—each of which could break, and eight of which were human.

I glanced occasionally at the tanks and the lordly men who ruled and serviced them. I had no excuse to take me beyond the women's apartment during daylight.

Excitement roused the women early, but there was little pretense of getting on with their lacemaking. They dressed, changed, primped—argued over rights to one bit of clothing or another—and primarily, they talked.

Lady Miriam was less a part of the gossip than usual, but she was the most fastidious of all about the way she would look at the night's banquet.

The tank lords bathed at the wellhead in the courtyard like so many herdsmen. The women watched hungrily, edging forward despite the scandalized demands of one of the older maids that they at least stand back in the room where their attention would be less blatant.

Curran's muscles were knotted, his skin swarthy. Sergeant Grant could have passed for a god—or at least a man of half his real age. When he looked up at the women's apartments, he smiled.

The truck returned in late afternoon, carrying the two soldiers and a third man in civilian clothes who could have been—but was not—the manager of one of the outlying estates. The civilian was closeted with the Baron for half an hour before he climbed back into the truck. He, Wolfitz, and the Baron gripped one another's forearms in leave-taking; then the vehicle returned the way it had come.

The tank lord on guard paid less attention to the truck than he had to the column of steam-driven produce vans, chuffing toward the nearest rail terminus.

The banquet was less hectic than that of the first night, but the glitter had been replaced by a fog of hostility now that the newness had worn off. The Baron's soldiers were more openly angry that Hammer's men picked and chose—food at the high table and women in the corridor or the servants' quarters below.

The Slammers, for their part, had seen enough of the estate to be contemptuous of its isolation, of its low technology—and of the folk who lived on it. And yet—I had talked with Lord Curran and listened to the others as well. The tank lords were men like those of the barony. They had walked on far worlds and had been placed in charge of instruments as sophisticated as any in the human galaxy—but they were not sophisticated *men*, only powerful ones.

Sergeant-Commander Grant, for instance, made

the child's mistake of thinking his power to destroy conferred on him a sort of personal immortality.

The Baron ate and drank in a sullen reverie, deaf to the lieutenant's attempts at conversation and as blind to Lady Miriam on his left as she was to him. The Chamberlain was seated among the soldiers because there were more guests than maids of honor. He watched the activities at the high table unobtrusively, keeping his own counsel and betraying his nervousness only by the fact that none of the food he picked at seemed to go down his throat.

I was tempted to slip out to the tanks, because Lord Curran was on duty again during the banquet. His absence must have been his own choice; a dislike for the food or the society perhaps . . . but more probably, from what I had seen in the little man when we talked, a fear of large, formal gatherings.

It would have been nice to talk to Lord Curran again, and blissful to have the controls of the huge tank again within my hands. But if I were caught then, I might not be able to slip free later in the night—and I would rather have died than missed that chance.

The Baron hunched over his ale when Lieutenant Kiley gathered his men to return to the gatehouse. They did not march well in unison, not even by comparison with the Baron's soldiers when they drilled in the courtyard.

The skills and the purpose of the tank lords lay elsewhere.

Lady Miriam rose when the tankers fell in. She swept from the banquet hall regally as befit her birth, dressed in amber silk from Terra and topazes of ancient cut from our own world. She did not look behind her to see that her maids followed and I brought up the rear . . . but she did glance aside once at the formation of tank lords.

She would be dressed no better than a servant later that night, and she wanted to be sure that Sergeant Grant had a view of her full splendor to keep in mind when next they met in darkness.

The soldier who had guarded the women's apartments the night before was on duty when the Chief Maid led her mistress out again. There was no repetition of the previous night's dangerous byplay this time. The guard was subdued, or frightened; or, just possibly, biding his time because he was aware of what was going to come.

I followed, more familiar with my route this time and too pumped with excitement to show the greater care I knew was necessary tonight, when there would be many besides myself to watch, to listen.

But I was alone on the roof, and the others, so certain of what *they* knew and expected, paid no attention to the part of the world which lay beyond their immediate interest.

Sergeant Grant sauntered as he left the vehicle where he was supposed to stay on guard. As he neared the staircase to the guest suites, his stride lengthened and his pace picked up. There was nothing of nervousness in his manner; only the anticipation of a man focused on sex to the extinction of all other considerations.

I was afraid that Wolfitz would spring his trap before I was close enough to follow what occurred. A more reasonable fear would have been that I would stumble into the middle of the event.

Neither danger came about. I reached the gutter over the guest corridor and waited, breathing through my mouth alone so that I wouldn't make any noise.

The blood that pounded through my ears deafened me for a moment, but there was nothing to fear. Voices murmured, Sarah and Sergeant Grant, and the door that had waited ajar for the tank lord clicked to shut the suite.

Four of the Baron's soldiers mounted the outside steps, as quietly as their boots permitted. There were faint sounds, clothing and one muted clink of metal, from the corridor on the Baron's side of the door.

All day I'd been telling myself that there was no safe way I could climb down and watch the events through a window. I climbed down, finding enough purchase for my fingers and toes where weathering had rounded the corners of stone blocks. Getting back to the roof would be more difficult, unless I risked gripping an out-swung casement for support.

Unless I dropped, bullet-riddled, to the ground.

I rested a toe on a window ledge and peeked around the stone toward the door of the suite the lovers had used on their first assignation. I could see nothing—

Until the corridor blazed with silent light.

Sarah's face was white, dazzling with direct reflection of the high-intensity floods at either end of the hallway. Her mouth opened and froze, a statue of a scream but without the sound that fear or self preservation choked in her throat.

Feet, softly but many of them, shuffled over the stone flags toward the Chief Maid. Her head jerked from one side to the other, but her body did not move. The illumination was pinning her to the door where she kept watch.

The lights spilled through the corridor windows, but their effect was surprisingly slight in the open air: highlights on the parked tanks; a faint wash of outline, not color, over the stones of the wall and gatehouse; and a distorted shadowplay on the ground itself, men and weapons twisting as they advanced toward the trapped maid from both sides.

There was no sign of interest from the gatehouse. Even if the tank lords were awake to notice the lights, what happened at night in the palace was no affair of theirs.

Three of perhaps a dozen of the Baron's soldiers stepped within my angle of vision. Two carried rifles; the third was Murphy with a chip recorder, the spidery wands of its audio and video pick-ups retracted because of the press of men standing nearby.

Sarah swallowed. She closed her mouth, but her eyes stared toward the infinite distance beyond this world. The gold signet she clutched was a drop from the sun's heart in the floodlights.

The Baron stepped close to the woman. He took the ring with his left hand, looked at it, and passed it to the stooped, stone-faced figure of the Chamberlain.

"Move her out of the way," said the Baron in a husky whisper.

One of the soldiers stuck the muzzle of his assault rifle under the chin of the Chief Maid, pointing upward. With his other hand, the man gripped Sarah's shoulder and guided her away from the door panel.

Wolfitz looked at his master, nodded, and set a magnetic key on the lock. Then he too stepped clear.

The Baron stood at the door with his back to me. He wore body armor, but he can't have thought it would protect him against the Slammer's powergun. Murphy was at the Baron's side, the recorder's central light glaring back from the door panel, and another soldier poised with his hand on the latch.

The Baron slammed the door inward with his foot.

I do not think I have ever seen a man move as fast as Sergeant Grant did then.

The door opened on a servants' alcove, not the guest rooms themselves, but the furnishings there were sufficient to the lovers' need. Lady Miriam had lifted her skirts. She was standing, leaning slightly backwards, with her buttocks braced against the bedframe. She screamed, her eyes blank reflections of the sudden light.

Sergeant-Commander Grant still wore his helmet. He had slung his belt and holstered pistol over the bedpost when he unsealed the lower flap of his uniform coveralls, but he was turning with the pistol in his hand before the Baron got off the first round with his mob gun.

Aerofoils, spread from the flaring muzzle by asymmetric thrust, spattered the lovers and a two-meter circle on the wall beyond them.

The tank lord's chest was in bloody tatters and there was a brain-deep gash between his eyebrows, but his body and the powergun followed through with the motion reflex had begun.

The Baron's weapon chunked twice more. Lady Miriam flopped over the footboard and lay thrashing on the bare springs, spurting blood from narrow wounds that her clothing did not cover. Individual projectiles from the mob gun had little stopping power, but they bled out a victim's life like so many knife blades.

When the Baron shot the third time, his gun was within a meter of what had been the tank lord's face. Sergeant Grant's body staggered backward and fell, the powergun unfired but still gripped in the mercenary's right hand.

"Call the Lightning Division," said the Baron harshly as he turned. His face, except where it was freckled by fresh blood, was as pale as I had ever seen it. "It's time."

Wolfitz lifted a communicator, short range but keyed to the main transmitter, and spoke briefly. There was no need for communications security now. The man who should have intercepted and evaluated the short message was dead in a smear of his own wastes and body fluids.

The smell of the mob gun's propellant clung chokingly to the back of my throat, among the more familiar slaughterhouse odors. Lady Miriam's breath whistled, and the bedsprings squeaked beneath her uncontrolled motions.

"Shut that off," said the Baron to Murphy. The recorder's pool of light shrank into shadow within the alcove.

The Baron turned and fired once more, into the tank lord's groin.

"Make sure the others don't leave the gatehouse till Ganz's mercenaries are here to deal with them," said the Baron negligently. He looked at the gun in his hand. Strong lights turned the heat and propellant residues rising from its barrel into shadows on the wall beyond.

"Marksmen are ready, My Lord," said the Chamberlain.

The Baron skittered his mob gun down the hall. He strode toward the rooms of his own apartment.

It must have been easier to climb back to the roof than I had feared. I have no memory of it, of the stress on fingertips and toes or the pain in my muscles as they lifted the body which they had supported for what seemed (after the fact) to have been hours. Minutes only, of course; but instead of serial memory of what had happened, my brain was filled

with too many frozen pictures of details for all of
them to fit within the real timeframe.

The plan that I had made for this moment lay so
deep that I executed it by reflex, though my brain
roiled.

Executed it by instinct, perhaps; the instinct of
flight, the instinct to power.

In the corridor, Wolfitz and Murphy were arguing
in low voices about what should be done about the
mess.

Soldiers had taken up positions in the windowed
corridor flanking the banquet hall. More of the Baron's men, released from trapping Lady Miriam and
her lover, were joining their fellows with words too
soft for me to understand. I crossed the steeply-
pitched roof on the higher catwalk, for speed and
from fear that the men at the windows might hear
me.

There were no soldiers on the roof itself. The wall
coping might hide even a full-sized man if he lay flat,
but the narrow gutter between wall and roof was an
impossible position from which to shoot at targets
across the courtyard.

The corridor windows on the courtyard side were
not true firing slits like those of all the palace's outer
walls. Nonetheless, men shooting from corners of the
windows could shelter their bodies behind stone thick
enough to stop bolts from the Slammers' personal
weapons. The sleet of bullets from twenty assault
rifles would turn anyone sprinting from the gatehouse door or the pair of second-floor windows into
offal like that which had been Sergeant Grant.

The tank lords were not immortal.

There was commotion in the women's apartments
when I crossed them. Momentarily a light fanned
the shadow of the window bars across the courtyard

and the gray curves of Sergeant Grant's tank. A male voice cursed harshly. A lamp casing crunched, and from the returned darkness came a blow and a woman's cry.

Some of the Baron's soldiers were taking positions in the West Wing. Unless the surviving tank lords could blow a gap in the thick outer wall of the gatehouse, they had no exit until the Lightning Division arrived with enough firepower to sweep them up at will.

But I could get in, with a warning that would come in time for them to summon aid from Colonel Hammer himself. They would be in debt for my warning, owing me their lives, their tanks, and their honor.

Surely the tank lords could find a place for a servant willing to go with them anywhere?

The battlements of the wall closing the north side of the courtyard formed my pathway to the roof of the gatehouse. Grass and brush grew there in ragged clumps. Cracks between stones had trapped dust, seeds, and moisture during a generation of neglect. I crawled along, on my belly, tearing my black velvet jacket.

Eyes focused on the gatehouse door and windows were certain to wander: to the sky; to fellows slouching over their weapons; to the wall connecting the gatehouse to the West Wing. If I stayed flat, I merged with the stone . . . but shrubs could quiver in the wrong pattern, and the Baron's light-amplifying goggles might be worn by one of the watching soldiers.

It had seemed simpler when I planned it; but it was necessary in any event, even if I died in a burst of gunfire.

The roof of the gatehouse was reinforced concrete, slightly domed, and as proof against indirect fire as

the stone walls were against small arms. There was
no roof entrance, but there was a capped flue for the
stove that had once heated the guard quarters. I'd
squirmed my way through that hole once before.

Four years before.

The roof of the gatehouse was a meter higher than
the wall on which I lay, an easy jump but one which
put me in silhouette against the stars. I reached up,
feeling along the concrete edge less for a grip than
for reassurance. I was afraid to leave the wall because my body was telling itself that the stone it
pressed was safety.

If the Baron's men shot me now, it would warn the
tank lords in time to save them. I owed them that,
for the glimpses of freedom Curran had showed me
in the turret of a tank.

I vaulted onto the smooth concrete and rolled, a
shadow in the night to any of the watchers who
might have seen me. Once I was *on* the gatehouse, I
was safe because of the flat dome that shrugged off
rain and projectiles. The flue was near the north
edge of the structure, hidden from the eyes and guns
waiting elsewhere in the palace.

I'd grown only slightly since I was twelve and
beginning to explore the palace in which I expected
to die. The flue hadn't offered much margin, but my
need wasn't as great then, either.

I'd never needed *anything* as much as I needed to
get into the gatehouse now.

The metal smoke pipe had rusted and blown down
decades before. The wooden cap, fashioned to close
the hole to rain, hadn't been maintained. It crumbled in my hands when I lifted it away, soggy wood
with only flecks remaining of the stucco which had
been applied to seal the cap into place.

The flue was as narrow as the gap between window bars, and because it was round, I didn't have the luxury of turning sideways. So be it.

If my shoulders fit, my hips would follow. I extended my right arm and reached down through the hole as far as I could. The flue was as empty as it was dark. Flakes of rust made mouselike patterings as my touch dislodged them. The passageway curved smoothly, but it had no sharp-angled shot trap as far down as I could feel from outside.

I couldn't reach the lower opening. The roof was built thick enough to stop heavy shells. At least the slimy surface of the concrete tube would make the job easier.

I lowered my head into the flue with the pit of my extended right arm pressed as firmly as I could against the lip of the opening. The cast concrete brought an electric chill through the sweat-soaked velvet of my jerkin, reminding me—now that it was too late—that I could have stripped off the garment to gain another millimeter's tolerance.

It was too late, even though all but my head and one arm were outside. If I stopped now, I would never have the courage to go on again.

The air in the flue was dank, because even now in late Summer the concrete sweated and the cap prevented condensate from evaporating. The sound of my fear-lengthened breaths did not echo from the end of a closed tube, and not even panic could convince me that the air was stale and would suffocate me. I slid farther down; down to the *real* point of no return.

By leading with my head and one arm, I was able to tip my collarbone endwise for what would have been a relatively easy fit within the flue if my ribs and spine did not have to follow after. The concrete caught the tip of my left shoulder and the ribs beneath my right armpit—let me flex forward minutely on the play in my skin and the velvet—and held me.

I would have screamed, but the constriction of my ribs was too tight. My legs kicked in the air above the gatehouse, unable to thrust me down for lack of purchase. My right arm flopped in the tube, battering my knuckles and fingertips against unyielding concrete.

I could die here, and no one would know.

Memory of the tank and the windows of choice expanding infinitely above even Leesh, the Lady's page, flashed before me and cooled my body like rain on a stove. My muscles relaxed and I could breathe again—though carefully, and though the veins of my head were distending with blood trapped by my present posture.

Instead of flapping vainly, my right palm and elbow locked on opposite sides of the curving passage. I breathed as deeply as I could, then let it out as I kicked my legs up where gravity, at least, could help.

My right arm pulled while my left tried to clamp itself within my rib cage. Cloth tore, skin tore, and my torso slipped fully within the flue, lubricated by blood as well as condensate.

If I had been upright, I might have blacked out momentarily with the release of tension. Inverted, I could only gasp and feel my face and scalp burn with the flush that darkened them. The length of a hand farther and my pelvis scraped. My fingers had a grip on the lower edge of the flue, and I pulled like a cork extracting itself from a wine bottle. My being, body and mind, was so focused on its task that I was equally unmoved by losing my trousers—dragged off on the lip of the flue—and the fact that my hand was free.

The concrete burned my left ear when my right arm thrust my torso down with real handhold for the first time. My shoulders slid free and the rest of my body tumbled out of the tube which had seemed to grip it tightly until that instant.

The light that blazed in my face was meant to blind me, but I was already stunned—more by the effort than the floor which I'd hit an instant before. Someone laid the muzzle of a powergun against my left ear. The dense iridium felt cool and good on my damaged skin.

"Where's Sergeant Grant?" said Lieutenant Kiley, a meter to the side of the light source.

I squinted away from the beam. There was an open bedroll beneath me, but I think I was too limp when I dropped from the flue to be injured by bare stone. Three of the tank lords were in the room with me. The bulbous commo helmets they wore explained how the lieutenant already knew something had happened to the guard. The others would be on the ground floor, poised.

The guns pointed at me were no surprise.

"He slipped into the palace to see Lady Miriam," I said, amazed that my voice did not break in a throat so dry. "The Baron killed them, both, and he's summoned the Lightning Division to capture you and your tanks. You have to call for help at once or they'll be here."

"Blood and martyrs," said the man with the gun at my ear, Lord Curran, and he stepped between me and the dazzling light. "Douse that, Sparky. The kid's all right."

The tank lord with the light dimmed it to a glow and said, "Which *we* bloody well ain't."

Lieutenant Kiley moved to a window and peeked

through a crack in the shutter, down into the courtyard.

"But . . ." I said. I would have gotten up but Curran's hand kept me below the possible line of fire. I'd tripped the mercenaries' alarms during my approach, awakened them—enough to save them, surely. "You have your helmets?" I went on. "You can call your colonel?"

"That bastard Grant," the lieutenant said in the same emotionless, diamond-hard voice he had used in questioning me. "He slaved all the vehicle trans-ceivers to his own helmet so Command Central wouldn't wake *me* if they called while he was—out fucking around."

"Via," said Lord Curran, holstering his pistol and grimacing at his hands as he flexed them together. "I'll go. Get a couple more guns up these windows—" he gestured with jerks of his forehead "—for cover."

"It's my platoon," Kiley said, stepping away from the window but keeping his back to the others of us in the room, "Via, *Via!*"

"Look, sir," Curran insisted with his voice rising and wobbling like that of a dog fighting a choke collar. "I was his bloody driver, I'll—"

"*You* weren't the fuck-up!" Lieutenant Kiley snarled as he turned. "This one comes with the rank, trooper, so shut your—"

"I'll go, My Lords," I said, the squeal of my voice lifting it through the hoarse anger of grown men arguing over a chance to die.

They paused and the third lord, Sparky, thumbed the light up and back by reflex. I pointed to the flue. "That way. But you'll have to tell me what to do then."

Lord Curran handed me a disk the size of a thumb-nail. He must have taken it from his pocket when he planned to sprint for the tanks himself. "Lay it on the hatch—anywhere on the metal. Inside, t' the right a' the main screen—"

"Curran, *knot* it, will you?" the lieutenant demanded in peevish amazement. "We can't—"

"*I* don't want my ass blown away, Lieutenant," said the trooper with the light—which pointed toward the officer suddenly, though the pistol in Sparky's other hand was lifted idly toward the ceiling. "Anyhow, kid's got a better chance'n you do. Or me."

Lieutenant Kiley looked from one of his men to the other, then stared at me with eyes that could have melted rock. "The main screen is on the forward wall of the fighting compartment," he said flatly. "That is—"

"He's used it, Lieutenant," said Lord Curran. "He knows where it is." The little mercenary had drawn his pistol again and was checking the loads for the second time since I fell into the midst of these angry, nervous men.

Kiley looked at his subordinate, then continued to me, "The commo screen is the small one to the immediate right of the main screen, and it has an alphanumeric keypad beneath it. The screen will have a numeral two or a numeral three on it when you enter, depending whether it's set to feed another tank or to Grant's helmet."

He paused, wet his lips. His voice was bare of affect, but in his fear he was unable to sort out the minimum data that my task required. The mercenary officer realized that he was wandering, but that only added to the pressure which already ground him from all sides.

"Push numeral one on the keypad," Lieutenant Kiley went on, articulating very carefully. "The numeral on the visor should change to one. That's all you need to do—the transceiver will be cleared for normal operation, and we'll do the rest from here." He touched his helmet with the barrel of his power-gun, a gesture so controlled that the iridium did not clink on the thermoplastic.

"I'll need," I said, looking up at the flue, "a platform—tables or boxes."

"We'll lift you," said Lieutenant Kiley, "and we'll cover you as best we can. Better take that shirt off now and make the squeeze easier."

"No, My Lord," I said, rising against the back wall—out of sight, though within a possible line of fire. I stretched my muscles, wincing as tags of skin broke loose from the fabric to which blood had glued them. "It's dark-colored, so I'll need it to get to the tank. I, I'll use—"

I shuddered and almost fell; as I spoke, I visualized what I had just offered to do—and it terrified me.

"Kid—" said Lord Curran, catching me; though I was all right again, just a brief fit.

"I'll use my trousers also," I said. "They're at the other—"

"Via!" snapped Lord Sparky, pointing with the light which he had dimmed to a yellow glow that was scarcely a beam. "What *happened* t' you?"

"I was a servant in the women's apartments," I said. "I'll go now, if you'll help me. I must hurry."

Lord Curran and Lieutenant Kiley lifted me. Their hands were moist by contrast with the pebbled finish of their helmets, brushing my bare thighs. I could think only of how my nakedness had just humiliated me before the tank lords.

It was good to think of that, because my body eased itself into the flue without conscious direction and my mind was too full of old anger to freeze me with coming fears.

Going up was initially simpler than worming my way down the tube had been. With the firm fulcrum of Lieutenant Kiley's shoulders beneath me, my legs levered my ribs and shoulder past the point at which they caught on the concrete.

Someone started to shove me farther with his hands. "No!" I shouted, the distorted echo unintelligible even to me and barely heard in the room below. Someone understood, though, and the hands locked instead into a platform against which my feet could push in the cautious increments which the narrow passage required.

Sliding up the tube, the concrete hurt everywhere it rubbed me. The rush of blood to my head must have dulled the pain when I crawled downward. My right arm now had no strength and my legs, as the knees cramped themselves within the flue, could no longer thrust with any strength.

For a moment, the touch of the tank lord's lifted hands left my soles. I was wedged too tightly to slip back, but I could no more have climbed higher in the flue than I could have shattered the concrete that trapped me. Above, partly blocked by my loosely-waving arm, was a dim circle of the sky.

Hands gripped my feet and shoved upward with a firm, inexorable pressure that was now my only chance of success. Lord Curran, standing on his leader's shoulders, lifted me until my hand reached the outer lip. With a burst of hysterical strength, I dragged the rest of my body free.

It took me almost a minute to put my trousers on. The time was not wasted. If I had tried to jump down to the wall without resting, my muscles would have let me tumble all the way into the courtyard—

probably with enough noise to bring an immediate storm of gunfire from the Baron's soldiers.

The light within the gatehouse must have been visible as glimmers through the same cracks in the shutters which the tank lords used to desperately survey their position. That meant the Baron's men would be even more alert . . . but also, that their attention would be focused even more firmly on the second-floor windows—rather than on the wall adjacent to the gatehouse.

No one shot at me as I crawled backwards from the roof, pressing myself against the concrete and then stone hard enough to scrape skin that had not been touched by the flue.

The key to the tank hatches was in my mouth, the only place from which I could not lose it—while I lived.

My knees and elbows were bloody from the flue already, but the open sky was a relief as I wormed my way across the top of the wall. The moments I had been stuck in a concrete tube more strait than a coffin convinced me that there were worse deaths than a bullet.

Or even than by torture, unless the Baron decided to bury me alive.

I paused on my belly where the wall mated with the corner of the West Wing. I knew there were gunmen waiting at the windows a few meters away. They could not see me, but they might well hear the thump of my feet on the courtyard's compacted surface.

There was no better place to descend. Climbing up to the roofs of the palace would only delay my danger, while the greater danger rushed forward on the air cushion vehicles of the Lightning Division.

Taking a deep breath, I rolled over the rim of the wall. I dangled a moment before my strained arms let me fall the remaining two meters earlier than I had intended to. The sound my feet, then fingertips, made on the ground was not loud even to my fearful senses. There was no response from the windows above me—and no shots from the East Wing or the banquet hall, from which I was an easy target for any soldier who chanced to stare at the shadowed corner in which I poised.

I was six meters from the nearest tank—Lord Curran's tank, the tank from which Sergeant Grant had surveyed the women's apartments. Crawling was pointless—the gunmen were above me. I considered sprinting, but the sudden movement would have tripped the peripheral vision of eyes turned toward the gatehouse.

I strolled out of the corner, so frightened that I could not be sure my joints would not spill me to the ground because they had become rubbery.

One step, two steps, three steps, four—

"Hey!" someone shouted behind me, and seven powerguns raked the women's apartments with cyan lightning.

Because I was now so close to the tank, only soldiers in the West Wing could see me. The covering fire sent them ducking while glass shattered, fabrics burned, and flakes spalled away from the face of the stone itself. I heard screams from within, and not all of the throats were female.

A dozen or more automatic rifles—the soldiers elsewhere in the palace—opened fire on the gatehouse with a sound like wasps in a steel drum. I jumped to the bow slope of the tank, trusting my bare feet to grip the metal without delay for the steps set into the iridium.

A bolt from a powergun struck the turret a centimeter from where my hand slapped it. I screamed with dazzled surprise at the glowing dimple in the metal and the droplets that spattered my bare skin.

Only the tank lords' first volley had been aimed. When they ducked away from the inevitable return fire, they continued to shoot with only their gun muzzles lifted above the protecting stone. The bolts which scattered across the courtyard at random did a good job of frightening the Baron's men away from accurate shooting, but that randomness had almost killed me.

As it was, the shock of being fired at by a friend made me drop the hatch key. The circular field-induction chip clicked twice on its way to disappear in the dark courtyard.

The hatch opened. The key had bounced the first time on the cover.

I went through the opening head first, too frightened by the shots to swing my feet over the coaming in normal fashion. At least one soldier saw what was happening, because his bullets raked the air around my legs for the moment they waved. His tracers were green sparks; and when I fell safely within, more bullets disintegrated against the dense armor about me.

The seat, though folded, gashed my forehead with a corner and came near enough to stunning me with pain that I screamed in panic when I saw there was no commo screen where the lieutenant had said it would be. The saffron glow of instruments was cold mockery.

I spun. The main screen was behind me, just where it should have been, and the small common screen—reading 3—was beside it. I had turned around when I tumbled through the hatch.

My finger stabbed at the keypad, hit 1 and 2 together. A slash replaced the 3—and then 1, as I got control of my hand again and touched the correct key. Electronics whirred softly in the belly of the great tank.

The West Wing slid up the main screen as I palmed the control. There was a 1 in the corner of the main screen also.

My world was the whole universe in the hush of my mind. I pressed the firing pedal as my hand rotated the turret counterclockwise.

The tribarrel's mechanism whined as it cycled and the bolts thumped, expanding the air on their way to their target; but when the blue-green flickers of released energy struck stone, the night and the facade of the women's apartments shattered. Stones the size of a man's head were blasted from the wall, striking my tank and the other palace buildings with the violence of the impacts.

My tank.

I touched the selector toggle. The numeral 2 shone orange in the upper corner of the screen which the lofty mass of the banquet hall slid to fill.

"Kid!" shouted speakers somewhere in the tank with me. *"Kid!"*

My bare toes rocked the firing pedal forward and the world burst away from the axis of the main gun.

The turret hatch was open because I didn't know how to close it. The tribarrel whipped the air of the courtyard, spinning hot vortices smoky from fires the guns had set and poisoned by ozone and gases from the cartridge matrices.

The 20 cm main gun sucked all the lesser whorls along the path of its bolt, then exploded them in a cataclysm that lifted the end of the banquet hall ten meters before dropping it back as rubble.

My screen blacked out the discharge, but even the multiple reflections that flashed through the turret hatch were blinding. There was a gout of burning stone. Torque had shattered the arched concrete roof when it lifted, but many of the reinforcing rods still held so that slabs danced together as they tumbled inward.

Riflemen had continued to fire while the tribarrel raked toward them. The 20 cm bolt silenced everything but its own echoes. Servants would have broken down the outside doors minutes before. The surviving soldiers followed them now, throwing away weapons unless they forgot them in their hands.

The screen to my left was a panorama through the vision blocks while the orange pips on the main screen provided the targeting array. Men, tank lords in khaki, jumped aboard the other tanks. Two of them ran toward me in the vehicle farthest from the gatehouse.

Only the west gable of the banquet hall had collapsed. The powergun had no penetration, so the roof panel on the palace's outer side had been damaged only by stresses transmitted by the panel that took the bolt. Even on the courtyard side, the reinforced concrete still held its shape five meters from where the bolt struck, though fractured and askew.

The tiny figure of the Baron was running toward me from the entrance.

I couldn't see him on the main screen because it was centered on the guns' point of impact. I shouted in surprise, frightened back into slavery by that man even when shrunken to a doll in a panorama.

My left hand dialed the main screen down and across, so that the center of the Baron's broad chest was ringed with sighting pips. He raised his mob gun as he ran, and his mouth bellowed a curse or a challenge.

The Baron was not afraid of me or of anything else. But he had been *born* to the options that power gives.

My foot stroked the firing pedal.

One of the mercenaries who had just leaped to the tank's back deck gave a shout as the world became ozone and a cyan flash. Part of the servants' quarters beneath the banquet hall caught fire around the three-meter cavity blasted by the gun.

The Baron's disembodied right leg thrashed once on the ground. Other than that, he had vanished from the vision blocks.

Lieutenant Kiley came through the hatch, feet first but otherwise with as little ceremony as I had shown. He shoved me hard against the turret wall while he rocked the gun switch down to safe. The orange numeral blanked from the screen.

"In the *Lord's* name, kid!" the big officer demanded while his left hand still pressed me back. "Who told you to do *that*?"

"Lieutenant," said Lord Curran, leaning over the hatch opening but continuing to scan the courtyard. His pistol was in his hand, muzzle lifted, while air trembled away from the hot metal. "We'd best get a move on unless you figure t' fight a reinforced battalion alone till the supports get here."

"Well, get in and *drive*, curse you!" the lieutenant shouted. The words relaxed his body and he released me. "*No*, I don't want to wait around here alone for the Lightning Division!"

"Lieutenant," said the driver, unaffected by his superior's anger, "we're down a man. You ride your blower. Kid'll be all right alone with me till we join up with the colonel and come back t' kick ass."

Lieutenant Kiley's face became very still. "Yeah, get in and drive," he said mildly, gripping the hatch coaming to lift himself out without bothering to use the power seat.

The driver vanished but his boots scuffed on the armor as he scurried for his own hatch. "Gimme your bloody key," he shouted back.

Instead of replying at once, the lieutenant looked down at me. "Sorry I got a little shook, kid," he said. "You did pretty good for a new recruit." Then he muscled himself up and out into the night.

The drive fans of other tanks were already roaring when ours began to whine up to speed. The great vehicle shifted greasily around me, then began to turn slowly on its axis. Fourth in line, we maneuvered through the courtyard gate while the draft from our fans lifted flames out of the palace windows.

We are the tank lords.

ROBERT A. HEINLEIN

"Heinlein knows more about blending provocative scientific thinking with strong human stories than any dozen other contemporary science fiction writers."
—*Chicago Sun-Times*

"Robert A. Heinlein wears imagination as though it were his private suit of clothes. What makes his work so rich is that he combines his lively, creative sense with an approach that is at once literate, informed, and exciting."
—*New York Times*

Seven of Robert A. Heinlein's best-loved titles are now available in superbly packaged new Baen editions, with embossed series-look covers by artist John Melo. Collect them all by sending in the order form below: